T0128917

Where Is Sara? transports you to the utopian, fortressed community of Brentville. While driving from a conference, Sara, a happily married mother and physician, happens upon this little town and discovers that she must participate in the life of Brentville in order to find her way out. As she adapts to this small village immersed in the 1950's, she begins a journey of self-discovery as she interacts with fascinating people and finds true faith. Cindy Kilpatrick tells a unique story filled with biblical truth. And you must read Where Is Sara? in order to find out how she escapes! If you do, I think you will agree with Harold, the godly elder in Brentville, who said, "You will be happified."

—Cynthia Heald, author of the "Becoming A Woman of..." bible study series.

Brentville's man made world of perfection and peace, is quietly undermined by a strange mystery, while the gentle unveiling of God's love, is revealed.

-Joan Hjalmquist, Teacher

Cindy Kilpatrick takes the reader on a fascinating journey to a place known only by its inhabitants. As a series of mysterious events unfold, Sara discovers something that brings profound meaning to her life. It's an experience that she realizes will forever change her. "Where Is Sara?" is a riveting read!

—Claudia Loopstra, author/speaker

Cindy has captured the nostalgia and feeling of a simpler time. Her story brought back fond memories from our past and accurately presented life as it used to be.

—Judy Tew, Retired computer professional and homemaker

Traveling with Sara through her unexpected journey was an opportunity to revisit my own realization of God's simple, yet powerful, offer of salvation through a loving Savior. I am so grateful for Cindy's imagination and ability to tell a story with truth and substance. Enjoy the journey!

—Annie Frost of Annie Ministries

WHERE IS SARA?

CINDY KILPATRICK

BALBOA.
PRESS
A DIVISION OF HAY HOUSE

Balboa Press books may be ordered through booksellers or by contacting:

Balboa Press
A Division of Hay House
1663 Liberty Drive
Bloomington, IN 47403
www.balboapress.com
1 (877) 407-4847

Print information available on the last page.

ISBN: 978-1-5043-7818-5 (sc)
ISBN: 978-1-5043-7820-8 (hc)
ISBN: 978-1-5043-7819-2 (e)

Library of Congress Control Number: 2017905478

Balboa Press rev. date: 06/29/2017

To my husband, George. His love for me and his love for Christ have made my life—and our marriage—a safe and wonderful place to be.

God has granted us three beautiful daughters: Amy (and her husband, Nick), Kim (and her husband, Richard), and Kristin (and her husband, Dan), who have enriched our lives beyond measure. So have our lovable grandchildren: Caleb (and his wife, Maddie), Haylee, Tyner, Ian, Brennan, Isaac, Hannah, Molly, Emma, and Evelyn, *and* the delightful great-grands, Eloise, Penelope, and Julianne. May God bless them all, holding their hands and their hearts during their own life journeys.

"It's folly to think we can predict what twists and turns our own journeys will take. How often has a person said, 'If anyone had told me that I'd be doing this, I'd have told him he was crazy'"?

It's only when we recognize that we do not have the control that we think we have, that we are neither the almost-perfect nor the totally worthless persons we've thought we were, we'll open up to God's intervention. Often, through seemingly unlikely people and in ways that can confound us, our Creator offers exciting new life!"

Willow Hadson, writer, in an oral presentation

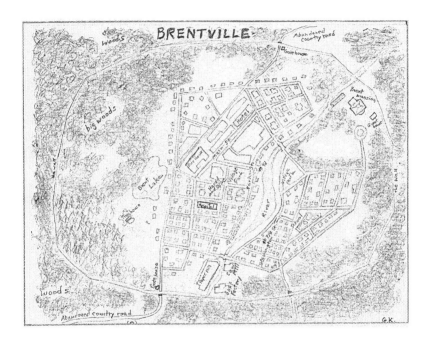

Mary and David's map of Brentville

Contents

ACKNOWLEDGMENTS

Thank you to my talented husband, George, who provided the map and sketches to help readers join Sara on her journey. Thank you also to Patricia Elford for her guidance and support and to my tech angel, Hillary Hale. I'm grateful to Gordon Bleich and Bob McKeen for their help in transcribing my song, "Forever." Thanks to A. Spencer, and everyone else at Balboa for their help. Finally, I thank my friend Ellen Schutter for her help with my final editing.

Unless otherwise indicated, biblical quotes are from the New International Version.

INTRODUCTION

Where Is Sara? tells of a significant journey within a journey. As readers travel with the narrator, they realize this pilgrimage is both unique and familiar, for such is the way in which God leads us.

Although there is truth in the telling, all characters and incidents are products of the author's imagination.

Fasten your seat belts. Here we go!

CHAPTER 1

Welcome to Brentville

As Sara drove down Route 3, the sun gently touched the leaves. Soft color filtered through the trees. It was like looking into the kaleidoscope on her coffee table back in Harleysville—a breathtakingly beautiful reminder that fall was upon her. *Where has summer gone?* she thought. *So many things left undone. As soon as I get home, I'll make a list and follow it through.*

Now that David, Debbie, and Susan were out on their own, Sara and Jim were enjoying a second honeymoon, a time when they could be alone to rediscover and enjoy each other. Sara still worked outside their home, so her life was very full—sometimes even hectic. Jim, a lawyer, worked at home. This plan had worked well when the children were young and still did, now that they were empty nesters. Jim still prepared most meals, which was a tremendous help to Sara.

Paying attention now to the highway exits, she wished she'd filled the tank earlier, when she'd been near a more populated area. It seemed more rural with every mile, and she decided she'd take the next exit she saw.

Okay, what's this? Looks like an exit coming up. Doesn't seem to be any sign in sight, but it's getting dark. I'll take that little winding road. *If I can't find a gas station, maybe I'll at least find a house. I've never thought that Wisconsin was this uninhabited.*

After driving for a few minutes, Sara realized she was on a dirt road. Because of all the flying stones and dust, she slowed the car to a crawl.

I'm lucky to have a mobile phone in my car; not many people do yet. Jim wants me to have everything available, to make sure I'm safe. He paid a lot of money to get me this newfangled mobile car phone. I guess I'd better be careful—the signal here is weak. Don't want to be uselessly calling for help.

Panic was setting in as she realized her situation. *This road is so narrow, I could never get the car turned around. Complete darkness now.*

The pitch-black woods and the tall, thick brush along the road were closing in on her. For the first time in her forty-five years, Sara was really afraid. She stopped the car to call Jim, but it was too late. No reception.

I should have flown to the medical convention.

Sara's fear of airplanes had dissuaded her from flying, and it made driving the miles from Harleysville, Pennsylvania, to Minneapolis, Minnesota, seem like a good idea. She had always wanted to see Minnesota and Wisconsin. With a two-week vacation, she could do so. The drive to Minneapolis had been a breeze. The return trip was turning out to be a little more complicated. *Right now, my options are few. I'll keep driving.*

After what seemed like many more miles, although the odometer said that it had been only fifteen since she'd left the highway, Sara decided to keep going. At about twenty-five miles, she thought she could see a dim light off in the distance. *Maybe it's just my imagination—wishful thinking. No, it's getting brighter.*

Sara could tell the road hadn't been used for years. The trees and bushes were getting closer to the edge, making it almost impossible to drive.

God was not someone Sara knew or thought much about. She was pretty self-sufficient; she had always taken care of things herself. But she found herself thinking that if she *did* have a higher power, this would be a good time to ask for help.

The light ahead was getting brighter. Sara was beginning to feel more relaxed. She could almost see where the narrow dirt road was leading her. *It looks like the Florida gated community where we lived for a few years.*

The first thing Sara came to was a very high concrete wall. *I don't see an entrance.* As she drove up to the high wall, an opening appeared, as if by magic. When she drove through the gap, she found the gatehouse just beyond the opening.

That's odd. In Florida, a gatehouse usually comes first, followed by a gate. As soon as she had driven through the opening in the big wall, it closed as magically as it had opened.

Sara was excited to have found some people, some light, *and—* she hoped—a town or village. *Maybe now I'll find some gas, some food, and someone to help me get my phone working.*

Stopping at the gatehouse, she rolled down the window of her new, light-blue Mercedes-Benz convertible. A nice-looking young man said hello through the gatehouse window. She could see his badge and "Walter Brent" on his nametag. As he rose to come to her car, she noticed his gun.

"Welcome to Brentville," he said with a warm smile. Sara observed that he was eyeing her brand-new vehicle.

"What are my chances of getting some gas, some food, and maybe even lodging for the night?" she asked. She was feeling somewhat shaky. The thought of a nice bed was definitely appealing.

He seemed delighted she had come.

He probably doesn't have many visitors at this time of night.

"Follow this road for around fifteen miles, and it will take you right into the center of Brentville. Stay on Main Street, and you will find everything you need, ma'am."

After taking her name, he gave her a ticket for the car window and motioned her on. Sara was relieved to see the road was paved. *It should be smooth sailing from here on.*

Again Sara could see nothing but trees and darkness. However, the guard had said she would find Brentville by staying on the road, so she did.

Funny, the radio station I've been listening to is no longer coming in. She tried looking for another station but could find only one. It was from Brentville and came in loud and clear. *Sounds like some kind of swap meet. Oh well, it's better than the silence.* She half listened to the young girl explaining why someone might want to buy her used bedroom furniture.

Soon Sara saw the lights of Brentville. What a welcome sight! The lights were warm and inviting—a safe haven away from the woods' darkness.

When driving right into the middle of the village, Sara noticed a few eating places, a hotel, a grocery store, a church, a fire station, and a gas station. None of those establishments had names she recognized. *No McDonald's, no Motel 6, no Weis Supermarket.* She guessed there might be around three thousand people in the cute little village. Even though it was 1980, Brentville made Sara feel like she was back in the 1950s. All the cars Sara saw were from the 1950s. As she pulled up to the only stop light in Brentville, she could see a 1950s pick up truck in her rear view mirror.

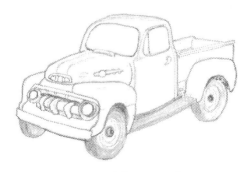

1950s pick up truck

4

Where are the malls? All the stores are on Main Street. Parking is the old diagonal parking with parking meters that seem to take nickels and dimes. I don't even keep my nickels and dimes anymore. Oops! My gas gauge says empty. I'd better stop at that gas station.

A gas station and repair shop attendant—Oscar, according to his nametag—ambled over to her car.

"How can I help?"

"I need gas."

"Well," he said, "I can help you with that, but first you'll need a converter. We don't have regular gas here. We've figured out a way to drive cars without it. We use natural gas. We have plenty of that here in Brentville."

The whole idea sounded kind of far-fetched to Sara. *Sometimes when I am in need of help with my car, repair people try to con me because I'm a woman. However, though I don't understand why, I feel pretty sure I can trust this man.*

"Yes, please. Install the converter."

"It'll take about a half hour."

Sara left the car, walked to the little cheese store, and did some window-shopping. *Before I leave this community, I'll stop here to buy some cheese for Jim.*

When she walked back to the gas station, she found her car ready for her. "How much do I owe you?" Sara asked, handing Oscar her credit card.

"Sorry, miss," he said, "but we only accept cash."

Sara had just enough in her wallet to pay him.

It was seven thirty, and Sara's stomach was growling, a reminder that she hadn't eaten since morning. When pulling up to the quaint hotel, she noticed a menu in the window, with meat loaf and mashed potatoes pictured on the cover. *Can't wait!*

She hurried up the brick-lined walkway and pulled open the glass door. The bell on the door announced her arrival. A young mom with two children pulling at her apron appeared at the desk. The children seemed to be about four years old.

"May I help you?" asked the distracted young woman.

Sara noticed a name embroidered on her beautifully tailored uniform. *Crystal, what a fitting name.* Crystal's sparkling eyes were sapphire blue. As her mothering instincts kicked in, Sara was immediately drawn to this young mom. "I'd like to get some dinner, and if you have a room available, I'll take it," Sara said. "I'll be leaving in the morning."

Crystal seemed happy to have some company. "All eight of my rooms are vacant right now."

Sara could see only a few couples in the tea room, and she noted that getting dinner should not be a problem. As Sara pulled her credit card out, she noticed a look of concern on Crystal's face. "I'm sorry, ma'am," Crystal said. "We only accept cash."

By then, the hunger pains were affecting Sara's thinking. All she could think about was that great-looking meatloaf. Pulling herself back to reality, she remembered an envelope she'd tucked away in her suitcase. Traveling with a large amount of cash wasn't the safest thing—she knew that—but she'd missed the banking hours before she left for the trip and hadn't had time to take the cash back home. She'd tucked the $1,000 (all in $100 bills) into an old envelope that she'd found in her purse and slipped it into her suitcase.

"Just a second," replied Sara as she looked for the key to her suitcase. Reaching into her crowded valise, she felt the envelope and pulled out a bill without disrupting any of the contents of her bag. She glanced around, hoping that no one in the tea room had seen her removing the money.

"Thank you," said Crystal, as she handed Sara seventy-five dollars in change. "This will cover you for one night and breakfast, and of course dinner tonight."

Sara smiled and took the table by the window. Even though it was dark, she could still see quite a bit. The streetlights were on. The storefronts were lit up so much it looked like Christmas. She noticed a young couple looking longingly at a beautiful handmade quilt hanging in the window of the hotel. It had a price tag she couldn't quite decipher. As she waited for her meal, the next thing she saw was a beautiful golden retriever. When he reached the door of the hotel, he gave the bell that was hanging on the doorknob a push with his paw.

Crystal's twins, introduced earlier as Joseph and Jenny, came running from the kitchen, shouting, "Sam!" They just about knocked each other down trying to see who could reach the dog first. When the twins returned to the kitchen, Sam was between them. *How cute,* Sara thought. *The Three Musketeers.*

When she opened the door of her room, Sara was pleased with the way it smelled and looked—very clean and inviting. It was furnished with furniture from the fifties. She had her own bathroom with a beautiful, old, claw-foot tub.

A rotary phone that looked very old was sitting on the end table by the bed. *That reminds me; I need to call Jim. I'll also have to plug in my car phone to get it charged up for tomorrow.*

As she picked up the old hotel phone, Sara realized she'd never used a rotary phone. *In that old Tracy and Hepburn movie, they dialed 0 for operator. Worth a try.* Putting her index finger on the 0, she pulled the dial clockwise until it would go no further. She took her finger out and let it click back to the original position, then listened.

"This is Mabel. May I help you?"

The reply caught Sara off guard. She cleared her throat to start talking to Mabel. "I want to make a call to Harleysville, Pa., can you help me with that?"

"I'm sorry, ma'am," Mabel said, "but this phone service covers only Brentville. Is there anyone in the village who I could connect you with?"

"No, thank you," Sara answered. Her voice was quiet; her disappointment dampened it. Sara was tired, worried, and dirty from her drive on that dirt road. *I hate to think what my car must look like!* But she was a strong woman. *It will take more than this to get me down.* As she slipped into her nice warm bath, she relaxed. *I'll try the mobile phone as soon as I'm done.*

I miss Marshmallow. If I were at home, my little white fluff-ball of a Maltipoo would be sitting by my tub. She never lets me out of her sight.

Wrapped in the pink chenille bathrobe that had been hanging in the bathroom, she curled up on the bed and tried her mobile phone again. Even though it was plugged into the charger, it was dead. *Oh, how I miss Jim. He'll be so worried about me.*

She was supposed to get home in two days. He would wonder why she hadn't called. But the day had been long, and she knew she'd done all that she could do. By ten, she was sound asleep, her tired body cradled in the ever-so-comfy feather bed.

Her alarm was a rooster crowing, followed by the smell of bacon then a quiet knock on her door. There stood Jenny and Sam.

"Mama says that breakfast is ready," said Jenny in a soft voice. She kept her arm around Sam's neck, although it didn't look like the dog wanted to go anywhere. Sam and the twins seemed to be close friends; in fact, they seemed inseparable. Sara was attracted to this little family. There didn't appear to be a dad in the picture, and Sara wondered about that.

"Okay, honey," said Sara to Jenny. "Please tell your mom that I will be right down."

The sun was shining in through the ruffled white curtains, and the room looked appealing. Sara decided to go down for breakfast before packing her bag.

The tea room was comfortably furnished, and the smell of roses filled the air. Crystal said she picked something from her flower garden each day to put on the tables. In the winter, she went to the greenhouse for flowers.

Breakfast consisted of eggs, bacon, toasted homemade bread, and some yummy homemade strawberry jam and tea.

Sara usually had a cup of coffee on her way to the hospital in the morning, but Crystal told her she didn't serve coffee. *I can't wait to get back on the highway to find a coffee shop.* She had been a doctor in the emergency room for the last ten years. She had about a half-hour drive to get from their restored Pennsylvania farmhouse to her job in the Philadelphia area and had come to rely on her morning caffeine fix.

Joseph, Jenny, and Sam were sitting on the floor in the middle of the tea room. The twins were brushing Sam's thick, shiny fur. As Sara took her last sip of hibiscus tea, she started thinking about her day. *Once I'm on the highway, I should be back in the Philly area in two days.*

After thanking Crystal and waving to the twins, Sara put her suitcase into her dirty convertible. She decided to take a quick drive around the appealing village. *Funny, I didn't see a Brentville on the Wisconsin map.*

Turning off Main Street onto Park Street, she was pleasantly surprised to see how nice the homes were. Most had porches with rocking chairs on them. Lots of picket fences framed the properties. Everyone had a garden. Most of the homes were the same, but on the outskirts of Brentville towered a mansion. It was huge, and the grounds were enclosed by what looked like an electric fence. She could see a pool. *Probably doesn't get much use. Not like my pool, because of our warmer weather in Harleysville.*

"Time to get going," Sara said out loud. "Guess I'd better find Main Street and head toward the road on which I came in."

She arrived at the gatehouse expecting to see the guard, but he was nowhere in sight. From that side of the wall, she couldn't tell there was a gateway. In fact, the more she looked, the more she was sure it didn't exist.

How can this be? This is the exact spot where I came in through the gate. I should be able to get out at the same spot, but it isn't going to work. Maybe there's another road that will take me to the exit gate. I did notice yesterday another road that headed toward the high wall. It looked as if it led out of the community.

Sara turned around at the gatehouse and got back on the road. Heading back into Brentville, she could feel some concern and fear bubbling up. *There has to be a way out! Be calm. You'll be fine.*

She turned the radio on. As had happened the day before, she could get only the Brentville station. Now they had some prerecorded stories, fifteen-minute segments of *Our Miss Brooks*, *The Shadow, Sky King,* and *Jack Benny.* Listening to the old-time story, she drove back into Brentville to begin her search for the other paved road she'd seen earlier.

As she drove around the community, trying to find that road, Sara remembered all the times she had given her husband grief because he wouldn't stop to ask for directions. *Well, I have a feeling the other road is going to get me back on the highway. If it doesn't, I'll stop to ask for directions.*

The next turn took her around a large lake. From the lake's edge, she could see a little paved road. She followed the road for quite a few miles. It was small and was also much too narrow to ever turn around on. It seemed to Sara that, once again, trees were pushing into the road.

She could see the very high concrete wall now. In front of the wall, she saw another gatehouse. *Whew, now we're getting somewhere!*

When she got right up to the gatehouse, the guard said she wasn't allowed to exit there. She could feel anger and frustration rising. But fear quickly overwhelmed her. *How am I going to get back on the highway?*

Sara tried in her most persuasive voice to get the guard to open the gate. Remembering the gun the first guard had carried, she decided to stop arguing, spun the car around, and headed back to the village—a place that just a few hours before had been an enjoyable spot to be in.

I wish I'd never seen Brentville!

The only person she knew there was Crystal, and her little blue convertible seemed to drive itself to the hotel. She barely remembered getting out of the car, talking with Crystal, or crawling into the same featherbed on which she'd slept so well the night before.

Next morning a faint knock on the door awakened Sara. It was Jenny and Sam. Jenny had a note for her: "Stay in bed. I'll bring breakfast to you. Crystal."

What a nice person. I don't want to be here, but I am. I'm grateful that I've met Crystal and her little family. I'll never give up on making an escape, but for now, I need to keep a level head and learn as much as I can. I can't believe this is happening! But it is. This family is real. Brentville is real. This bed is real.

Sara drifted back into a fitful sleep.

CHAPTER 2

Finding Her Way

The rooster crowed. Sara stirred in her sleep. Breakfast aromas opened her eyes enough for her to realize she felt good in the soft, warm bed. Light was peeping through the gleaming windows. She felt happy.

A quiet tap on the door brought her back to what she was facing. *I'm a prisoner in this lovely place. It doesn't seem lovely anymore.*

Crystal entered the room with a large tray in her arms. Sara didn't have an appetite for breakfast, but because Crystal was being so considerate, she took a few bites.

Crystal sat down on the edge of the bed and looked at Sara with sadness in her eyes. "I'm sorry, Sara," lamented Crystal. "I'm sorry that I didn't tell you." Tears were rolling down her cheeks. Soon Sara was crying too. "Sara, even though I've been in Brentville for five years, there are days when I still can't believe my plight."

"There is so much I need to know," cried Sara. "I want to know who I'm dealing with and what." *I'll never accept that I can't get out of this place.*

Crystal dried her eyes. "I'll help you, Sara," she said compassionately. "I'll tell you all I know. I'll also offer you this room. It's yours until you get yourself situated, and I don't want you to pay for it."

Sara's head was full of worries. *No way to get word to Jim. No way to let the hospital know they need to get a replacement for me. The kids will be worried as soon as they hear I didn't make it home. What's going to happen when my money runs out? And my Marshmallow will be so sad without me!*

Sara couldn't remember anything in her life that had been so unacceptable, so wrong, so frightening. Not even bothering to dress, she spent the whole morning curled up in a fetal position in the bed. It was a huge dilemma, and she needed time to process everything.

By midafternoon, Sara felt ready to get up. She went downstairs to find Crystal, heard voices in the kitchen, and decided to wait before entering. She stood in the empty tea room, trying not to eavesdrop; yet her curiosity got the best of her.

There were two voices coming from the kitchen, and they seemed to be discussing something important. Crystal was in deep conversation with someone named Oliver. The conversation led Sara to believe that they were close. When Oliver said his good-byes to Crystal and left via the tea room, Sara noticed that he had warm-looking eyes and the body of someone who worked out. *If not, he has a job that keeps him fit.*

Sara gave Crystal a few minutes to regain her composure. Then she went in to ask for a cup of tea, hoping to have some time with her. Two hours later, Sara and Crystal were still talking. Sam was curled up on Crystal's feet, and the twins had napped longer than usual. Both Sara and Crystal were thankful.

During their conversation, Crystal offered, "I came in on the same dirt road you came on, five years ago. I was traveling back home to my husband. I didn't know it, but I was pregnant. Sam was then a puppy I'd purchased to take home as a surprise for my husband. Mr. Brent, the founder of Brentville, took me under his wing and helped me to get a start. When I first came, I stayed in bed for three weeks. After I realized my predicament, I didn't want to live."

Sara learned that Mr. Brent had given Crystal the hotel, fully furnished with a fully equipped sewing room, and a backyard garden.

"The hotel is used predominately by people who need care after surgery or after a hospital stay. My own living quarters are right off the kitchen. I have a wringer washing machine in the cellar and a clothesline out back."

Sara discovered later that Mr. Brent had brought the old wringer machines because he knew he wouldn't be able to fix or replace a modern one. There would be too many complicated parts. He felt his handyman could keep the old washers running forever. And so far, he was right. It had been thirty years since he'd pulled the gates shut around the village.

Brentville's lack of coffee was due to the fact that growing coffee plants hadn't worked out. They'd tried in the greenhouse, but due to a faulty watering technique, all the plants were lost. Once they were gone, there was no way to get out to the outside world to replenish them. Crystal was told that the residents of Brentville took some time to adjust to not having their caffeine. Once all the coffee cans that had come in with the people were empty, Brentville had some grumpy men and women.

Sara would never give up on the idea of getting out of Brentville, even though Crystal's own story and her accounts about others made being trapped there forever seem to be the final truth.

The next day, Sara drove out to the two gatehouses and then found a third road. This road led her to another manned gate house. There was no possible way to open it from the inside. She was discouraged and was covered with a layer of dust. Sara drove back to the hotel, climbed the stairs to her room, pulled down the shades, and retreated to her bed. *Staying in bed for three weeks might not be such a bad idea.* She drifted into a heavy sleep.

The next morning, Crystal suggested, "Maybe it's time to call Mr. Brent. There's an unwritten rule: Don't just show up on his doorstep. You call and make an appointment."

"Okay," replied Sara. *Maybe it is time to meet the man who's keeping me here against my will. Crystal is in awe of him. He did so much for her, giving her anything she needed. Now her mind's being tricked into feeling beholden to him rather than remembering that she's his captive.*

It reminds me of the abuse cases at the hospital—the abused repeatedly go back to the abuser. I guess it's a matter of survival for Crystal. As long as she doesn't face the reality of it, she can survive.

At ten the next morning, Sara, Crystal, Jenny, Joseph, and Sam all stood on Mr. Brent's doorstep.

When Crystal had arrived in Brentville, she'd stayed with Mr. Brent until after the twins were born. They hadn't left until the twins were two, so they all felt at home there. Crystal never had the run of the house but was allowed to live in the heavily guarded guesthouse.

Maggie, the housekeeper, opened the door. The twins squealed with delight. She had been like a grandmother to them for as long as they could remember. Sam drooled for the treats he might receive.

"Mr. Brent is in the den," Maggie said as she pointed to the room around the corner. Crystal entered ahead of Sara and guided her to the sofa.

Mr. Brent jumped up from his desk and gave Crystal a big hug. "So good to see you, my dear. Please introduce me to your friend." He reached out his hand to Sara.

Her first impulse was to pull away, but she thought better of it. *Not good to bite the hand that may be feeding me.*

Sara and Crystal visited with Mr. Brent for an hour or so. He was very good at conversation and at getting information about Sara that she had not meant to share. She was surprised that she was having a pleasant chat with him, but under the circumstances, she knew it was the only way to go. *I have to play along, but I must always remember that this man is not my friend.*

"I'm pleased to know you are a doctor," said Mr. Brent. "Our hospital had only two doctors, and we lost one last week. The one doctor we have is in need of help, and certainly the people of the village need that too. Poor Dr. Adler died of old age and pneumonia. He was well liked and was quite an expert in natural medicine, using herbs and plants to take the place of many drugs you're used to using."

He continued. "Dr. Ted Barone is the other doctor, and he knows quite a bit about natural healing as well. We have five physician's assistants who have never been to college but have been trained by Drs. Barone and Adler. I would love it if you would consider joining the team."

Sara thanked Mr. Brent, smiled, and said she would consider his offer. *That's a laugh. Of course I don't want to consider your offer! I want to go home to Harleysville. I want to work in my own hospital.*

Mr. Brent asked if he could set up another appointment for Thursday morning at ten. She said that would be fine, at which point, Joseph and Jenny and Sam bounded through the door. Sara could tell that Mr. Brent was genuinely glad to see them.

Sara had put her convertible top down to make room for Crystal, the twins, and Sam. It was the first time her four passengers had ridden in a convertible. She could tell by the giggles that they loved it. Sam was in the middle of the back seat, flanked by a twin on each side. The rearview mirror reflected big smiles on all their faces. Yes, with the help of the wind, even the dog was smiling.

On returning to the hotel, they found Oliver waiting for Crystal. *The way Oliver's eyes soften when he looks at Crystal certainly spells love,* Sara thought.

Apparently, they'd been a couple for a year. According to Crystal, she had feelings for Oliver but was dragging her feet for two reasons. One was that she was still married, although she had given up all hope of being reunited with her husband. The second was that Oliver was one of the second-generation townies. He'd been born in Brentville thirty years before. It was just Oliver and his mom, and he'd grown up taking all the handouts Mr. Brent offered, thinking he would be looked after forever. He didn't know about all the freedoms and liberties that had been taken from him. And he didn't seem to mind being controlled by Mr. Brent. Crystal had fallen prey to this faulty thinking to some degree, but there was still a part of her that was hanging on to her old life and beliefs.

Sara took the children and Sam in to get lunch started. Crystal and Oliver sat in the big, old-fashioned bench swing in the front yard. Crystal had said there were many like it in Brentville. They were easy to make; without any connection to the outside world, things had to be kept simple.

Bench Swing

Before lunch was served, Crystal pulled Sara aside to speak to her privately. "Oliver asked if I would spend more time alone with him, now that you're here and might look after the kids. The two of us would like to go for some picnics at the lake. In the meantime, there's something we'd like you to do *with* us today, Sara. Would you like to watch the Brentville Day Parade with us? It's a yearly fall event. It's something everyone looks forward to, and we spend many hours preparing for it. I have a friend ready to look after the hotel's front desk so the twins and I can enjoy the parade."

Sara agreed to join them. They grabbed a blanket from the sofa and went out to find the chairs that Crystal had set up in front of the hotel earlier in the afternoon. Sitting in front of the hotel would allow them the best view in the whole community.

The parade started on the other side of the village. By the time it got to the main section, the bands, the floats, and the marching groups were pulling out all the stops. The trumpet players were showing off; the people on the brightly colored floats were throwing candy. There was even a barbershop group singing old loved songs everyone seemed to know. It was a sight to behold—enough to send shivers up Sara's spine.

As she sat enjoying the splendor of it all, Sara was remembering all the parades she'd enjoyed as a child and then with her own family in the Harleysville area. The unbearable reality of her situation began to overwhelm her. Choking, she excused herself to run up the stairs to her room. Sara closed the door and locked it. She needed time to be alone.

Just when she thought she was finished crying, another round of sobs shook her.

Two hours later, the church chimes awakened Sara. *Six o'clock! I've missed helping Crystal with the dinner crowd.*

A few minutes later, Crystal appeared with her dinner tray. "Thought you might like to eat in your room," she said.

18

After dinner, Sara decided to take a walk up and down Main Street. It was a happy-looking business section. Everything was bright and cheery. To Sara it was apparent that the picturesque community had funds for keeping things painted and looking good. Crystal had told her that everyone paid a small tax that went toward the upkeep of the properties on Main Street. They had no say in choice of colors. That was up to Mr. Brent.

Sara window-shopped until she noticed an open drugstore with a lunch counter. *I'll just go in to see what they have.* As Brentville was a self-contained community, everything had to be made inside its walls. Sara already knew Brentville had a smelly paper mill, hidden back in the woods. There was also a soap factory on the outskirts of the village.

"If you get too close to either one of them, or if the wind happens to be blowing the wrong way, you have to hold your breath," Oliver had warned.

While checking the drugstore shelves, Sara found soap wrapped in a crude and primitive way, not like she was used to seeing in the Philadelphia area. *Mmm. It smells like lavender. I'm sure Debbie would like it, regardless of the wrapper.*

Next to the drugstore was a shoe store, complete with a highly polished old leather boot hanging in front of it. *Oh, yes, Crystal said that Mr. Brent brought a shoe cobbler and his family when he started the village. The cobbler gets his materials from the tannery, another small business on the outskirts of the community.*

Each day, Sara became more amazed at what she learned about all the people there, whom Crystal called "townies." They had come when the village was established. Apparently, they were people who, for one reason or another, were easy prey for Mr. Brent. He was able to talk them into giving up freedom for all the promises he was to offer them.

Granted, he's made it pretty nice—free stuff and the promise of more when that's gone. They must have been so disillusioned with their old lives that his new one sounded like something they wanted.

Everyone I've met so far is true to Mr. Brent. By pulling them from the depths of their misery, he's become their savior. He gave them what they needed with one hand and took away their freedom with the other. He did it with such finesse, they don't seem to realize, or care, that it had happened.

After leaving the drugstore, she heard the ten o'clock whistle that went off every night to get people off the streets. Everyone had five minutes after it sounded to get home. Offenders received a fine or jail time.

It seemed that most people in Brentville had a bicycle. You could walk or ride your bike to most places. When the whistle blew, bikes sped every which way, all riders trying to get home before the curfew.

Made it! Oh, this pillow feels good. Sara started planning the next day's activities. Though she put on a good face, her insides were always crying; there was a constant sadness in her soul. Quiet times were the worst, so she tried to keep busy.

See Mr. Brent at ten. Work on my escape. That's as far as she got. No more worries or thoughts until morning, only dreams. Most were nightmares.

Sara had been helping Crystal with the morning crowd. She was enjoying it, thankful to engage in conversation with some of the local people. *There must be some clue, something that might help me to find a way out of Brentville.*

Crystal had a pretty steady and loyal group for breakfast.

"Good morning, Hank," said Sara, her smile warm. "What can I get you?"

"The usual, please," he answered. Hank was one of those individuals she couldn't help but like. He always had a happy face. *Hank is someone I want to get to know. His happiness is contagious.*

He has what I want. Hank worked in the sawmill and had a wife and baby. *There's something about this young man that draws me to him.*

Maggie answered the door. Sara knew from what Crystal had said that Maggie was the only worker allowed to be alone in the big house.

"Good morning, Maggie," said Sara. "I'm here for my appointment with Mr. Brent."

"Welcome," said Maggie, giving Sara a hug. She was a round, soft, plump woman, sixty or so years old. She wore a plain housedress. Sara thought, *She looks like an ideal 1950s grandmother—warm, cuddly, modest.* "Mr. Brent is upstairs. I'll let him know you're here. Why don't you come into the living room and make yourself comfortable?"

Sara was very curious as to how this man lived. *What makes this multibillionaire do what he does?* After working in the emergency room for so many years, Sara was pretty good at analyzing people at first meeting.

"Hello there," greeted Mr. Brent. Fixing his brown eyes on Sara's, he shook hands with her and then headed toward the white leather chair.

Sara watched as he settled his thin, well-formed body into the chair. He was wearing slim tan pants and a long, brown, tailored shirt that reflected his eyes and suited his graying sable hair. Mr. Brent was an attractive man who seemed composed and genuine.

But underneath it all, there's a man with an array of complex defects. Assessing him and focusing on how to get back to Jim and her world was helping Sara survive.

"Let me tell you what I will offer you," stated Mr. Brent in a direct, no-nonsense way.

No niceties here. No small talk that could lead me to much-needed information.

"I want you on the staff at the hospital," he said abruptly. "I will pay you well. The facility is very well equipped. When I came thirty years ago, I made sure we had what we needed. It won't be what you are used to, but we do have a good system going, with all the herbs and natural ways of doctoring."

Mr. Brent didn't give her time to respond. He took a breath, smiled, and continued. When he talked, he had a voice and a way of articulating that made her listen, not wanting to miss a word. "There are five houses available in Brentville at the moment. You will have your choice. Each house is furnished with everything you could ever need. One of the perks of living in Brentville is that you don't have to pay for your housing. You have to pay for the heat, water, and electricity, but that will be minimal. We have well-run plants for all these utilities."

He added, "You will have lawn care, a garden, a clothesline—we even make our own clothespins in Brentville."

Mr. Brent appeared to stop to check if she was on overload yet and decided to continue. "There will be a small maintenance fee, a small property tax, and a small tax is figured in on everything sold in Brentville. You will soon learn that we also do a lot of bartering."

He thinks of everything. I wonder if he tells me when I can have a bathroom break. It would have been funny if she hadn't felt too afraid to laugh.

"I know that I have given you a lot to think about, so please do take some time to make your decision," said Mr. Brent. "I admire your brand-new blue convertible," he added. "It's been thirty years since I've had a new car, and yours is the first that has piqued my interest. I would pay you well."

Sara's mouth dropped open. She tried not to show her cards. "Well," she stated, "thank you for all your generous offers. I'll take some time to think about it. But I can tell you today that the job sounds good to me." She had been away from her life's passion of helping others for a while now and thought, *How I miss it!*

"I can start this week if you want me to. I think I'd like to stay with Crystal for now. I need to be with people." Then she added, "And I will have to think about the car."

Mr. Brent served her a piece of the apple pie Maggie had brought in and a cup of herbal tea. *This pie is delicious,* Sara thought. *Probably made with some of the early apples I noticed ripening on the trees in his yard.*

It was August and almost harvest time for Brentville citizens. Crystal had explained that most citizens had gardens and fruit trees and canning equipment. The community's cannery also provided jobs and food all year long.

Sara thanked Mr. Brent, said good-bye to Maggie, and left with a head full of questions. *What drives this man? What can I learn that will get me out of here?*

She felt tired and overwhelmed but hadn't given up the hope that she would see her Jim again, would hug her three kids again, and would hold her sweet Marshmallow.

CHAPTER 3

Riding into New Experiences

On her way back to the hotel, Sara decided to stop at the bicycle shop. *I'll find a bike I'll feel good riding. I used to love riding bikes, but that was a few years ago. Can I still ride one properly?*

That's where she met Harold Turner. He was in his seventies and had white hair and twinkling blue eyes. It seemed he could fix anything. He was not an original townie, she learned, and he had been in Brentville for only ten years.

He'd started working in the shop when he first came and had been there ever since. He also had a clock repair shop in his home. Harold and his wife, Olive, had been traveling east to visit family when they noticed their gas gauge was on low. When they saw the road that went to Brentville, they decided to follow it to see if they could find a gas station. When they were almost to the big wall, they ran out of gas, so they continued on foot until they found the wall. As they stood in front of the gate, it opened, and they found the guard. The guard drove them into Brentville.

"It's a decision we feel we'll regret for as long as we live," he concluded.

"Would you mind if I took a bike for a ride?" asked Sara. "I want to see if I can still ride before I get one."

"That would be fine."

Sara could tell Harold was one of the nice guys, and she tucked that notation down into her heart. *I need good things to hang on to. Harold is a good thing.*

She picked a bike that reminded her of one that she had owned as a child: no gears, just a big, heavy red bike. Mr. Turner told her to keep it for a couple of days to see what she thought. He put it on the back of her car, tied it down, and waved her on. Sara waved back, sent him a smile, and headed to the hotel.

Crystal had finished up with the lunch crowd when Sara arrived, and the twins had completed a short nap. "Grab your bikes!" Sara yelled as she ran up to her room. "I'm going to learn how to ride a bike again." After running back down the stairs, now wearing sneakers and shorts, Sara rounded up the crew. Off they went to the lake.

Sara was in good shape. And the white shorts and pink top she'd chosen showed off her good looks. Her long blond hair was shining in the sun.

That smooth walking path around the lake will be a good place to practice, she thought.

The twins were giggling as their new friend Sara tried to ride the bike. Crystal expressed joy at seeing her in such a good mood. Sam seemed more than ready to have some fun with his family. His wagging tail and occasional veer toward the lake's edge hinted that he'd like to be having a swim.

Sara was wobbly on the first try, but before long she was gliding along with nostalgic memories of her childhood. With her long blond hair blowing in the wind, she looked—and felt— sixteen years old. *What a thrilling ride!*

Bike

Sara awoke, a little sore but cheerful, on Sunday morning. She thought, *Visiting the one church in the community might be a good idea. Meeting people and hearing stories might help with my escape plan. I've been listening to the clock chimes coming from the church ever since I arrived.* The clock chimed every hour on the hour, with as many chimes as it took to count off the time. Everyone always knew what time it was, and just in case they wanted more information, it struck a single chime each half hour.

Pretty good idea, unless you can't sleep at night. Then counting chimes can be very frustrating.

Entering the church, Sara could see that Mr. Brent had spared no expense when he designed the beautiful building. The many windows had amazing stained-glass artwork, and they added to the brilliant colors throughout the sanctuary. *The pews were designed for comfort and beauty,* she thought as she slipped into the back row.

The service hadn't started yet, and Sara could hear organ music coming from the pipes that were across the front of the sanctuary. There were song books but no hymnals and no Bibles in the bookrack on the back of each pew.

Sara knew from talking with Crystal that the reverend was a townie and a good speaker. And he did give a positive and interesting talk. She guessed that he was seventy. *I wonder why he consented to giving up his freedom thirty years ago.*

After the service, there were refreshments in a fellowship hall. Everyone who'd come to church stayed after for food and conversation.

Walking the two blocks back to the hotel, Sara couldn't help thinking that the church was more like a club than a church. *I guess it's a much-needed outlet for Brentville citizens. They told me about dances, food sales, dinners, etc. I don't remember hearing any mention of God. Not that I'd know what church should be like. I never attend church in my world. And I certainly didn't like the way one of the men looked at me.*

Sara needed Sunday evening to prepare herself for the first day of work at Memorial Hospital. She had the new stethoscope she'd purchased just before she left home, along with many samples that she had acquired at the medical convention. Sara thought about giving all the samples to the hospital, but something held her back.

I'll just tuck them away in my closet. I can always take them in at another time. She had a sixth sense about things and was learning to listen to such nudges.

CHAPTER 4

The Hospital—On the Job

It was eight o'clock on Monday morning. On that beautiful August day, some leaves had started to change color. The mums and the hydrangeas were in full bloom.

Sara was on her way to the hospital to meet with Dr. Barone. She knew that to survive this new life she had fallen into, she needed to work. Work had always rescued her from negative emotions, made her feel good about herself, and given life meaning.

Sara had decided to walk the few blocks to the hospital. It was apparent that villagers in Brentville all took pride in their yards. As she walked, she was greeted with smiles and nods. Most of the porches had rocking chairs. She couldn't remember a time since her arrival when she hadn't seen neighbors out rocking.

Rocking Chairs on Porch

As she opened the door to Memorial Hospital, on which a wall plaque indicated it had been built in 1953, Sara was hit with a feeling of nostalgia and familiarity. The smells and the overall looks were the same, but the faces and the old-fashioned appearance of the building were different. For a few seconds, a feeling of sadness overwhelmed her. Determined to be strong, Sara pulled herself together.

March on, Sara! She had always marched on her own through life. Wiping away a tear, she looked for a directory and found Dr. Barone's name. "Suite 106," she read aloud. She followed the arrows to his wing.

"Good morning." Dr. Barone, who looked to be in his early sixties, greeted her with a smile and gestured for her to take a seat. Sara had been busy noticing that Memorial Hospital and its equipment, offices, and cafeteria appeared to be just the same as the day the building had been constructed. She found a comfortable chair and switched her attention from furniture to the doctor.

"Please call me Ted," said Dr. Barone. "And may I call you Sara?"

She nodded and smiled.

"My book learning stopped in the 1950s," continued Ted, "so, as you can imagine, I am anxious to hear what you have been up to. We have had a few nurses who came as you did and who have been very helpful in our quest to update our hospital. As I'm sure you remember, thirty years ago, medicine had the artificial heart program, reproductive technology that gave many couples hope, and lasers for surgeries. Alternative medicine was becoming popular."

"But," he continued, "I'm certain you have much knowledge about so many new discoveries. I can't wait to pick your brain."

Sara was impressed by this humble man, and she found herself feeling sorry for him. *What could have hurt so much, those thirty years ago, to have made Ted leave his world to come to Brentville?*

"To tell you the truth," stated Sara, "I'm not very happy to be here. But I am glad to meet you and am looking forward to working with you. I need to be busy, and I yearn to be helping others again."

"That's fine," said Ted. "I will teach you all I know about alternative medicine and how we do things around here. You can fill me in on what I've missed for the last thirty years. I think we'll make a smashing team."

Sara's interview lasted a couple of hours. Then Ted gave her a tour of the forty-bed hospital. During the tour, he asked, "Would you like to work Monday through Thursday with on-call duties every other weekend?"

Sara said that would be fine, shook hands with Ted, and walked back out into the sunlight. As she headed back to the hotel, she noticed again how the folks in Brentville seemed to love their porches. *There's so much I want to know. How did these people come here? What do they do for a living, for entertainment? Why are they so content, given the fact that they're prisoners here?*

But the biggest question was always on her mind: "How can I get back to Jim?"

Each day Sara recognized more faces and learned more names. She was drawn to the friendly smiles, and as she walked past the porches, she was usually welcomed with a wave.

One day, when Harold waved and smiled, she stopped for a chat. He had come home from his bike shop to eat lunch. *What a genuinely happy man! He exudes joy and always seems so full of hope. Meeting a person like Harold makes each day bearable.*

Sara had been feeling more loss every day, but she knew that she had to stay strong. "I miss my Jim and my family," she lamented tearfully.

When she opened the door of the hotel, she could hear Crystal's sewing machine whirring in the sewing room as she was working on Sara's hospital apparel. It had been a few years since Sara had worn a uniform or white jacket to work, but she hadn't had time to talk to Crystal about scrubs. *Next time, I'll help her make a pattern for scrubs.*

After dinner, Sara took Sam for his nightly stroll. Her feet seemed to head automatically toward Harold and Olive's house. *I don't know what it is, but I do love this couple.*

Seeing their smiling faces and the inviting porch, Sara headed Sam toward the vacant rocker. He found a spot on the braided rug, and Sara started rocking. "Why is it that, in thirty years, no one has spotted Brentville by air?" she asked. "You would think that by now it would have been spotted by a satellite or aerial photographers."

"We asked the same question," answered Harold.

"Yes," agreed Olive, "and what we learned will help you appreciate Mr. Brent's intelligence.

"And how he'll go to any length to make his kingdom work," added Harold.

Sara stopped rocking. She was all ears.

"You see, dear," said Olive, "Mr. Brent had unlimited funds and a friend who was ahead of anyone in experimenting with different ideas. His scientist friend, who was definitely a brilliant creative thinker, developed a substance that goes from the top of the high wall and stretches above the whole enclosed area. It's a permanent mist."

"Nothing under the substance can be seen from above," Harold added. "But everyone under the veil can see through it. So we can see the overhead planes and clouds without any problem. The snow and rain and sunlight go through the veil. I can't explain it, but I understand that is how it works."

Sara was shocked. *Hard to believe—but, then again, how can any of this be happening?* She continued her rocking, a little more rapidly, while Olive and Harold rocked and remained quiet.

Harold interrupted the quiet, wanting to share something he'd once heard. "Worry is like rocking. It gives you something to do, but you don't get anywhere."

Olive had no doubt heard him say that before, and she just smiled. Sara, on the other hand, thought it quite funny, and she laughed out loud.

"You always make me laugh," said Sara. "Thank you. I need some laughter in my life."

Thanking Harold and Olive for the visit, she stood up. Sam arose, stretching. Sara extended a hand to the couple, but Harold and Olive both gave her a friendly hug. She emotionally accepted it. *How long has it been since I've trusted and felt close enough to someone to let my guard down like this?*

When they reached the hotel, Sam rang the bell with his paw. The twins, in their footed pajamas, padded to the door. With joyous smiles, they greeted Sam and Sara.

Roosters were crowing, and alarms were ringing—time for Sara to get herself out of the warm bed. Looking at the old-fashioned windup alarm clock, she noted that she had only an hour before she was to be at the hospital. One thing she was finally getting used to was winding the clock every night before bed.

Apparently, Mr. Brent had expected that batteries would be nonexistent and had decided to bring only clocks with springs and pendulums. Harold and a few others had clock shops and were able to repair any and all clocks.

Sara had decided that walking back and forth to the hospital would be the best plan. She thought that keeping her convertible out of sight as much as possible was probably a good idea too. She wasn't ready to sell it to Mr. Brent, and she wasn't sure what others would think of so modern a car. Walking would mean allowing an extra ten minutes each way for getting to and from work, depending on how many porches she visited on her way home.

Sara spent much of the first week getting used to the layout of the hospital, settling into her office, and trying to remember the names and faces of the staff. She was most intrigued with the natural healing department and all the pharmaceutical products that were manufactured from the plants that were grown in the in-house greenhouse. Fortunately, there was a comprehensive manual that helped her learn what she needed. She was going to have to find things to replace medicines that she had used in her former life.

Her first patient was an eight-month-old baby girl with extreme diaper rash. Sara grabbed the well-used manual and found a chapter on diaper rash. She instructed the young mom to go home and let the baby play in a bath of oatmeal and tepid water for ten or so minutes. Sara also gave her a jar of salve. The salve, which had been manufactured in the hospital's pharmacy, contained dried marigold flowers, sunflower seed oil, and beeswax among its ingredients.

Sara was relieved to have found an answer for her first patient, and the new mom seemed relieved to have found a doctor she liked and trusted.

What a great start to my first day!

Sara opened the door to her next patient. This boy of seven had been shot near his eye with a BB gun. It seemed that almost all the boys in Brentville had BB guns, thanks to Mr. Brent. Apparently, he thought that all boys should have one, so he had come with a large supply of Daisy BB guns—enough to last for years. The fathers all passed them down to their sons. This boy had been playing out in the fields with a few of his older brothers and friends. The other boys didn't hang around after the boy was taken home to his mom. *I imagine his mother will have something to say when she has him back there!* Sarah mused.

The week flew by. Sara met each new patient and each new problem with care and concern, but there was a sadness and fear in her that she could not shake. *Living here in Brentville will never be okay.*

Because Sara was a practical and usually calm person, she had decided to make the most of her predicament. Most days she was able to get through the day without dissolving. She hadn't given up her plan to escape, but she knew that she had to be levelheaded about it and stay calm.

On some days, she felt as though she couldn't stay in Brentville for another minute. She just had to get away from the anguish and the heartache that filled her soul. Those were the days that she felt like kicking and screaming her way back to her world. But she was reminded that, like the moving rocker, that would get her nowhere. She knew that she had to stay calm and alert, and keep looking for clues. *Surely soon—very soon—I'll be driving my little blue convertible right out of Brentville.*

Sara's convertible

34

It was Sara's weekend off, and she was walking with Sam. The sun was warm, the leaves were colorful, and the apple trees were heavily laden with fruit. After the cooler weather of September, she was enjoying the magnificent day of Indian summer. *I can't believe it's October.*

Harold was resting in the swing in his front yard. He had raked a big pile of leaves but hadn't moved them to the compost pile yet. Sara loved being with Harold in his swing, and she always looked forward to their conversations.

Sam jumped up onto the middle platform of the swing, curled up, and rested his head on Sara's feet. Harold handed Sara a four-leaf clover he'd just found. She was impressed and said, "I've never found one."

"You just have to look," Harold replied. "They are there."

Sara learned later that Harold had an uncanny ability for finding four-leaf clovers. He frequently presented someone with a clover he'd just found.

Every Wednesday night, in the central park, a group of musicians set up their instruments in the bandstand and played all kinds of glorious music. Harold and Olive had taken her when she first came, and they hadn't missed a Wednesday night since. Olive had told Sara that she loved seeing Harold enjoying the music. He could sing along because he knew all the parts by heart and by ear.

"How much longer can we enjoy the band concerts?" Sara asked.

"Another couple of weeks and they'll be calling it quits until spring," answered Harold. "I think the Harvest Festival is the last concert."

Sam scrambled through the neatly piled leaves to chase a squirrel on the other side of the yard. Harold smiled. "By the way, Sara, we're having a few friends over for Thanksgiving. We'd love to have you join us."

Sara felt like hugging the old gentleman, but instead she gave him a smile and a quiet thank-you. She knew the holidays would be hard and was thankful to have a place to go. She expected Crystal and the twins would be spending Thanksgiving with Oliver and his mom.

Sara walked home with a lighter heart. And she realized that she had been dreading the holidays. *I don't suppose I'll ever have a real happiness again*, mourned Sara *But having Harold and Olive and Crystal is helping in that department.*

As Sara and Sam reached the hotel, she could see that Crystal was busy with the dinner crowd. She knew that Crystal could use her help, and she knew that keeping busy helped her blot out her sadness. She had almost completely given up on an escape plan, partly because Olive had told her of someone dying while trying to get over the wall. She had heard of an electric fence; but this one didn't just give you a severe shock, it killed.

Getting Joseph and Jenny bathed and tucked in for the night seemed like an enormous job to Sara. She hadn't been sleeping well, and the church clock that counted out every hour and half hour didn't help.

I just need to get a good night's sleep.

Sara filled the big claw-foot tub with hot water and lavender, and gradually let her body sink into the inviting water. Resting her head on the tub pillow that Crystal had made, she closed her eyes and thought of her old life. Tears coursed down to her chin as she thought about Jim, the kids, and Marshmallow. *She'd be sitting right here beside the tub. She was my buddy.*

CHAPTER 5

The Harvest Festival— Despair Eased

Sara had been in Brentville for a few months, and her feelings of despair seemed to be worsening. During the day, Sara loved the chimes reminding her of the time. Nighttime was a different story. Her nights consisted of counting the hours each time a new hour chimed. Her fretting always took her to Jim and her kids and to thoughts of how she might find a way to be reunited with them. She decided to try to learn more about the mansion.

Maybe there is some underground tunnel. Maybe Mr. Brent left a way to be in touch with the outside world, something that he did years ago when he developed this place, something that only he knows about.

It would be wonderful if Jim or the police could retrace my steps and be miraculously led to the same dirt road that I took that fateful night. I cannot lose hope!

Sara drifted back into a light and fitful sleep.

Although Sara often felt mornings would never come, they always did. Smells of breakfast cooking came drifting through her half-opened door. No one else was staying in Crystal's hotel, so Sara had fallen into the habit of leaving her door open at night. She loved the impromptu visits from the twins and Sam.

The twins arrived, as they did every morning at six, carrying her morning tea. Her thoughts gradually came to the day—and what was in store.

It was Saturday, and Harold had convinced her to attend the Harvest Festival with them. *I'm so glad to have something to look forward to, a reason to get up. Harold and Olive and their friends seem to have a joy about them. I don't understand how it can be. They're living in the same circumstances as I am. I like them; I feel at home with them. I want to learn more about the peace they seem to feel.*

It was another beautiful Indian Summer morning. The air was dry and warm, with the scent of freshly raked leaves. Sara could smell the barbecued chicken that was being prepared in the park. Apparently, this was a big day in Brentville, and residents had been working around the clock, getting things ready.

After giving the twins a hug, Sara grabbed her sweater and ran out the back door. Crystal was hanging sheets on the clothesline. With one clothespin in her mouth and one hand holding the end of the sheet, she smiled and waved to Sara.

"See you later," said Sara as she headed down the alley toward Harold and Olive's house. She felt so at home in this house, she rarely knocked, but gave a tap, stuck her head in the door, and asked, "Is anyone home?" She was always welcomed with "Come on in, Sara," and was always given a big hug.

Olive was in the kitchen, busy with last-minute details. She was concentrating on pulling a golden apple pie from the oven. Sara could see two apple pies, two pumpkin pies, and one cherry pie that Olive must have baked earlier. The house smelled heavenly.

Oscar, the young man Sara had met at the gas station when she first came to Brentville, was there with his wife. They were among the friends whose companionship Harold and Olive enjoyed. *I can understand why. They're all friendly. They seem to genuinely like being together—and they laugh. They enjoy each other and have fun. Under these circumstances, though, how can they be so happy?*

Harold was busy piling supplies out by the road. At nine, someone with a horse and wagon would stop by to pick up all the pies, food, tablecloths, tables, and anything else that was to be taken.

"What can I do?" Sara inquired.

Harold's blue eyes twinkled as he thanked her for offering. "We'll put you to work when we get there," he replied. "We will probably need you in one of our booths for part of the time, but I want you to be free to enjoy the festivities today. Take some time to get to know some of our citizens."

The horse-drawn wagon was on its way to the park area. Sara, Harold, Olive, and friends walked the few blocks. The bandstand was right in the middle of the park, and music was already filling the air. The first group to play was the village band. They were playing a John Philip Sousa march as Sara's group entered the park.

Harold couldn't seem to contain himself. He smiled at Sara with a look that no one could resist and headed toward the bandstand. Sara's feet marched right along beside him, her small body and short legs marching double-time to the pace of his lanky torso and long legs.

After about ten minutes of enjoying listening to the band and hearing this handsome, white-haired man humming along to all the different parts, Sara's conscience prodded her to find Olive to see if she could help with anything. Sara wasn't sure how many miles she would have to walk to get from one end to the other, because the park was big.

The sun was feeling very good on her sun-starved body. *I think I'll walk the perimeter of the park until I find Olive.*

The first attraction she reached was the Taffy Pull. It was the booth of a mom-and-pop business that made all kinds of candy. That day they were selling only taffy, which they were making right at the park.

Sara remembered that sweet smell from fairs in the sixties. She stood for a few minutes, watching the couple as they put the taffy on a hook and pulled it back and forth until it was the right consistency. Then they placed it out on the counter and cut it into rectangular pieces. They wrapped each piece in wax paper.

She just had to try a piece, and she thought as she chewed, *The taste really brings back memories!*

In talking with the young couple, she learned that they were friends of Harold and Olive and that they went to their house once a week for a book club.

Next to the Taffy Pull was a pizza booth. Pizza was new in America in the fifties, so when Mr. Brent established Brentville, he made sure to bring along someone who knew how to make pizza. Thirty years later, the same family was still making pizza. Rocco and Maria were relaxing on lawn chairs, enjoying the pizza, while their boys were creating the secret recipes. Newcomers from the outside world had given them a few tips from recent changes in pizza making.

But really, Sara thought, *how much can you change and improve pizza?* She loved the smell and the taste, and she savored a piece as she walked to find Olive.

Being the animal lover she was, Sara was drawn to the next section. It was a fenced-in area with small animals—a perfect area for children. They were also offering pony rides.

Sara thought she caught sight of a young girl she'd taken care of at the hospital a few days before. The fourteen-year-old had been heavy on her heart and mind, since the teen had come in with abdominal pain and bleeding. After doing an internal examination, Sara had all kinds of questions, but the girl's parents were not about to answer any, and they would not allow the girl to be alone with Sara. The best she could do was send her home with some natural antibiotics and hope she would heal.

Sara decided to recheck the pony rides because she thought that was where she'd seen the girl. She didn't see her again, but she did see a man in charge of the pony rides who looked familiar to her. *I can't remember just where I've seen him, but I'll file it away in the back of my mind. I hope it will come to me.*

Just beyond the pony ride was a baseball field where the youngsters were warming up for a game. There were games for all ages scheduled throughout the day. Sara chatted with a few of her coworkers who had children playing.

Next in line was something comparable to the 4-H club Sara had been in as a child. Planting and growing food was a very important part of survival in Brentville, so the children were encouraged at quite a young age to learn all about the process and to help with it. Sara enjoyed looking at all the articles of clothing that they had made.

The more Sara talked with folks, the more she noticed that the children were also encouraged, while still very young, to think about what they would like to do in life. The medical, legal, dental, plumbing, storekeeping, and other professions and trades each had an active apprenticeship program that Mr. Brent had started so many years ago. He had made a big effort to bring in many books and teachers.

"Oh, there's a coin toss!" Sara delightedly exclaimed aloud. *How hopeful I was when I used to go to the fair and toss pennies, hoping they'd land in a dish.* Nostalgia swept over her as she remembered being twelve and running home to place dishes in a box—her first hope chest—that she had tucked away under her bed. She had kept a couple of her fair dishes with her dishes in the dining room. *Oh, how I miss my dining room!*

It had been an hour or so since she'd left Harold at the bandstand. *I need to stop my tour of the park and find Olive. She may need some help.*

Sara scooted through the middle of the park, landing just about on target. Harold, Olive, and six or so other couples were in charge of a desserts booth. Hank and his wife were there, and Sara was glad to know that Hank was a friend of Harold and Olive. She had gotten to know Hank at the hotel, as she waited on him for breakfast. Pies, cookies, squares, and other treats beckoned. Nearby was another booth with hamburgers and hot dogs, one booth that was a book swap and newspaper stand, and beyond that, a popcorn machine with popcorn and caramel corn. The enticing smells blended.

The Harvest Fair had started at ten and was to go until dusk. Then there would be entertainment and a bonfire. Almost everyone had brought a foldable wood-framed, canvas chair as well as a blanket, and planned to stay for the duration. It was an event most people anticipated and wouldn't miss. Arriving early to claim a place near the bandstand seemed crucial; everyone had scurried around in the morning, trying to find the best spot.

Olive asked Sara if she would mind going with Harold to the booth selling barbecued chicken to pick up some dinners for their group of friends. Sara was happy to have an excuse to be with Harold. She seemed to have adopted him as her dad and Olive as her mom. *Goodness knows, if there had ever been a time that I needed a mom and dad, it's now.*

Harold grabbed the wooden wagon and started pulling it toward the chicken. Sara ran to catch up. Seeing her over his shoulder, he slowed down a little.

"This is the best day," Sara said to him. A familiar, seductive aroma coming from the barbecued chicken reached her. "Harold, how do they make that sauce?"

He went into great detail about how they made it and about how it had first been created at Cornell University in Ithaca, New York.

"No wonder I recognized the aroma!" cried Sara. "My husband and I both did our undergraduate work at Cornell. This chicken recipe was used at many of our college backyard parties—oil, vinegar, salt, pepper, poultry seasoning, and egg—so simple and so good!"

At three, it was time for their late lunch. Sara had been helping Bob and Jan with the book swap and newspaper booth.

"I'm ready for some chicken," remarked Jan.

"Me too," answered Sara. "I've been getting whiffs of the meal ever since we brought it back," she said as she opened the white cardboard box. Two pieces of yummy chicken, mashed potato, gravy, and salad stopped the conversation for a while. They were all ready for a break, and they enjoyed the meal.

With no television and no news to listen to on the radio, many relied on reading to pass the time. The book swap booth turned out to be a very popular one. Even all the newspapers were bought. Granted, it was only news of the community, but Bob and Jan were creative writers. The villagers looked forward to sitting down with the fresh newspaper every Wednesday. Sara discovered that an elderly gentleman did an admirable job of creating cartoons, and everyone appreciated his humor.

Jan and Bob, who had a blanket laid out by the book swap booth, had two daughters: Donna, eight, and Marion, seven. The girls had just eaten their chicken, and Jan had persuaded them to rest for a while before running around the park with their friends. Jan had a little box of paper dolls out for them, but both the girls were lying on their backs, looking at the white puffy clouds.

"Oh, there's a horse," cried Donna. Marion spotted a puppy. There were just enough breezes to keep the cloud game interesting.

Sara remembered being enchanted and captivated by the clouds. *When I was eight, my imagination ran wild, seeing all those cloud figures in the sky. As much as I want to be back in Harleysville, I know everyone there today would be much too busy to be checking out the clouds. Life in my old world was so hectic, so very busy.*

Sara decided to catch a glimpse of the rest of the fair. There were pumpkins and apples for sale as well as crafts. There was even a booth where a family was making and selling musical instruments. *Amazing, the talents that come to the surface when there aren't so many other distractions clogging the mind.*

At five thirty, the booths were being disassembled. The big horse-drawn wagon would be around soon to pick everything up. The materials would all be left in front of the houses from which they had come. Tomorrow, each family would store it away until next year.

While helping to take down the booth, Sara came upon a few books that she thought she might read in her spare time, maybe even that night, when she tired of counting the church bells. One book, down at the bottom of a pile, was *The Screwtape Letters* by C. S. Lewis, and beneath it lay a Bible.

Crowds headed to the bandstand to find the spot they had staked out earlier in the day. Sara was nestled in with Olive, Harold, and a group of their friends. Some had children; some didn't. Sara looked around appreciatively. *How comforting to be included and accepted by this affectionate group.*

A huge bonfire had just been lit. It was far enough away to be safe but close enough to enjoy. Right ahead of her was the bandstand. There was an ensemble singing songs like "You are My Sunshine," "Mocking Bird Hill," "Up a Lazy River," and "The Tennessee Waltz." The people knew all the words and were singing along. Even the children knew every word.

After the bonfire, a couple of Sara's new friends walked her to her door. Sam followed her up the stairs to her room and went to sleep on the rug by her bed.

CHAPTER 6

A Meaningful Thanksgiving

Two more days until Thanksgiving. I told Olive I'd bring a couple of pumpkin pies. I'm working today and tomorrow, so I'll wait until Thanksgiving morning to do the baking. Crystal has a well-stocked kitchen and has canned her own pumpkins. That should work.

There's been a change in Crystal. It seems as though she's letting go of the concerns about Oliver. I wouldn't be surprised to see them getting engaged one of these days. The twins love him, and Crystal is becoming more dependent on him.

The church clock was counting out the hour as Sara walked to work. The seventh bell was chiming just as she opened the door to the hospital.

I like the seven-to-three shift. I meet more people and enjoy the walk home. Almost everyone's out on porches at that time of day. It's early enough for me to stop to visit a little. If I were asked, "Which is your favorite stop?" I'd immediately answer, "It's with Harold and Olive."

The hospital was busy. Most Brentville citizens knew who Sara was, and she was beginning to put names with the faces.

There was another fourteen-year-old girl in that day with her parents. Sara could tell she wanted to talk and to answer Sara's questions, but her parents would have nothing to do with that. They made sure they didn't leave the girl alone with her. So once more, all Sara could do was to put the girl on the natural antibiotics, tell her to rest, and encourage her to come back if she needed more help.

If I were back in my world, I'd be reporting these cases to the authorities. But, here in Brentville, who can I trust? She carried a heavy heart for these girls. *And if there are babies involved, where are they?*

Crystal and Oliver were on a date, and Sara was holding down the fort. The dinner dishes were all put away, and Sam had been walked. Remembering the Bible that she'd picked up at the fair, she ran upstairs to get it.

Sitting down on Crystal's sofa, she decided to look it over. There had been one Bible in Sara's old world, but she had never opened it. She had been too busy and felt no need for it.

It's probably sitting on the shelf in my lovely home in Harleysville, Pennsylvania, right now.

Opening the Bible to Genesis, Sara started reading, "In the beginning..."

Though she had been wondering about God lately, she wasn't getting too much from those first few pages. Soon she was nodding off. She finally closed the book and wrapped herself in the afghan that Crystal had made.

Bible in her lap, Sara awoke only when Crystal and Oliver came into the room.

Sara plodded through work on Wednesday, stopping in to chat with Harold on her way home. She had seen a Bible in Harold's house that looked used and worn, so she made mention of her new purchase. Harold looked at her with an approving smile. "Nothing like the Good Book," he commented.

It was Thursday morning, and Thanksgiving was upon her. Sara's morning was busy. Not having made pies in a while, she had to wrack her brain to remember how to make the crust and the exact measurements for the filling.

Sara finally found an old *Better Homes and Gardens Cook Book*. Every kitchen in Brentville was said to have one. *How could I miss it with that red-and-white-checked cover? It's just like my own copy and the one Mom had.*

A couple of hours later, two pumpkin pies were baking, and the kitchen smelled like Thanksgiving. She'd also made a tiny little pie for tasting. *Just to be sure it is acceptable.* Sara smiled.

Before leaving for Harold and Olive's home, she took a bite of the cooled little pie. Memories of her Thanksgivings with her family engulfed her. It was almost more than she could bear. Her tears overflowed, so Sara was grateful to be alone in the inn. Feelings of defeat and surrender overwhelmed her. *Who would have thought that a little piece of pie could do this?* The floodgates were opened.

Sara found her way to the den, closed the door, and sat down on the sofa. Noticing the Bible that she'd left there, she picked it up and held it. "Oh, God," she cried, "I don't know you, but if you're really there, I need you." That's all she could say. No fancy words—just "Help! I need you."

Sara was unaware of the length of time she spent in that room. It was the first time in her life she'd surrendered to something other than herself. She was realizing that she could not handle life with her strength alone.

Sam had climbed up onto the couch and was licking her tears away. "I know," said Sara. "I know you care." Sam's tail started to wag. "Your tail is definitely attached to your heart," Sara said as he rested his head on her lap.

The church bell began chiming two. *It's time to meet at Harold's!* Sara splashed cold water on her face and changed into a cheerful-looking red dress. She placed the pies into her wagon, called Sam, and they were off.

Because of the way Harold and Olive looked at her, Sara knew they'd both noticed her red, swollen eyes as she'd come through the door. Giving Sara a hug, Olive quietly asked if she was okay. Sara nodded and said she would talk about it later. Right then, she knew it was time for everyone to celebrate Thanksgiving. She didn't want to be a wet blanket, and she was glad to be a part of their day.

Sam's twitching nose hinted that he appreciated the food smells. There seemed to be quite a few children there. The crumbs would be falling soon, and Sam would be a very grateful dog. His would be a happy Thanksgiving.

As she carried her pies to the dessert table, Sara noticed she was acquainted with almost everyone present. There were eight couples and ten children.

She was the only woman without a husband, but the women were all busy getting the meal ready, and the men, when not asked to help, were relaxing in the living room and on the porch. Harold led what they called the Porch Game on the veranda. Some of the men were attempting to impress the others with the number of times they could get the ring—attached to some kind of fishing line—over the hook on the opposite corner of the porch. It was a game Harold's father had played when he was in the Pacific during World War II.

Sara had become pretty adept at this game. Most of her stops to chat included a try or two with the ring game. The clang of the ring going down over the hook was music to her ears.

Olive had baskets of nuts and nutcrackers out on the porch. In the living room, she had dishes of dates and figs, candy and nuts. Sara was amazed at the food that was grown in the area. She'd learned that there were heated, covered areas where they grew produce that would usually be found only in warmer climates. Keeping the greenhouses up and going was a very important industry for Brentville. Having supervisors in charge of the gardens and the canning industry, and having others in charge of planting and nurturing trees, provided important jobs.

Olive's now-crowded kitchen was full of good aromas. All the dessert creations were in dishes on the small table where Sara had already placed her pies. The pots and pans containing turkey, gravy, and mashed potatoes were on the stove. Squash, green beans, gelatin salad, lettuce salad, cranberries, and pickles were in bowls on the countertops.

In the living room were enough tables and chairs so that everyone could sit. What a feast! Sam, wise dog, was under the children's table.

After Harold had thanked God for the nourishment they were about to enjoy, everyone took a plate to the kitchen to fill it with the wonderful food Olive had so beautifully arranged. It was a gathering of people from all walks of life. They all seemed to care genuinely for each other—and for Sara.

Oscar and his wife were sitting by Sara. He was the young man who had the gas station and the repair shop that she'd visited that first night. Now she learned a little more about them. Sharon, his young wife, was a teacher. Before they'd landed in Brentville, Sharon had taught for two years in a grammar school. Sara was guessing the couple to be in their early thirties, and they had been there ten years. Sharon was now teaching at the Brentville Grammar School.

When Sara glanced out the front window, she noticed four old-fashioned ice-cream makers covered with newspaper. Olive told her that the ice cream was just sitting there in the corner of the porch, hardening—waiting to be eaten. "I prepared it last night and had it waiting in my refrigerator. Then, as the children gathered this morning, I had them help me layer the ice and the salt around the container with the ice cream in it. Then I assigned them turns at rotating the handle until the ice cream was firm and the handle couldn't be turned anymore. Next was the goody that the kids eagerly awaited. I pulled the paddles from the middle of the containers—covered with thick ice cream. I put them on a dish out on the back picnic table. All ten children—even the two-year-old—went running, with spoon in hand, to taste-test this treat. Then I put the cover back on the containers, added more ice around the container, and covered the whole thing with newspapers, leaving it to harden—or ripen, as they say."

Almost everyone had finished eating. Some went back for seconds, but Sara was content to have had a delicious meal shared with good companions. And she wanted to save room for one piece of pie and a scoop of that ice cream.

Everyone wanted Harold to play his piano. It was a very special part of the day. All were happy and ready to relax. Harold played for a while, and the faces in the group showed how much they appreciated it. Then he played a few songs with which most sang along.

Maybe these are hymns, Sara thought, since she heard the words *Lord* and *God* in them. Never having been a churchgoer, she didn't know. She did recognize "Amazing Grace" and joined in on that one.

After the singing, the children gathered into little groups to play. There were boxes of paper dolls for the girls. One table had been cleared for a puzzle. Four children were enjoying a Monopoly game set out on the floor in a corner of the living room. The adults sat and chatted. The perishables had been put away. And the pies were in serving dishes on the dining-room table, but so far, everyone was too full to think about dessert.

Before everybody left, most prepared a turkey sandwich. Olive had made numerous loaves of her scrumptious homemade white bread, and it was all sliced and ready to go.

Sara was on the sofa talking with David and Mary. Olive was in the chair next to them.

"How are you doing?" Olive asked Sara.

"Okay," she replied, "although I had some bad moments before coming to your house. I've never felt so down—and overwhelmed. I even cried out to God. I cried out for help. I don't know God, or even if there is one, but I did call to him."

Mary heard the despair in Sara's answer, reached over, and put her arm around Sara's shoulder. "There is a God, and he loves you, Sara. He knows you and wants you to know him. You have taken that first step. You are crying out to him." She added, "I would love to meet with you once a week to help you get to know him."

Touched by Mary's caring way, Sara replied, "I would be delighted to do that." They decided that Saturday afternoon would work for both of them and that they would meet at Mary's house.

Sara's first Thanksgiving in Brentville had been better than she expected. And, for the first time ever, she had a very real desire to learn about God. Sara drifted off to sleep with a newfound glimmer of hope.

She didn't hear the church clock once until it was chiming six. She was grateful to hear it, because she had forgotten to wind her alarm clock, and she needed to be at the hospital by seven.

CHAPTER 7

Surrendering

I'm glad I have only this one day to work before the weekend. I don't really understand it, but I'm looking forward to my appointment with Mary on Saturday afternoon. Since experiencing her time of surrendering the day before, Sara's spirits were a little lighter. *That tiny ray of hope seems to be growing in my heart.*

Crystal had honored her request for scrubs, and Sara was wearing them for the first time. She was already receiving some attention because of her outfit. Though not formfitting, the scrubs fit well enough to show off her fit body. The pink color complemented her tanned skin and her braided blond hair.

Sara had no more than walked through the door when two or three of her coworkers noticed the scrubs and wanted to know where they could get some. In her office, a few more people asked the same question.

Until then, in Brentville Memorial, the nurses and doctors had all worn white coats and white uniforms. Everyone knew of Sara and of the fact that she had not been away from her world for very long. They all wanted to try out the new fashion. Sara couldn't wait to tell Crystal that she had an idea for a new little business for her. She thought, *It will be a great way for Crystal to earn some extra money. I can envision it spreading to the dental offices as well.*

That day started slowly at Memorial. Sore throats, a couple of cases of chickenpox, and then, at around one o'clock, Sara was treating the young girl who had been in the previous week. She was quite weak.

"I think you need to be in the hospital today," Sara told her. "I believe you'll need to have a D&C."

The girl's mother had come with her, and Sara could tell that she was very worried. When the mother agreed to the procedure, Sara called for help to get the operating room ready. She was afraid that if she didn't do it right away, the mom would change her mind.

Sara was supposed to leave at three but stayed with the girl until she was settled in her room. Sara knew that the mother would be in a hurry to get her daughter away from any questions that might lead to the truth about what had happened to her child.

Sitting with this young girl, Sara made a pledge to herself that she would somehow get to the bottom of this mystery. *There is something going on in Brentville that is very wrong. I'm not sure yet who might be involved in it, but this girl is definitely a victim of whatever it is.*

On the Saturday mornings when Sara didn't work at the hospital, she helped Crystal change sheets, bake, do the wash, and hang clothes on the line.

Wringer washer

On that particular morning, Sara was down in the cellar doing some wash in the wringer washer. It had taken a while for her to get a routine going, but now she felt herself to be quite the expert. There were eight long clotheslines strung up in the cellar. During winter and stormy weather, all the clothes were to be hung there. Crystal told Sara stories about when the twins were small and of how she'd brought many a frozen diaper in from the outside lines and bent them over the radiators to dry.

Despite the laundry setup's antiquity, it had been well planned. There were two big sinks with good drains, and the washing machine was sitting between them. The clean water was easy to get. The dirty water went right into one of the sinks. After she fed the clothes into the wringer, they dropped into a big wicker basket. Shaking each washed piece, whether it was a blouse, tea towel, or sheet, was important. Sara had learned that the hard way. Much less ironing was required when she shook them first.

Crystal also showed her the little tricks for hanging clothes, arranging them on the line so they would get better aeration, for example. Sara smiled as she remembered Crystal showing her the ropes.

Carrying the clothes to the clothesline was a job in itself, usually requiring two or three trips up and down the cellar stairs. The weather was sunny, with crisp air and a little breeze, so by afternoon, the clothes would be ready to be taken down and folded.

Sara's appointment with Mary was set for two. The day before, she had stopped at the gas station to find a map of Brentville. Someone had made one, and Jan and Bob had printed it off and distributed it to the gas stations. Sara was used to finding free maps of the different states in gas stations. There she found only one map—a map of Brentville.

Looking at it, Sara figured that it would probably take her twenty minutes or so to reach Mary's place. It was on the other side of the village, just across the big river. Sara grabbed her new wool jacket, and with map and Bible in hand, she headed for the bike. Harold had put a basket on it so she could easily carry books and other items. He took very good care of her bike yet never charged her. He did the same for most of the youth in Brentville. They all called him Grandpa Turner.

How fortunate I am to have Harold and Olive in my life.

As she rode her bike to Mary's, she recalled her first visit to Harold's house—how he'd asked in an almost bashful way if she would like to look around. *They're a very humble couple. I couldn't imagine them bragging or even wanting to.*

The little house was beautiful. There was one room where Harold kept all his clocks. It seemed he hadn't met a clock yet that he couldn't fix.

There was a piano in the living room. The kitchen and dining room were well stocked, furnished, and decorated to Olive's liking. She said she loved having guests, and they entertained at least once a week.

The most interesting and somehow exciting thing Sara saw on that first visit was Harold's shed—or as they called it, his house. It was his little hideaway, a place where he could go to be quiet, to read his Bible, and to write poems and songs.

Harold's shed

It was just a tiny building out behind the flower gardens, but when Harold built it, he'd added good insulation. In it was a wood stove, a typewriter table with a typewriter on it, an old wooden chair that he used when he did his typing, a small piano, and a cot. A bookshelf and a few musical instruments hung on one wall. It was the perfect spot for him, a place where he could be still—and be Harold.

It's nice to have a place to just be, thought Sara.

As she rode her bike over the bridge, she decided she should start paying attention. *No more reminiscing.* The map indicated that Mary's house was coming up soon. One turn left, and she was at 714 Washington Street.

The wind was blowing just the right way, so she could hear the church clock. Funny that no matter where she was, she always knew what time it was. *Right on time: two o'clock.*

Mary's house looked a lot like all the others, but Sara was sure that Mary would have added her little personal touches to make it her own.

Mary had told Sara a little about herself and David. *Let's see what I remember. They're both in their thirties. They've been in Brentville for around ten years. When they entered Brentville, they were traveling to a church to work with its minister and laypeople regarding a mission project. Needing gas, they left the highway and drove through that gate, never to return to their old life.*

The couple had arrived in a Winnebago that was loaded with Bibles, Bible study books, a printer, paper, pens and pencils, and other useful items. Some of those things Sara would soon be using to help her in her study of the Bible. The young couple had dedicated their lives to serving the Lord and had accepted the place in which they'd found themselves as being part of God's plan for them.

Number 714 was an attractive gray house with yellow trim. There was a bike rack just off the side of the front steps. Sara was reaching out to knock on the yellow door when Mary yelled from across the street.

Sara sat down in the white wicker rocking chair on the big front porch and watched Mary as she ran to join her. "Hi there," said Mary as she opened her arms to Sara and gave her a hug. "So glad you're here. I've just come from my neighbor Susan's house. She's ill. When I phoned to ask what I could bring her, she wanted some of my homemade soup. I was happy to know what I could take to her. Come on in. I'll show you around."

When Mr. Brent had arrived in the fifties, he had contracted to have the houses built. They all had hardwood floors. Many of the kitchen countertops were covered with tiles or linoleum—no quartz or marble, which Sara's home in Harleysville had. The kitchen floors and the bathroom floors were linoleum or tile. Apparently, most of the homes had the original wool rugs over a good portion of the hardwood floors.

In the fifties, Mr. Brent had all the furniture shipped in after they had the houses built. The men and the trucks that delivered all the goods never left. Thirty years later, in the cases that Sara had seen, the furniture and the houses were still in pristine condition. Mary's was no exception.

Sara was once again finding it interesting to see how each person made his or her house look a little different.

Mary offered Sara a cup of tea. "Thanks," answered Sara. "I didn't realize it was this cold. Guess I'll need mittens soon."

Mary and Sara sat and talked for a few minutes. Then Mary said, "Why don't I tell you my story? I would love to hear about you too."

"I never attended church as a child," Mary said. "My dad was an atheist and an alcoholic. My mom was too afraid of him to go to church. But when I was in college, a friend got me involved in Campus Crusade.[1] It was there that I realized a need to have God in my life. And there I met my husband, David. He had been a Christian since he was a little boy, and he had such a heart for missions! He became interested in becoming a minister in college."

Then she sighed. "I just knew that I had a big hole in my heart. I tried to fill it with many things—alcohol, cigarettes, sugar, work, and people pleasing, to name a few. By the time I was nineteen, I'd realized that nothing was working. Nothing satisfied. I always needed more. I called what I had The Disease of More. When my friend asked me if I wanted to meet Jesus, I was ready.

"My friend explained to me how God cannot tolerate our sin and that God sent us his son, Jesus, who died on a cross for me and for you, to atone for our sins. She told me, 'He gave his life so that you can live. By asking him for forgiveness and asking him into your life, you are saved—saved from hell. She also said, 'You will spend the rest of your life on earth with him, and you will be in heaven with him when you die. That's a promise!'

"I was so ready. I went immediately to my knees and asked Jesus into my life. Soon after that, I met David. He had two more years left in seminary. I had one year until I would graduate with my bachelor's degree. As soon as I graduated, we were married, and the rest is history.

"My life isn't totally free of problems, but it is free of worry. I have a heavenly Father who is always with me. He will always take care of me. What a magnificent promise to be able to count on!"

Sara didn't know what she'd expected Mary to say, but it wasn't that. She sighed. "I never really thought about God until I got to Brentville. I was a strong person and always seemed to be able to do things for myself and by myself. I've always tried to be good, to do the right thing. So, because of that, if there was a God and a heaven, I guess I thought I would end up there with him."

She continued, "On Thanksgiving morning, I *did* cry out to God. I didn't know him, but I knew that if he was there, I needed him. I wanted to know him."

Tears were rolling down Sara's cheeks. First Mary handed Sara a handkerchief then used another one to wipe her own eyes. "Sara, would you like me to pray with you?" whispered Mary. Sara nodded and buried her face in her handkerchief. "Dear Lord," Mary said softly, "I come to you today with my friend Sara. You know that she needs you and wants you in her life. Even though she is a good person, you tell us in your Bible that we are all sinners. We know that even a bad thought is a sin in your eyes, Lord. We know we all need you, Jesus. Please hear Sara now. Give her your Holy Spirit so she can understand and love you. In Jesus's name. Amen."

Sara joined in. "Please forgive me, God, for all the wrong things I have done and said and thought. I want to be your child. Amen."

Sara dried her eyes again and thanked Mary.

"Did you say that you have a Bible, Sara?"

"Yes."

"Then why don't you read the Gospel of John this week?" Mary said. "Read it through and then through again if you want to. We'll meet again next Saturday afternoon, and we can talk about it."

It was after four and would soon be getting dark. Sara said her good-byes and jumped on her bike to head back over the bridge to the hotel. *I just need to be by myself tonight.*

Sara stopped to say hi to Crystal, ordered some dinner to take to her room, and said her early good night to the twins.

Sara slumped in the big overstuffed chair by the bed, where she ate the chicken noodle casserole and salad, drank her tea, and got ready for bed.

Crawling into bed, she opened the Bible to the Gospel of John. She didn't stop reading until she'd finished reading it. She closed the Bible, turned off her light, and slept all night. No bells disturbed her sleep.

CHAPTER 8

The Book Club

Sara's mind was full of questions. Her once-a-week study with Mary was helping, and she couldn't wait to get to her Bible every night after dinner. She was learning of God's wonder-filled grace.

It's so hard to understand that Jesus's death on the cross is for me—me individually—not just for others. God loves me so much that he gave Jesus. Jesus died for my *sins. I've never thought much about my sin. I've been doing good things. I've believed that God—if there was a God—would take that into consideration when I died. I've been so unaware.*

My time with Mary and my reading the Bible is making it clear that God can't tolerate sin. The Bible shows me that sin in God's eyes can be anything from a bad thought to murder. I've not murdered anyone, but I've certainly had some bad thoughts!

So, Jesus is the bridge I've had to cross to get to God, to be saved from the hell of eternal separation from God. It's so amazing! As soon as I asked God to be in my life and asked him to forgive my sins, I was saved. It has been done.

Mary explained that, as God promises, he has given me his Holy Spirit. That must be the reason I now have such a thirst for the Bible. It must also be why I'm starting to understand more of what I'm reading.

Sara was very happy to be in that incomparable place of grace. She was feeling God's presence and was filled with His peace. She was just beginning to understand and appreciate that this plan of salvation in which God, in his goodness, had included her, was the best and biggest gift she would ever receive.

On Saturday morning, Sara tiptoed out of the maternity ward. There were six babies, and they were all sleeping. "See you tomorrow," she whispered. *There seems to be no shortage of babies in Brentville—just another way in which Mr. Brent's plan seems to be working.*

Next Sara wanted to check on Lucy, her young patient from the day before. As she went around the corner, she could see Room 4. She had placed Lucy in it because it was near her office. She'd thought maybe she could keep better track of her.

As she approached the room, a man was leaving. He moved like one in his forties or fifties, but she couldn't see his face. He was hurrying toward the back door.

Entering Lucy's room, Sara could see that she was upset. Her face was tear-streaked. As she handed Lucy a tissue, Sara was struck with the severity of the situation. She could see that her life in Brentville was not only to be as a doctor; she also needed to be Chief Detective Sara Saunders. *That's a sign I can't hang on my door! I need to be very quiet about my self-appointed additional position. I also need to rely on all my instincts and experience.*

The good news was that Lucy was physically doing much better—no fever, and all her vitals were good. Sara gave the nurses orders to discharge Lucy later in the day.

The church bell struck the half-hour chime as she walked home from work. *Must be three thirty.*

As she turned the corner to Harold's street, she caught a glimpse of him sitting in his swing. The mums in his yard were still beautiful, and the leaves had turned a brilliant red. Many had fallen from the trees. *There are little leaf piles on the lawn. Harold has been raking.* Sara plunked herself down across from him in the swing and said, "I hope you know how much you mean to me. I always look forward to this time of the day when we can sit and chat. I dread having the cold weather come. Soon it will be too cold to be sitting out on your swing."

"We do have a nice warm house," Harold responded with a chuckle. "We hope you'll stop in every day." His blue eyes had a way of drawing a person in, especially when he smiled.

Sara was filled with gratitude as she thought about how much this gentleman and his affectionate wife had come to mean to her. *Yes, they've definitely become my Brentville Mom and Dad.*

Sara and Harold sat in the swing, gliding slowly back and forth. "You know," Harold said, "having God in my life has happified my world. Yes, I've been truly happified."

Sara looked at Harold and smiled. *I love the way he uses all those old-fashioned expressions. I might have to look this one up in my trusty dictionary. Perhaps he invented it. It's a good word, regardless.*

Harold's eyes were not smiling as he broached the next subject. "I think, Sara, that it's time to tell you of our secret church. As we've discussed before, the church in Brentville is very liberal. The gospel of Jesus is never heard, and the Bible is not believed to be the true Word of God. We've heard some worrisome rumors about the church, but up to this point have not been able to verify them.

"You might wonder why we feel the need to keep our church a secret. The answer is Mr. Brent. He wants only one church in Brentville, and he wants to be the leader. Our secret church consists of about eighty Brentville residents. We meet in small groups at members' homes on different nights, so as not to raise suspicion.

"We meet under the guise of book clubs. If neighbors inquire, we just say we're hosting a book club. In truth, it is *The Book* club, and Mary and Jim are in charge. They help plan what all the different houses are doing. We have different leaders at each home."

Sara sat very still as she listened to Harold. In fact, she was hardly breathing. She didn't want to miss a word.

"We meet at seven thirty in the evening. Most ride bikes in the summer," continued Harold. "In the winter, we bundle up and walk. We try to keep each meeting place as near to a member's home as we can. When night comes in the winter, it can be pretty cold to be out walking.

"We keep each group's membership to about twenty. We meet once a week, and every month we try to get all eighty members together somewhere."

Harold seemed to be trying to read Sara's face to see whether or not he should continue. He thought he knew that he could trust her not to share the secret, but he didn't seem to know how much he should give her at one sitting.

Even though Sara and Harold were wearing jackets, the nippy air was starting to affect them. Olive stood at the door with a cup of tea in her hand, waving them in. Her cheery flowered apron was a good indication that she must have been in the kitchen, preparing dinner.

"Come on in," invited Olive. "Can you eat supper with us, Sara? We'd love to have you."

As soon as Sara entered the house, she was taken by the aroma of something baking in the oven. *It must taste really scrumptious!* Sitting in the swing with Harold, she had been getting whiffs of it. *How can I say no? I can't.*

A few hours later, Sara was thanking her friends for the meal and for trusting her enough to include her in the book club.

"Your club meets on Friday nights. That's tomorrow! I'm looking forward to meeting everyone then," Sara warmly exclaimed.

Later, as she sat in her room with her Bible and her questions for her Saturday study, she decided to answer a couple of questions. Then, feeling tired and ready for sleep, she put her Bible by her chair. She got ready for bed, said good night to Sam, who had settled on the rug by her bed, and crawled between the soft sheets. *No counting clock chimes tonight.* With her head on her pillow, she thanked God for an overwhelmingly satisfying day. She was sleeping before she could say amen.

CHAPTER 9

A Unique Church Experience

Friday night had arrived—time for Sara to have her first church experience with Harold and Olive. She had been looking forward to it. *I want to be around others who believe as I do now. There's so much I want to know—so many questions. There's so much excitement bubbling up in my soul!*

Mary had explained that God fills the God-shaped hole that all have in their hearts. Sara had admitted that, before this, she had tried to fill that space with work and busyness, attempting to control things on her own.

Sam seemed to go everywhere with Sara. As they strolled along the well-lit sidewalk, she looked at him. His eyes returned her glance. She felt such comfort, knowing Sam was by her side, paying attention to what was going on. He was her trusted friend.

Sara and Sam walked up the steps of the Turners' house. She gave a couple of taps on the door, and they walked in. She guessed around fifteen participants were there. Apparently only a few more were expected. As usual, Olive's house smelled inviting. There always seemed to be something baking in the oven; that night was no exception.

Group members gathered around to welcome Sara—some she knew and some were new faces. *More names to learn.* Sara jotted a few of them in her notebook. The chairs were arranged in a semicircle, allowing everyone a view of Harold's piano.

There were some handmade hymnbooks that Harold had put together. He'd included a lot of hymns from hymnbooks the missionaries had brought when they'd arrived in their van and some hymns that Harold had composed.

The first song they sang was "What a Friend We Have in Jesus."[2] Reading the words and singing along, Sara was moved to tears. Thinking about how Jesus had died on a cross for her reminded her of what he had been through. *Anything I might go through, he'll certainly understand, because of his own suffering. Now I know I can talk with him about anything. No appointment needed—just call out his name.*

After the first hymn, everyone settled down in a chair with a Bible and a notebook in hand. There were a few announcements. A collection was taken. Harold explained to Sara that the money was offered to the host for the evening, to cover any expenses incurred. If the host didn't want it, the money was put into a fund for anyone who ran into hard times.

They sang another hymn. The new-to-her songs touched Sara's freshly softened heart.

One of the announcements caught her attention, and she made a note to ask Harold or Olive about it later. A committee was being formed within the Bible study group to look into some rumors about a few of the Brentville church members. *I wonder if this will shed some light on the mystery I've run into at the hospital.*

William, a slim, gentle man, was the leader for the evening. He'd taken his place just behind the piano, which he used as his podium. He set his notes and Bible on the top of it.

"Hi, folks," his baritone voice greeted them. "Tonight we're beginning the study of Matthew. Please open your Bibles to Matthew."[3]

William asked a young brunette woman to read the entire first chapter aloud. Then he led them back to reading verse by verse, talking about and explaining what each verse meant. Even though Sara had to look in the index of the Bible to find the different books of the Bible, she was sure she was going to like this kind of church. Harold had told her that this was called expository teaching. She loved it already.

As soon as the church time was finished, Harold practically scampered downstairs to the cellar to get some Limburger cheese. Sara learned later that it was a playful thing the men did on occasion, so that the strong odor would make the women go crazy. He placed it on a cutting board, put a few crackers in a serving bowl, and located the mustard.

Laying it all out on the table, Harold waited for the reaction. With a twinkle in his eye, he asked, "Would anyone like some cheese and crackers?"

Most of the men wanted a piece. Sara was told that some of the children were learning to like it too.

Dorothy, the woman who had read the Bible chapter aloud, said, "It's almost like a passage into adulthood for the children. If they come to like it, the men clap and carry on, and the kids feel very important. As you see, most of us women run to another room, holding our noses." Sara discovered that, though the cheese came out periodically, dessert and tea were always served after the service.

At nine, participants were beginning to leave. Group members left quietly, no more than two or three left at one time. *I don't quite understand all the fuss about being secretive, but I know it's important, so I will definitely follow the rules.*

At nine thirty, Sara and Sam hurried along. The ten o'clock curfew would be sounding soon. At ten, the police force would be out on their horses, riding up and down the streets, looking for lawbreakers who dared to be out past curfew. Though she hadn't been there long, Sara had heard stories about citizens being put in Brentville's large jail because they stayed out after curfew time. Sara didn't care to spend the night there.

It was nine forty-five when Sara and Sam arrived at the hotel. All the lights were still on. Even though Sara was anxious to get into bed and read as much of the book of Mathew as she could, she also wanted to say good night to Crystal.

Hearing her in the kitchen, Sara plopped her book bag down on the stairs and hurried to join her there. Crystal was preparing for the morning crowd. She seemed to be in a world of her own. Coming closer, Sara noticed a brilliant diamond ring on Crystal's left hand.

"Oh, Crystal!" squealed Sara. "What is this?"

Dreamy-eyed, Crystal looked at Sara. "Isn't it gorgeous?"

"I'm so happy for you!" exclaimed Sara. "Let me look at that ring. Wow, it's perfect."

"The ring belonged to Oliver's grandmother." Crystal was happy and excited. She wanted to talk. Sara pulled up a chair, and the chatting began.

A few hours later, Sara knew Crystal's heart and plans. Crystal had finally given up hope of ever getting out of Brentville.

She truly does seem to be in love with Oliver. He's a fine young man, and he seems to love the twins. Crystal is young; she deserves a full life. She deserves a husband who loves her, a husband who will help her and be her partner in every aspect of life.

Even though Sara was happy for Crystal, she felt a twinge of jealousy. *How I miss Jim, my lover, my companion, my best friend. I could never marry again. I just couldn't. I will never give up hope!*

Dropping into bed, Sara was too exhausted to read Matthew. *Sorry, God. I will read your book first thing tomorrow. I can't wait to find out more about you.*

Saturday morning, Sara awoke rested and happy. As she rolled over in bed, she felt her Bible under her ribs. She propped herself up with Crystal's hand-embroidered pillows to read the whole book of Matthew.

Once she had completed her reading, she helped Crystal with the Saturday chores. Then it was time to go to Mary's for their Bible study time. God had placed a thirst in her for his truth, so Sara wanted to know everything she could. She wanted to know God, Jesus, and the Holy Spirit.

The love that was growing in her heart for Jesus wasn't something she could explain, but she knew Mary, Harold, Olive, and all the other friends at their church felt that same love. She was beginning to realize how important it was to be surrounded by like-minded people.

"Come on in," waved Mary at the door. She was another safe person in Sara's life. Her home was a warm and welcoming place to be.

That week Mary had Sara learning and studying the prophecies about Jesus Christ. She taught her how fulfilled prophecy helps verify the fact that Jesus is the son of God. "All those prophecies preceded Jesus by hundreds of years. The ways in which Jesus fulfilled them show the authenticity of Jesus," Mary summed up.

"Mary," Sara sighed, "given the fact that I had never even opened a Bible, I'm in awe of how God is calling me to him. I am so humbled."

When the lesson was finished, Sara asked Mary, "Can you shed any light on what was said at the church meeting regarding the Brentville church?"

"Well," said Mary, "starving people do desperate things. I doubt that many in that church know Christ as we know him. They aren't people who love God as you now do. The church is a social club, filled with those who are starving for Christ, but they don't know it. Some are seeking to satisfy that hunger with things that are bad.

"We believe that a few of the men in the church are doing things they would never do if they had God in their lives," continued Mary. "I think it's safe to say that very few of the Brentville church members have a Bible or believe it to be true. They don't know, or love, Jesus. Therefore, the few bad men are able to spread their lies as truths.

"We believe that this darkness that is being encouraged is in a growing sect and is not seen directly in the Brentville church; but small groups are popping up around the community, made up of members gathered from the Brentville Church. "We think that there is some kind of satanic movement happening. Our committee has been looking into it for a while now, but we have no proof. Even if we had proof, we're not sure how we would handle it."

Mary continued, "Mr. Brent may know about this activity and may even be at the head of it—or he may know nothing about it. We just don't know who to trust, and until we do, we're treading very carefully."

"Thanks for your honesty," said Sara. "I would love to be on that committee. I have questions of my own. Things I have run across with my patients at the hospital have me concerned."

Chief Inspector Dr. Sara Saunders had just gone from wondering to being on high alert. Her antenna was up as far as it could go.

"Be careful," warned Mary. "Remember, we don't know who is trustworthy."

Sara waved good-bye to David, who had just finished mowing the lawn with an old-fashioned manual lawn mower. *Brentville has a lawn service that's included in our taxes. I guess David isn't happy with the way they do it, or maybe he likes the exercise and feeling of accomplishment. Mary and David have adjusted so well to their life here in Brentville. They're a perfect example of what it is to trust in the Lord.*

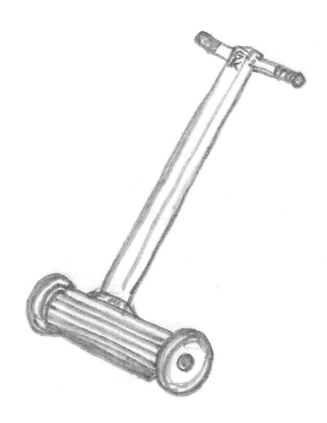

Manual lawnmower

CHAPTER 10

Wedding Plans

Crystal told Sara that she and Oliver had decided to have a Christmas wedding. Actually, it would be on Christmas Eve. Crystal's romantic side had taken over. Her starry eyes were picturing a candlelight wedding with horse-drawn sleighs to transport the wedding guests.

She was already sewing the dress created from the design she had sketched and made into a pattern. The twins and Sam would be wearing the outfits that Crystal had already made. Sara was to be maid of honor, but Crystal still needed to meet with her to measure and produce a pattern.

Crystal asked Harold to give her away. The reception would be at the Brent mansion, and it would be a grand night. There would be six or seven horse-drawn sleighs lined up to take guests from the church to the mansion and back. Maggie would be a part of this wedding. To most in the community, Mr. Brent was seen as royalty, and being invited to the mansion was almost unheard of.

There was not much time left; it was already the first week in December. But Crystal seemed to have an aura of calm around her. She said that Maggie and Mr. Brent were doing all the reception planning and preparation. The Brentville church was available at six thirty on Christmas Eve. Crystal's favorite singer would be there to sing a solo. Everything seemed to be coming together.

Sara found her mind wandering. *Too bad it's not summer. Crystal could have had the twins catch fireflies for the wedding. Sitting out on the back porch of the hotel on summer evenings is a favorite pastime for the family. Seeing the fireflies twinkling at night is magical. I've heard that the male twinkles to the female and then she twinkles back. The kids also could have hung some jars of those glowing fireflies around on the trees.*

Oh well, snow is good too. Gently falling snowflakes and candlelight can be very romantic.

Am I actually feeling relaxed enough to think of fun and such trivial things? The heavy heart that before thought only of my old life, escape, and hospital problems is being lifted—lifted right into God's loving arms.

"Where will you go on your honeymoon?" Sara asked suddenly. She had just realized that there was really no getting away from Brentville, no flying off to a warm beach somewhere.

Crystal put her arm around Sara's shoulder and smiled. "Don't worry. We have it all worked out. Oliver's mom has a cabin on Lake Brent. It's winterized and has a good wood stove. We thought we'd spend a few days there. His mom has offered to take care of the twins. By the way, would you be willing to take Sam?"

"For sure," answered Sara. "You know I love being with Sam."

The dinner crowd had come and gone. The hotel was almost empty. Sara helped to get the dishes done and the preparations for the next day completed.

"I think I'll close the hotel for a couple of weeks around my wedding time," said Crystal. "Maybe the week before and the week after."

"Good idea," said Sara. "You'll need it."

"Oliver has decided to move in with us so I can keep running the hotel," said Crystal.

"I've been thinking," Sara mused. "It may be time for me to get my own house. It's something that's available to me now that I'm considered a citizen here. I wanted to stay with you until I got my feet on the ground. Now I feel that I have been in Brentville long enough to be able to make it on my own. Being here with you has helped me survive. You will always be my family, but you and Oliver need your space, and I should be finding mine too."

Crystal looked surprised.

Sara understood. *Other than Oliver, I've become the most important adult in Crystal's life. I'm her very best friend, and she'll miss me. I'll miss her. But if Crystal thinks about it, she'll realize she and Oliver need their own space. And it isn't as though I'll be moving far away.*

"I will miss having you here, Sara. The twins will too. And by the way, I learned today that Sam is going to be a father. Do you remember Julie? Well, her dog, Sissy, and Sam were together a while ago. We were hoping it would work out that puppies might come from the encounter. Julie just told me today that I'll be getting half the litter. Now that you're planning to get your own home, would you like one of the puppies? Or maybe you'd rather have Sam."

The generous offer overwhelmed Sara. She jumped to her feet in excitement, gave Crystal a hug, and thanked her for her kindness. "I would love to have Sam."

Sara had become so attached to Sam and he to her that she had been wondering how she would manage without him.

There weren't many bare roads in Brentville during winter. Villagers who owned cars tended to put them away for the winter. A horse and buggy, horse and sleigh, or bundling up and walking were the transportation choices.

Most of the household garages had a space for the car, and in the back of the garage was a spot for a buggy or sleigh, or both, and horse stalls. *Quite an ingenious setup, really. I'll probably want to get a horse and sleigh once I'm in my own house.*

When Sara let Mr. Brent know she was ready for her house, he was more than happy to oblige. "Just call my office in the morning, and we'll get everything started," he said, beaming.

Sara found his smile troubling. Part of her would like to be caught up in his charismatic presence. Part of her would like to be taken care of, without a worry in the world. But that part was a tiny part.

The bigger part of Sara's psyche was getting its sea legs, was feeling stronger, and was never going to let go of finding a way to escape. Most significantly, she was basking in her newfound faith. She was coming to understand that the most important thing in her life was God and her relationship with him: her Father, her Friend, her King.

Even though Sara had not known the Lord long, God was showing her that he could—and would—use her right where she was. She also realized that there was so much more that she wanted to learn. But she didn't hesitate for a minute to share what she already knew. And that was Jesus and his love. Yes, she had become a contagious Christian.

CHAPTER 11

House Hunting

On Friday afternoon, Sara met with one of Mr. Brent's right-hand women. Ginny had worked for him for the last ten years and seemed very competent. She took Sara to all four of the available homes, which were very much alike. Other than furniture, color, and address, the first one was pretty much identical to the last.

After they visited the houses, Sara was a little overwhelmed. "Would you like to come back and bring a friend to help you decide?" asked Ginny.

"Yes," answered Sara. "I think I should do that."

Ginny gave her all four keys. "You can return these this weekend after you've made a decision."

The next morning, Sara got up early. *I'll run over to Olive and Harold's house. Maybe they will help me with this decision.* She opened the door and in a quiet voice said, "Yoo-hoo, anybody home?"

To her surprise, Olive and Harold were on their knees in the dining room. They explained that for years one of their daily practices had been to kneel by a dining room chair, resting their open Bible on its seat.

Sara was embarrassed to have walked in on their intimate family time. However, Harold jumped up, got another chair, and motioned for Sara to come kneel and pray with them.

Sara knelt on the floor between Olive and Harold. Leaning on the chair seat, she bowed her head, closed her eyes, and thanked God silently for those beautiful friends. Sara, Harold, and Olive continued with their prayer time and read a few verses from the Bible. After "Amen," they stood up, exchanged hugs, and went to the kitchen for a cup of tea, and Danish pastry.

"Tell me," inquired Olive, "what brings you out so early in the morning?"

"I need your help in making a decision on my house," answered Sara. "You have been here long enough to know what to look for and what to avoid. I thought maybe you could go and look at them with me."

"Oh, we'd love to," Harold and Olive both blurted out at once. Olive asked, "When do you want to go?"

"Anytime today," answered Sara. "I have the keys to all four houses."

"We're free this morning," said Olive. "Let's do it now."

"That's perfect," said Sara. "I have my car. I figured, since the roads are free of snow, I'd take my car for a little spin. It doesn't get driven much anymore."

Harold climbed into the back of the convertible and folded his long body into the small seat. Olive sat in the front with Sara, holding the keys and the addresses for the empty houses.

They made a quick run-through at each address. Then they stopped at the drugstore. After pulling stools up to the counter, they started discussing what they had seen. As they enjoyed their root-beer floats, they laid out all the addresses in front of them.

"Is there one you liked better than the others?" asked Harold. "I don't think so," Sara answered. "I am most concerned with the location. I would like to be as near to the hospital as I can and, of course, to you. That would mean picking the house on Park Street. Is there anything about that one—or any, for that matter—that might be a problem?"

Olive was the first to utter an opinion. "The one near the edge of the woods might not be your best bet. We're concerned about what might be going on in that wooded area. The committee is working on it, and we have nothing concrete, but I would stay away from that one. Actually, I think the house on Park Street would be perfect. You would be smack-dab between our house and the hospital."

Harold added, "We would be near enough to let Sam out if you ever got delayed at the hospital."

"Okay then," announced Sara. "I have picked my new home. My new address will be 42 Park Street." She dropped the key to her new home into her purse. The other three keys she slipped back into Ginny's envelope.

Pulling up in front of the Turner home, Sara was feeling a sense of relief. It felt good to have made the decision. Harold unfolded his six-foot-two frame from the back seat. And Olive went running up the steps. "I plumb forgot that I have some bread rising!" she said as she opened the door. "The smell of the yeast and rising bread tells me it's time to put the bread in the oven."

Sara drove to Ginny's to drop off the keys and to claim her house at 42 Park Street. She filled out the paperwork, signed the papers, and came away with more papers to read—instructions for care of the house and information on the small maintenance fee that she would be paying. She was to have the house until her death. Then it would go back on the market.

Sara felt comfortable about her finances, as the hospital was paying her very well. She had opened a bank account, and her savings account was already growing. She now had a checkbook that was accepted in Brentville. Mr. Brent had developed a good system of government; they even printed Brentville money, which looked like United States currency. They also accepted US currency, of which Sara still had five hundred dollars.

I'll have the maintenance fee, water, electricity, Brentville community tax, and a few other expenses for the house, but I'll be well within my budget. It's amazing how this village works. Mr. Brent has thought of everything, from the windmills to the dam on the river for our electricity and the water that is piped into the homes.

Next stop was the hospital. Sara was on call that weekend.

"New patient in ER," yelled Nurse Mitchell from across the hallway. Sara let go of new-house thoughts and prepared herself for this most recent emergency. The hospital ran reasonably smoothly without her on weekends. It was fully staffed, and there were quite a few physician's assistants who could do almost everything she could. She was required to check in twice a day. Because she was there, they were assigning this case to her.

As she entered the emergency room, she could hear a man moaning. His chart and X-ray indicated he was suffering from a broken arm, and his face was battered.

Sara gave orders to have the operating room ready, called for the people in charge of anesthesia, and called for the best "stitching-up" nurse they had on staff. She was always surprised when she saw how well all the natural medicines worked, even to the point of putting this man, Ian MacPherson, to sleep while she set his broken arm. The nurses put his arm in a sling, woke him up, and settled him into a bed. Sara would check in on him before leaving.

She picked up the phone in her office and asked the operator to get Mary on the line.

"Guess I won't be able to get to our study today," she told Mary. "I've had a pretty busy day already, and now I'm tied up at the hospital. I'm hoping to move into my house tomorrow. Come and see me. It's at 42 Park Street."

"Sure will," said Mary. "I'll come tomorrow to help you move. See you around ten."

This move will be easy compared to moves in my old life. The only things I have to move are the things I can carry in my car.

Ian MacPherson was resting in his room when Sara got back to him. "Good afternoon," greeted Sara as she extended a hand to his good arm. "My name is Dr. Sara Saunders. I hope you're not too uncomfortable."

He tried to smile but obviously found it too painful with all the bruises and stitches on his face.

"I am going to keep you here overnight," said Sara. "I would think that by tomorrow you could leave. Where is your car?"

Ian told her of how he had been looking for gas, much like she had been, and of how he had found the gate into Brentville. "After I talked with the guard at the gatehouse, I started driving toward Brentville. Next thing I remembered I was going too fast on the small winding road, and I hit some trees. Luckily, the guard found me and brought me to the hospital. My car has been towed to the repair shop."

"Okay," said Sara, "then take this phone number. It's Crystal's hotel. I can vouch for the fact that it is comfortable. And she serves very good food. I have been staying there for a while now. It's not far from the repair shop. I will see you in the morning, and if you'd like, I can take you there. Rest now. I'll talk with you in the morning."

Driving back to the hotel, Sara was agonizing over how to handle the Ian MacPherson situation. *Do I try to explain what he has gotten himself into, or should I let him find out by himself? He is a fifty-six-year-old veterinarian. Mr. Brent will be pleased. Brentville needs another animal doctor. With all the horses and the cattle and other livestock, keeping them all healthy is a big job.*

Meeting Ian today has put a damper on the excitement I've been feeling about getting into my own place. I feel as though I've been hit on the head with a two-by-four. It reminds me in a very clear way that I'm still a prisoner in Brentville. It's becoming a more comfortable place to be, but I'm still being held against my will.

When she arrived at the hotel, it was four o'clock. She stopped to tell Crystal about the house and that she planned to move the next day. She took her dinner up to her room.

Sara was anxious to get into her prayer chair and open her Bible. Putting her dinner aside, she sat down with her Bible and her questions for the day. They were from the study book that she was completing with Mary. It showed her how God helps us live above our circumstances—not below them in deep despair—but above them, with hope for what is yet to come.

"Thank you, dear Lord, for helping me to live through this terrible time with hope in my heart. I yearn to be with Jim and back in my old life, but if that doesn't happen, I know I have you in my life now. My eternity with you has already begun, and I will be with you in heaven, forever and ever. Amen."

After opening the dinner-tray dishes, she enjoyed Crystal's home-cooked meal. *I will miss this tomorrow night—and the next night and the next night. One more bath in the beautiful big tub and one more night on this featherbed. Then I have to be a big girl and be in my own house.*

Sara did some packing and was asleep by nine.

At six the next day, she was up and dressed and on her way with Sam to 42 Park Street. By eight, she had all the car's contents carried into the house.

Sara showed Sam his new house. *It's pretty amazing to be in my own space again.* Her space was a three-bedroom, three-bathroom house with living room and dining room. The two-story house had hardwood floors except in the kitchen and bathrooms, where there were tiles. The many windows provided lots of light.

There were two bedrooms with a bath upstairs, one large bedroom with a bathroom and another guest bathroom downstairs. It was fully furnished. New towels and sheets lay in the linen closet, still in their packaging.

The kitchen had everything that she could think of and more: beautiful hotel-style Syracuse floral china, everyday silver, electric fryer, and an ice-cream maker, to name a few items. Everything was there that she would need for canning the vegetables from a garden.

Sam wasn't particularly interested in canning, but he loved the braided rug under the big old oval table and chairs in the middle of the kitchen. The cupboards were painted white; the countertop was a pretty yellow tile.

In the pantry, she noticed a yellow metal stool. It had two steps that folded out, so that she could use it for a stepstool. *Good thing. These cupboards are pretty high. I've been used to having Jim around to get into the high places.*

Kitchen Stool

She sat for a few moments on the living room sofa, appreciating the presence of a piano, a brick fireplace, some comfy-looking overstuffed chairs, a record player with lots of old LP records, and a radio. Sara couldn't help thinking that Mr. Brent had really outdone himself with those beautiful houses and the contents within.

There was a cream-and-blue antique rug in the middle of the room. Large windows reached across the room's front. The dining room was right off the kitchen and next to the living room. The dining room held a large buffet and an oval antique table that could seat eight, as well as a walnut cupboard full of fine Wedgewood-blue china and enough fine silver to serve eight.

The bedroom that she would be using was a room of about twenty by twenty feet. There was a black walnut featherbed flanked by two large windows, two antique dressers, and two end tables with converted oil lamps. The four windows in that room had white ruffled curtains and white pull shades. Her black-and-white tiled bathroom was huge. It had a shower and a big claw-foot tub that she hadn't noticed when she'd first toured. *It's just like the one at Crystal's!*

Sam followed her down into the large basement with a wringer washer and six clotheslines so she could dry her clothes in inclement weather. She found a door in the cellar that went out to the yard. Hanging clothes outside would be very convenient. Sara also remembered that there were two big porches, one on the front of the house and one on the back.

"Okay, Sam, now let me show you the outside." Sara opened the door to the back yard. A swing set like Harold's sat amid apple trees, a cherry tree, and a peach tree. There was a brick patio just off the back porch.

I thought I saw a charcoal grill and charcoal down in the cellar, along with a wagon and a wheelbarrow. I can put those on the patio.

There was a large flower garden, an even larger vegetable garden, a clothesline, a two-car garage that had a big area on one side that would be suitable for a horse, a buggy, and a sleigh. There was also a good-sized pasture available for horses.

"In a few weeks, we'll get a couple of horses," Sara told Sam. He wagged his tail and looked at her with what she was sure were approving eyes.

"You're such a good boy," she said. Sam wagged his tail again.

"Oh, I hear our new doorbell," said Sara. Sam was not a barking dog, but she knew from when she'd lived with Crystal that he did go to the door when the doorbell rang or when he heard someone approaching.

"Welcome, Mary," Sara said, her smile sincere. "You are our first guest."

Mary was all bundled up with mittens, a heavy coat, and a hat. She had walked, pulling her wagon. It was full of fruits, vegetables, homemade bread, butter, cheese, jam, milk, eggs, homemade soup, tea, and a meal that was all prepared, ready to be popped into the oven.

"Oh my goodness!" Sara shouted excitedly. "I was dreading going to the grocery store. Now I can wait until tomorrow or even the next day to do that. You are a sweet friend, and I thank you with all my heart."

Sara enthusiastically showed Mary around her new home.

"Now I have to get over to the hospital. Let's put your wagon into the trunk, and I'll drive you home."

"We had another person come through the gate last night, an Ian MacPherson," Sara began as she started the car. "He ran into some trees on his way to Brentville, and he doesn't know yet that he can't get out. I'm releasing him from the hospital this morning and will take him to the hotel. He will know soon enough, but I'm thinking I should sit him down and tell him the truth—his new truth."

Before Mary got out of the car, she prayed with Sara. "Please help Sara do the best thing for Ian this morning. Help him to be able to accept his situation. If he doesn't know you, Lord, help him to surrender himself to you as Sara and I have, for we know this surrender has brought us a total freedom. In Jesus's name we pray. Amen."

CHAPTER 12

Meet Ian

Sara drove to the hospital at around noon. Not yet wanting to leave Sam alone in the house, she told him to come along. He loved riding in the car. When she'd parked, she rolled the window down a crack. *He should be fine waiting there for me.*

She checked her office messages then went directly to Ian's room. The nurse's report looked good, and his vitals were normal.

"Well, what do you think?" Sara asked him. "Are you ready to be sprung? There's no hurry. I could easily keep you here for a few more days."

"No, Doc," replied Ian with a crooked smile. "I'm ready to leave. To the hotel it is!"

"Okay, I'll sign your release forms, put you into a wheelchair, and run out to get my car," said Sara. "I'll ask the nurse to take you to the front door. Did you bring any belongings from your vehicle?"

"No," answered Ian. "but the gas station attendant brought my suitcase and my briefcase over to me."

"That was nice of him,. I'll have someone bring those to the front door."

***

"Meet Sam," Sara said as she opened the door for Ian.

Getting a six foot four man with a full cast and his briefcase into the car was not an easy feat. They finally figured a way to protect his arm while settling his long legs and torso down into the rather small front seat. Sam and the briefcase took up the back seat. Sara shoved the suitcase into the trunk, but she couldn't get the trunk closed.

"Never fear," she said. "It's not far."

Ian watched Sara slide her five-foot-two frame into the driver's seat. "Perfect car for a cute little doc," he said. "I wouldn't last long in it. I'll stick to my trucks."

A couple of blocks later, they were at the hotel. They had to reverse the entering procedure. Sam patiently waited for them to get all the body parts out before he pushed his way up to the front seat and out the door. Sara assisted Ian into the hotel and helped him into a chair in the dining room.

She had talked with Crystal earlier in the day about his arrival. Crystal had told her to give him Sara's old room. "I will have it all ready," she said.

As Sara came in with the suitcase, the briefcase, and Sam, Crystal poked her head through the kitchen door. "This is Ian MacPherson," she said.

The twins came running from the kitchen. "Ian, meet Crystal and her twins, Joseph and Jenny."

"Sorry to hear about your accident," said Crystal. "Let me help you get settled into your room." They guided him up the stairs and got him to an overstuffed chair.

"Tonight and tomorrow, Ian will need room service," said Sara. "After that he should be able to come down for meals. He's right-handed, and it's his left arm that's broken, so he should be able to eat." She turned her attention to Ian. "Maybe Crystal will rig up a few shirts that will fit over your cast. She is an outstanding seamstress."

Crystal nodded. "I'll work on it after the evening customers have left. I've just hired someone to work in the kitchen, so that will be a big help. I'm also going to hire someone to help with laundry and the cleaning. By the time Oliver and I are married, I expect to have more free time."

"I will help get you into bed, Ian," offered Sara. "You should probably be resting."

She found some pajamas and helped him get them on. After he'd been to the bathroom, she made sure he got safely into bed. She gave him something to help him sleep, although he probably didn't need it. As soon as he put his head on the pillow, he was asleep.

I can't burden him with his plight when he's in this condition. No, I'll come back tomorrow.

After turning out the lights, she quietly went downstairs to talk with Crystal, and said, "I've decided to wait until tomorrow to tell Ian about Brentville. I'll leave for work early and come over to check on him. I will tell him then."

She turned and said, "Come on, Sam, let's go home. Oh, and by the way, Crystal, when do you get your new puppies?"

"Not sure," she answered. "Should be fairly soon. Sure you don't want another puppy? Sam would love it."

Sara just smiled as she headed out.

"Okay, Sam," said Sara, "this is our first night in our new home." Too tired to get dinner, she decided on some homemade soup, bread, and cheese. Mary had tucked a bag of dog food in her "wagon from heaven." Thanks to Mary, they both had a good meal.

The doorbell rang, and Sam was wagging his tail by the door. *Who could that be?* Sara wondered.

Olive and Harold were on the porch. "We've just stopped by to see if you have everything you need," Olive said.

"Welcome to our new home," said Sara. "You are our second guests."

"I want to make a porch game for your new house," said Harold. "On which porch would you like me to put it?"

"I think the back one would be good," Sara responded gratefully. "Oh, thank you so much! I will love having one of my own."

"Okay then," he said. "I'll come over tomorrow to put it up for you."

Olive took her warm, freshly baked apple pie to the kitchen and put it onto Sara's new table. "For you dear," she said. "I know you'll be too busy to do much baking."

"Before you go, I want to talk to you about something," said Sara. "Please, come sit in my new living room. I'll share the pie with you while it's still warm."

Then she told them about Ian and that she was going to tell him about Brentville the next day. "I've been thinking that when the time comes and he's ready for a house, maybe he'll choose the one by the edge of the woods. It would be a great opportunity for us to learn more about what was going on in the woods. I realize that we'd have to wait until he can be trusted, but he might be just the ally we need to break this case wide open. So far, he seems like a nice guy."

She continued, "At first, I will give him the facts of Brentville. As we get to know and trust him, we can let him into our inner circle. The more individuals on our side, the better it will be. What do you think?"

After a few seconds, Olive said, "Sounds like a plan, Special Detective Sara Saunders. Glad you're on our team."

Harold agreed and added a warning. "We must not move too fast. We also have to be very careful about giving out information regarding the satanic activity that the committee is investigating."

Sara agreed. "Thank you for listening and for supporting me. I'm on a mission on behalf of the young girls I've treated. I know I must be very careful in my quest for pieces of this ugly puzzle."

Early the next morning, Sara was not looking forward to her first stop. *Trying to explain to Ian that he might be stuck in Brentville forever isn't something I expect to be easy. I feel genuinely sorry for the poor man. Not only that, it's bringing up the pain of my own unfortunate confinement in Brentville.*

Sara pulled up into the alley behind the hotel, parked her car, and entered the back door of the hotel. It opened into the kitchen, where she found Crystal working with her new employees. One looked to be in her twenties and the other Sara thought might be in her fifties. *This will be good for Crystal's new life. She deserves and needs more help.*

Slowly climbing the stairs to her old room, Sara said a prayer. "Please, Lord, give me the words. If Ian knows you, I ask that your Holy Spirit help him wrap his mind around the unreal experience in which he is now involved. "And, Lord, if he doesn't know you as his Lord and Savior, please open his heart to your calling. In Jesus's name. Amen and amen."

Sara gave a soft tap on the half-opened door. Then she heard Ian arguing with Millie, one of the local phone operators. "But there has to be a way to make a call to Minnesota from Brentville. This doesn't make any sense. We're not that far away."

He made eye contact with Sara, rolled his eyes, and hung up. "Can't believe this!" he blurted out to Sara. "No one has this kind of antiquated phone system any longer!"

Sara sat down on the chair next to his. "How are you feeling this morning?" she asked.

"A lot better, but still pretty shaky," he answered.

"You'll probably want to stay at the hotel for a week or so. You'll receive good care, and it will probably take that long to get your truck fixed."

She could tell he was not pleased at the thought of being held up in Brentville for a week. "I have a busy veterinary practice back in Minnesota," sputtered Ian. "I can't just not show up!"

Sara remembered the same frustration that was now welling up in Ian. *It's time to start telling him about Brentville.* "Ian," she stated, "I'm afraid I have some startling news for you. No, don't worry. It's not about your health. Except for being somewhat battered, you seem to be in fine shape. You've found yourself in the same situation that I found myself in five months ago. I, like you, needed gas, took that little dirt road, and the rest is history."

She told him a brief story of her journey into Brentville, of how she'd been dealing with it, of how she'd reached the bottom of life and called out to God. "God is helping me now as I try to live above the circumstances instead of under them."

Seeing that Ian was becoming agitated, she stopped to ask if he wanted to say something. "I thank the Lord," said Ian, "that God has used this to get you to your surrendering point. I am a Christian and have loved the Lord for many years. However, I'm having a hard time trying to grasp the fact that we're all prisoners here in Brentville. I won't believe that we can't get out."

"I know," responded Sara, her voice sympathetic. "I was the same way, but I've tried every which way to escape. I still will never give up trying or give up hoping to be reunited with Jim and my family. I pray for that and for them to know God through Jesus, as I now do."

Ian said, "I lost my wife to cancer a couple of years ago, but I have three children who've kept pretty close track of me since then. They will be worried sick!"

Sara told him what she knew of Mr. Brent and the mansion, and added, "I find him to be a very egotistical person. He has formed this marvelous isolated village and is in total control of everything that goes on here. One thing Mr. Brent *can't* control is his death and the timing of it. He seems to be tuned into reality enough to realize that eventually death will come his way.

"There was a boy whose parents were killed in a logging accident. I've been told that Mr. Brent decided to adopt Walter to be his successor. Walter was two at the time. Mr. Brent has been grooming him all these sixteen years—the perfect arrangement. He has had the boy to mold and indoctrinate into his way of thinking. Walter is now eighteen—a son who could take over for his father at any moment.

"Walter was the first person I met as I drove through the gate and into Brentville. I gather that Mr. Brent feels a hands-on approach is very good for the young man, so Walter goes back and forth with a variety of duties. The more I learn, the more I can see Walter's large reach into the community.

"Mr. Brent, along with his brilliant scientist friend, thought of everything when they planned Brentville—everything, that is, but the corruption and sin that lives in the hearts of folks. There is something very dark that is going on around here. I don't know whether Mr. Brent is involved in it or not."

Ian seemed to be at a loss for words, so Sara continued.

"There are many amazing things here. Everything is well organized, works smoothly, and is well maintained. We have natural gas, rivers for water power, windmills, enough forest land with well-run replanting schedules, deep wells with pure water, and very successful greenhouses. They are large and well cared for and grow things in winter, like lettuce and vegetables.

"We have a glass-blowing factory, a bowling alley, a movie theater with many old movies that have been stored away, a playhouse theater where you can go to enjoy good plays, an ice-fishing industry, and a large food-canning factory. There are also rules and regulations about taking care of all these things. As far as I can see, everyone complies.

"There's a stinky paper mill out on the community's edge. Once in a great while, if the wind is blowing just right, you might get a whiff. Right beside that is a soap factory—the building where they render the fat is quite smelly. I try to stay away from that end of the village.

"Mr. Brent has a loyal group of second-generation Brentville men and women surrounding him. All work hard and seem very motivated to stay with the cause. There are three or four of the original townies involved in the government of this community, but as they die or get too old to be useful, I imagine this might be cause for a weakening of the psychological walls of this well-structured village.

"I've learned that as human beings become more and more accustomed to being taken care of, they also lose the incentive to work. They get spoiled and rebel for more free stuff, and give up thinking for themselves altogether.

"There are rumors that there is a child at the mansion, too. No one is aware of the particulars, but knowing as much about Mr. Brent as we do, it wouldn't surprise any of us to learn that he has managed to find a child for himself, or for Walter. It just makes sense that he wants another child to be groomed to be a successor or partner for Walter."

Ian was immobilized. His body had already been hurting. Now his mind was in pain too. "This can't be happening!" he moaned. "Maybe the drugs are making me delusional."

Sara gave him more pain medicine and said, "I'm sorry, but I have to get to the hospital for rounds. Eat, drink lots of water, and sleep as much as you can, Ian. I will come by again, early tomorrow morning, before I go to the hospital."

Crystal was in the kitchen. Sara gave her quick directions for the patient before she turned toward the back door. "Oh, and I've told him a lot about Brentville," said Sara. "I think he probably won't be able to believe me and will want to be doing some investigation on his own as soon as he's able."

Sara made her rounds at the hospital and was able to get back to her own new hideaway soon after they were completed. Sam was waiting on his rug, right by the door. The door had a large window, which enabled him to keep an eye out for her return. He seemed to trust that she would return. Seeing that good part of Sam's character reminded Sara that she must never lose hope either.

Her little house was beginning to feel like home, a refuge from the crazy world in which she'd landed. It was nice to be arranging things to her liking. *Think I'll go to the Christmas tree farm to get a tree. I have that stand, those beautiful antique tree decorations and icicles—even the string of lights I found in the attic.*

"Time for bed," announced Sara. Sam's ears perked up; he got up from his rug in the kitchen, stretched, and headed for the bedroom. Sara had a dog bed for him right beside her own bed. Grabbing for the toothbrush, Sara noticed that the store-bought toothpaste with which she'd arrived was almost gone. *Guess I'd better reread those instructions for making toothpaste. I think it was baking soda, peppermint oil, and salt. I'll check in the morning.*

At that point, she had only enough energy to read a few verses in the Bible and talk with God. She did that in her prayer chair in her bedroom, the same place that she went to answer her Bible study questions.

Mary had suggested that she find a place where she could always go when she wanted to have some time with God—not that she couldn't talk with God anywhere, but Mary had explained to her that it is good to have a specific place to go to, out of habit. That night, Sara was glad she'd chosen the chair instead of the bed. *When I'm as weary as this, if I sat in bed, I'd be asleep before I even had a chance to say hello to God.*

The neighbors on either side of Sara had chickens, so mornings were announced by roosters crowing on both sides. Sara didn't mind; in fact, it reminded her of her childhood spent growing up on a farm.

By six, Sara was up and dressed. She had eaten breakfast, walked Sam, and was answering her morning study questions. This time, the questions focused on 1 Peter 1:3-9.[4] It spoke to her of new birth—her spiritual rebirth. It was definitely an encouragement to her to read the apostle Peter's words of joy and hope in her time of trouble. She knew Peter was basing his confidence on what God did through Jesus.

I now have a living *hope of eternal life, as I've trusted Christ and joined God's family. I'm experiencing how God is helping me with the hard time through which I'm traveling. What joy to understand that my eternal life with God has already started right here on earth!*

"Thank you, God, for this wonderful gift," she prayed as she walked to the hotel to check on Ian. *Without God in my life, I would have crumbled by now.*

"Good morning, Crystal. How did our patient do?" Sara asked.

"Not a peep out of him," answered Crystal, "and he ate all his breakfast this morning. I wouldn't be surprised to see him out and about today. You were right; I think that he'll want to do some investigating himself."

"Thanks, Crystal," said Sara as she headed up the stairs.

"How's the patient this morning?" asked Sara. "I hear you still have your appetite."

"Yes, Doc. I'm your model patient. I'm doing so well that I plan to get out and check on my truck today." He paused. "By the way, I was traveling with cash that I had withdrawn for Christmas gifts for my kids and family. It's a thousand dollars, so I can pay my way here for a while. I'm quite confident that I will find a way out but was wondering how much it costs to stay here."

As Sara heard him talking, a wave of sadness and sympathy washed over her. *Oh, Ian, you're beginning the long process of grief and shock that I've experienced since landing in Brentville.* She placed her hand on Ian's good shoulder as she reassured him. "Don't worry about running out of money here. Crystal will not throw you out, and God will provide. Let's pray before I head out to the hospital."

Sara pulled a chair up to the bed and put her hand over his. "Lord," she prayed, "please take care of my dear brother in Christ. Help him to heal quickly, and please direct him to safe places. We ask that you guide us both as we look for clues to getting back to our families. In Jesus's name we pray. Amen."

"Don't get any crazy ideas of getting over the wall," she warned as she walked toward the door. "I've heard of a couple of deaths of would-be escapees who tried that."

Ian gave her a three-quarter smile in response. His lips were getting back to normal size, and the swelling on his face was going down.

CHAPTER 13

Settling In

At times Sara felt content in her new home. She was doing things she enjoyed. Even hanging clothes out on the line and bringing them in frozen didn't seem so bad. *I think maybe I'll cut back on my hours at the hospital. I need more time now that I have my own house, and I could certainly use more time to concentrate on my escape from Brentville.*

Sara bent a few pieces of frozen laundry over the radiators before she took the rest down to the cellar to dry. *I suppose I should have put them down there in the first place, but it was hard to resist that beautiful sunshine. A casserole in the oven and the laundry off the line—I have about an hour to run over to see Harold and Olive.*

"Knock, knock," she called, as she stepped into the hallway, followed by Sam.

"We're in the kitchen," shouted Olive. "Come on in!"

Harold and Olive were busy canning tomatoes. "We were over to the vegetable greenhouse. We bought a bushel basket of tomatoes," Olive explained.

Sara counted at least two-dozen jars of tomatoes on the counter. She heard the ping of a few of the tops going down while she stood there.

"Have a seat," invited Harold. "Come, chat with us while we work."

"You guys never quit," commented Sara. "But I guess you can't, can you? There's always something that needs doing when you have a house—which brings me to Ian. Remember? He's the gentleman who came through the gate last week."

"Oh yes," replied Harold. "How's he doing?"

"He's mending well," answered Sara, "but he's just getting into the shock and horror of what is actually happening in his life."

"Poor guy," said Olive.

"He is one of our brothers in Christ," Sara confirmed, "so I was wondering if we could include him in your Friday-night Bible study/church? What do you think? Do you have room for one more? I really think that he can be trusted not to say anything to the wrong person."

"I think he'd be a big asset in our search for information about what's going on in Brentville," continued Sara. "I hope that soon he will be ready for a house, and I hope he'll agree to live in the one by the woods."

Olive and Harold gave each other one of those looks that only couples who have had fifty-five years of marriage under their belts understand. "Yes," answered Harold, "it will be a pleasure to get to meet and worship with another one of God's children."

"Thank you!" said Sara. "Come on, Sam. We need to get home to our casserole."

Sara bundled up with her coat, scarf, and mittens, and gave her lovable friends a hug. She let Sam and herself out to brave the cold for the few blocks to their inviting little white home with black shutters and a red door.

Sara had just come into the house and turned on a few lights when the doorbell rang. "Well, if it isn't my model patient! Come on in," she said as she opened the door.

"Hi, Doc," greeted Ian. "Do you have time to talk? I'm full of questions."

"Certainly," answered Sara as she noticed that Ian wasn't wearing a coat. *I suppose he couldn't figure out how to get it to fit with his oversized arm.* "Come into the living room and sit by the fire. She had started the fire before going to Harold's. It was about ready for a new log. The popping and crackling of this new log added to the ambience of her living room.

"Have you had dinner?" she asked.

"Not yet," said Ian.

"Well then, please join me. We'll have one of Olive's casseroles," said Sara. "Casserole and salad is all there is, but I think you'll like it. Oh yes, I also have some homemade bread and apple pie."

"Sounds good," replied Ian. "Apple's my favorite. I just bought some cheese at the cheese shop. I'll get it out of the truck—should go well with the pie."

Sara and Ian started chatting like old friends, and she was glad she could be there for him. *I know firsthand what he's experiencing and what is yet to come. He's in the very beginning stages of the dilemma. Actually, I'm not that far ahead of him.*

"As you can see," said Ian, "I got my truck today. The damage wasn't too serious, and they had what they needed to fix it. I gave in and let them put the converter on after I found out that it was the only option for Brentville driving."

"I know," said Sara. "I couldn't believe it when they told me. What a shock!" She paused. "I want to tell you something, but you cannot tell anyone."

"Okay," answered Ian. "I'm all ears."

"Being a Christian in Brentville is not something we advertise," Sara confided. "There is an underground church, more like a Bible study, that meets in homes around the village once a week. The townies think that they're book clubs. When I first landed here, I didn't know God and didn't think I needed him. I was introduced to Jesus, and now I don't know what I would do without him.

"Praise God!" said Ian. "I can't even imagine being without him. The blessing is that we'll never have to imagine that, because it will never happen."

"Yes," agreed Sara. "What a promise! And I would love it if you could join me tomorrow night. I go to Harold and Olive's for the study every Friday night. I've told them about you, and they want very much to have you come. Oscar, the man who fixed your truck, is also a believer. He's part of the same group. And it would be nice for you to be with other Christians and to get to know more about the village. Also, Harold and Olive have impressed upon me how very important it is to be secretive about these meetings. I haven't even told Crystal."

As Ian's eyes widened, Sara could tell he was digesting more than just the food. "Well," he said, "I hate that I'm in this situation, but I'm glad to know that there are others here who believe in Jesus Christ. Yes, I would love to join you. Thank you for putting your trust in me."

He added, "Crystal told me today that she knows Mr. Brent quite well and that she knows he would like to have me working at one of the animal hospitals. She acts as though I will never leave Brentville." He sighed.

"I felt the same depression," said Sara. "But I was glad to know that I could work if I wanted to do so."

Ian nodded.

"Did Crystal tell you that once you are a resident of Brentville, you are offered free housing?" asked Sara.

"No," Ian answered with surprise.

"Well, you are. I opted to stay with Crystal until now. It took me five months to be ready to get a house. Sometimes a heart needs time to accept what a mind already knows." She said sadly, "I don't want to accept any of this, but on some level, I have to accept my situation, and make the most of it. However, all the while, I'll be looking for a way to get back to my family."

"It is time for me to go back to the hotel," said Ian. "I need some more pain medicine and some talking with the Lord."

"Do you have a Bible with you?" enquired Sara.

"Yes," answered Ian. "I keep one in the truck at all times. Never know when you might need some of God's medicine."

Sara said her good-bye to Ian and went to the kitchen to clean up. Next on the agenda was a walk around the block with Sam. She enjoyed the crisp air and the smell of the neighborhood fires burning.

I can see that with each day, Ian is handling his new reality much faster than I have. He's still trying to think of ways in which he can escape, but at the same time, within the Brentville confines, his mind seems to be set on getting a house.

He's facing the present problem head-on. He seems to feel that this is going to help him take charge and figure out a way to get back to Minnesota. Who knows? Maybe he will.

As she drifted off to sleep, Sara prayed, "Thanks for allowing me to help Ian adjust to Brentville."

Friday's rounds were almost completed when Sara heard the emergency calls. *Must be an accident. They're calling for all doctors. Must be bad!* She ran to the ER.

The gurneys were coming in, and she counted four. *Good thing the ER is well equipped and that there are six separate rooms for patients.*

"Ice-fishing accident," said the head nurse. "One was DOA, and the others are in pretty bad shape."

It took a few hours to get everyone taken care of. One of the patients looked familiar. At second glance, she remembered him from the fair. *He's the man I saw that day by the pony rides.* Suddenly it occurred to Sara. *On my first and last visit to the Brentville Church, this is the man I felt uncomfortable being around.*

Chief Detective Sara Saunders was now on duty. Her brain had just switched gears, and she was on the case. *At least I'll have his full attention for a while. He has broken legs, a broken arm, and some fractured ribs.*

Sara knew that ice fishing was a big industry and sport in Brentville. She learned that these four men were working for the village. They had misjudged the thickness of the ice and gone through with a horse, wagon, and four new icehouses. Emergency workers were able to rescue the horse and the men. Everything else was lost in the very deep lake. James Ross died on the way to the hospital.

Ross—I know that name. "Someone please bring me Mr. Ross's belongings," Sara requested. Going through his wallet, she saw a picture that made her heart sink. It was Mary Jane, the fifty-something woman Crystal had just hired. *Mary Jane Ross. Mrs. James Ross.*

"I know where Mr. Ross's wife is right now, so I'll walk over to the hotel to let her know about her husband's death," said Sara. "Someone has to do it, and I know her situation."

***

"Hi, Doc!" Ian said as Sara strode swiftly along the street. He'd pulled up beside her in his truck. "Want a lift?"

"That would be great," Sara answered.

"I hardly recognized you," he said. "With that big coat, the hat, and that scarf wrapped around your face, my only clue was your height and your doctor's bag."

"Glad you recognized me. I'm sorry to say that I'm headed to the hotel to tell Mary Jane that her husband just died in a fishing accident."

"Fishing accident?" asked Ian, surprised. "It seems a wee bit early for fishing. I am a big ice fisherman, and in Minnesota anyway, it would be too early."

"You're probably right. I just know that as part of their job for the village, they were trying to set up four new icehouses."

"Would you like to have me go with you?" asked Ian.

"When she's ready to go home, maybe you could take her," Sara replied. "But wait. What am I doing? Are you sure you are up for this? You are still recovering physically, and your head must be swimming."

"Yes," Ian immediately replied. "My head is swimming, but I know I'm better off helping others."

"Okay," Sara replied. "You're on."

Ian was able to give Sara a full smile, since the swelling on his lips and face was almost completely gone.

Ian drove up to the back door of the hotel. *Even with his broken arm, he's still a gentleman*, thought Sara as he walked around to open her door. Getting out of the truck took some doing for Sara. Ian held out his good arm to steady her as she stepped onto the running board.

Crystal and Mary Jane looked up in surprise when they noticed Sara and Ian entering the kitchen.

"Hi, you two," said Crystal. "We weren't expecting you, especially at this time of day."

"I'm afraid we have some bad news," announced Sara.

Both Mary Jane and Crystal looked fearful. Sara asked them both to sit down.

"You probably heard the siren a little while ago," she began. "There was an accident on Lake Brent. Mary Jane, I'm sorry to say that your husband died on the way to the hospital."

"Oh no!" Mary Jane cried.

Fortunately, Ian was standing beside her chair and caught her as she slipped toward the floor. With his good arm, he carried her to the sofa in Crystal's apartment. Sara pulled her smelling salts from her bag and swished them under Mary Jane's nose.

Mary Jane began sobbing uncontrollably. Sara gave her a very weak herbal sedative and covered her with a blanket as she went to sleep. "Does Mary Jane have children?" she asked.

"Yes," answered Crystal. "Two girls: an eighteen-year-old and a twenty-year-old."

"We need to find them before they hear this from someone else," said Sara.

"I think I know where they work," said Ian. "Mary Jane was telling me all about them this morning.

"Okay, let's go," Sara said to Ian. "Crystal, we'll be back soon to get Mary Jane."

Ian helped Sara up onto the big running board and into the truck. They headed toward the huge greenhouses. Both girls had jobs working in the big indoor gardens.

Telling Mary Jane's daughters was a sad job. The girls stayed strong for their mother and went to the hotel to pick her up.

It was already time for dinner and then Friday-night church. "Would you like to come in for dinner before we go to Harold's?" Sara asked Ian.

"I owe you one," he said. "Let me take you to the pizza place."

"Sounds yummy, but first I need to feed Sam and let him out."

Sitting in the pizza parlor, Sara and Ian discussed all that had happened earlier. "I have an appointment with the big man tomorrow," Ian said.

"I guess you're talking about Mr. Brent," laughed Sara.

"Yes, I'm actually looking forward to it. I want to see and talk to the man who seems to be my biggest enemy. Don't worry," he added, as Sara's face showed her concern. "I'll be very careful."

"See that you are," said Sara. "I don't want any more bad news around here. And besides, you and I are becoming a good team. When you're around, I feel myself believing that we will be free again."

After playing a few songs on the jukebox, they went directly from the pizza parlor to the Bible study/church.

"Welcome, son," Harold greeted, with outstretched hand. "So glad you've come. I've been looking forward to meeting you." Ian appeared to be immediately drawn to Harold. There was a genuine love in Harold that attracted people.

Nine o'clock came too quickly. Ian had connected with the group on many levels. As he paused at the door, it was clear that he hated leaving. "Thanks, everyone, for being so open to accepting me into your Bible study/church. It's been amazing."

"It looks as though we'll be getting some snow," said Sara to Ian. "I need to get my horse and buggy and sleigh this week. Maybe I could ask you to help me out with that. Are you thinking of starting work soon? It looks like the house by the woods is still available if you have a desire to get your own place."

Ian smiled his whole smile. "Sleep well."

The next morning, Sara realized that her weather prediction had been correct. Eight inches of snow had come during the night, and it was still snowing. Through the window, she saw a man standing on a moving V-shaped wooden plow. He was grasping a bar with his left hand and holding the horse's reins with the right. *Quite a sight, seeing this man cleaning off sidewalks this way. Great invention.*

As she opened the front door to take Sam out for his morning exercise, Sara noticed that the milkman had made his delivery. She'd ordered two quarts of milk and one pint of cream.

In Brentville, they didn't homogenize the milk, so when the milk arrived, it always had a couple of inches of cream on top. They could either take the cream off the top and use it as cream or shake the bottle well to get the cream and the milk blended.

Sara appreciated that the milkman, who delivered with horse and buggy, gave all his customers a little metal box to put on their front porch. It was insulated to keep the milk from freezing in the winter and to protect it from getting too hot in the summer. Sara was impressed with the way most things worked in Brentville.

Since it's turned cold, I've been longing for a cup of hot chocolate. Seeing this milk makes me think that maybe today is a hot chocolate day! Even though it isn't my choice to be here, I can feel myself settling in to some degree. Yes, on some level, I am at peace. I know it is because of my newfound faith.

Having Ian here is making me think more about Jim's absence. Having someone of the opposite sex around to talk with is nice and having someone to help with decisions—things from "What's for dinner?" to getting a house, is nice too.

It's stirring feelings that I haven't felt for a while. How I ache for the intimacy, the beautiful physical closeness that Jim and I've shared. And I need to be careful with Ian. He's a lovable man, and he's in a vulnerable position, too. I don't want to lead him on in any way.

I am a married woman, and I will never give up hope that I will be with Jim again.

CHAPTER 14

Plans and Plots and More Plans

One and a half weeks until Crystal's wedding. As far as I can tell, everything is going smoothly. Oliver's mother is having the shower for Crystal on Saturday night. Everything seems to be falling into place.

Mary Jane had decided to get right back to work. Staying home all day was harder for her than working. After her husband's funeral, she said she needed to be around people. And goodness knows, Crystal required all the help she could get.

Sara and Sam were at the hotel for some of Crystal's great home cooking, but the real reason Sara had come was to see the new puppies. Three darling, wide-eyed golden retrievers had been delivered to Crystal the day before.

Ian was checking them over. As soon as he put one down, Sara picked it up. "Oh my goodness, I want them all," she sighed.

"Well, my friend, I have promised one to Ian," Crystal said. "And I'm keeping one for the twins. The third one is yours if you want it."

"Hadn't considered having two dogs," answered Sara, "but these sweet little faces are making me think." In the next breath, she said, "Okay, I've finished thinking. I'd love to have one." With her new puppy in one arm, she hugged Crystal with her free arm and smiled at Ian, who was holding the other two puppies.

Mary Jane was trying to help Ian figure out how to get his coat over his enlarged arm. "Hey, Doc," yelled Ian. "How much longer do you think I'll have to put up with this cast?"

"Why don't you come to the office tomorrow," answered Sara. "Maybe we can figure a way to make a more coat-friendly cast. I've heard that Mary Jane is good with thread and needle. Maybe she'll make you a few things that will fit around the cast."

"I'd be glad to try," said Mary Jane.

Sara took the royal-blue dress Crystal had made for her for the wedding and went up to one of the spare bedrooms to try it on. *Perfect fit.* She called Crystal to come and look. They laughed and cried together. "I've never had a more beautiful dress," Sara said. It was form fitting, ended just above the knees, and went very well with her blue eyes and golden curls.

"I will take it home tonight. Thank you, Crystal!"

"Almost nine," announced Ian, calling up the stairs. "Why don't you let me take you home, Sara?"

"I'll swing back around at about nine thirty," he told Mary Jane, "to get you home by ten."

Sara grabbed her dress, called Sam, and started toward the truck. "I'll pick up the puppy in a couple of days," she said to Crystal. "Thanks for the delicious food."

Ian seemed glad to have a few minutes alone with Sara. He had news to share. "I'm going to start working four days a week at one of the animal hospitals. Just after the wedding, I plan to move into the house by the woods. I hope that, by being in that area, I'll see any things that might shed some light on this mystery you talk about."

"Be careful," Sara reminded him. "We must be cautious. We don't know who is trustworthy."

Ian once more assisted her in her departure from his oversized truck. Sarah thanked him and said, "See you tomorrow!"

One oversized truck plus one very petite lady was an interesting combination. Sara was learning that the running board was her friend, and she'd almost mastered the entering and exiting maneuver. Sam continued to be the gentleman that he had been. He always waited for her to get in or out before he leapt to join her.

Inside her home, Sara hung her dress carefully in her echoing closet then invited Sam to walk around the block. "We need to be planning a space for our puppy," she told Sam.

The wind was howling and the walkways were slippery, so she shortened the walk. Sam seemed as eager as Sara was to get back into a warm house.

The first thing Sara did at the hospital the next day was to look in on her suspect, John Morrison. She wasn't sure why she was suspicious of him. Something just didn't seem right. With Ian in Brentville now, and with the committee helping her, Sara was hopeful. *With God on my side, I can be hopeful.* "Help me, Lord," she prayed. "Please help me be open to any clues that I need to be seeing regarding this case."

Sara gave a few taps on the door then entered to find Mr. Morrison in deep conversation with Mr. Brent. Sara thought she sensed a little look of guilt on Mr. Brent's face, as though he were afraid Sara might have overheard something. He quickly regained his composure and turned into his steady, charismatic self. "Just checking on one of my employees," he announced. "Sorry to hear that we lost Mr. Ross."

"Yes," Sara said. "His wife and daughters are missing him too."

"A very tragic accident," added Mr. Brent. "Well, I should probably leave to let you check on your patient. It's good to have you here at the hospital. I'm hearing fine things about you."

Sara forced a nod and a smile his way. Pretending around him was not getting any easier, but she had a very practical side. *Even though my face feels as if it's cracking every time I smile at him, it's a necessary exercise.*

Holding her clipboard, Sara pulled a chair up to Mr. Morrison's bed. "How are you feeling today, Mr. Morrison?"

"Not so good," he answered. "Can you give me something a little stronger for the pain?"

"I don't see why not. I will check my *Natural Healing* book and get back to you as soon as I can."

"Thanks," he whimpered. "I really need something."

On the way back to her office, Sara met up with Ian. He had come to get a new cast. "You're just the man I want to see," said Sara. "Come in and close the door." Ian could see that she was excited about something, and he couldn't wait to get in to hear what it was all about.

"I'm pretty sure John Morrison is part of our mystery," confided Sara. "It's just a small thing, but my radar is rarely wrong. This is what I need you for this morning: Mr. Morrison is in a lot of pain and is asking for more pain medicine. I've discovered that one of the herbal meds for pain that I have been using on patients seems to make them talk—I mean, talk as in a truth serum. I've seen that if I ask them questions when they're under the influence of this drug, the answer is quite different from the answer I get when they're off the medicine.

"I don't dare call Harold, because I'm afraid the operator might be listening in," Sara continued. "Another thing is that he has a party line, so a couple of the neighbors on that line could also be listening. I'm asking you if you would drive over to Harold's place and ask him to get someone from the committee—or maybe come himself. They know the case better than I do and might have some pertinent questions for Mr. Morrison. I have a few myself, and you might want to be here too, Ian."

"I'm on it, Doc," said Ian. He seemed eager to do anything he could to help.

Within fifteen minutes, he was reporting back for duty, with Harold by his side. "Great work!" Sara exclaimed. "Now here's the plan. I will go in and administer the shot to Mr. Morrison. After a few minutes it will take effect. I will ask him a few questions that I have regarding Lucy. Then you guys come in. I'll stay in the room but will be watching the door to prevent any interruptions. If someone comes, I'll say you're visiting, and I'll try to divert them in some way."

"What a team!" Harold exclaimed. "When I tell the rest of the committee about this, they'll be glad that you're both on our side, and they'll want you on the committee for sure."

Sara had already gone to the hospital pharmacy to pick up the drug she needed. She entered first, while Harold and Ian sat outside the door. There were chairs in the hallway with books to read. They would just be seen as visitors sitting in the waiting room.

Mr. Morrison couldn't wait to get the shot. Within three minutes, he seemed to be asleep. Sara knew that the drug had kicked in and that he was ready to do some talking.

"Lord, guide me," she prayed. "Mr. Morrison, can you hear me?" she asked.

"Yes, ma'am," he answered.

"Is Lucy your daughter?"

"Yes."

"Did Lucy have a baby a few months ago?"

"Yes, ma'am."

"What happened to the baby?"

"That was handled by Frank."

"Have other girls in the church had babies?"

"Yes." He nodded.

"And what happened to those babies?"

"They were taken by Frank, the head of our group."

"Were those babies killed?"

"Yes, ma'am."

Sara left the bedside to get Harold and Ian. She was visibly shaken, and her normally pink cheeks were as white as the sheet on the bed.

As soon as they entered the room, they led Sara to a chair by the door. "What happened?" Ian whispered.

"My suspicions are true," she answered quietly. "I think there may be some very dark satanic rituals going on with some of the members of the Brentville Church. I think there may be babies being sacrificed!"

"You can ask him your questions now," Sara added. "Just make them direct and simple. He won't remember this. In a few hours, he'll wake up as if nothing has happened. I will stay here to try to keep others out of the room."

A few minutes later, Sara's color was back. A nurse came to the door to take Mr. Morrison's vitals, and Sara said that she would do it. When Mrs. Morrison came, Sara took her back out to the hallway, saying that she needed to talk with her. Mrs. Morrison complied without questioning Sara's motives.

Sara told Mrs. Morrison how her husband was doing and wondered aloud if she had any questions. Fortunately, she did. Sara took her time in answering. She was getting the impression that Mrs. Morrison didn't have much to say about anything in that household with its six children, three of whom were teenage girls.

Harold and Ian felt that they had questioned the patient long enough and decided to leave. "He seems to be too sleepy to talk," Harold said to Mrs. Morrison. "We'll be leaving." Then he added as he passed her in the hallway, "Sorry to hear about the accident, Mrs. Morrison."

"Thank you for stopping by," said Sara to Harold.

Then she turned to Mrs. Morrison. "John was in so much pain, I gave him a shot that should help him sleep for a while. Come on in. I will take his vitals, and then you can sit with him."

Ian and Harold were waiting for Sara in her office. "Wow!" exclaimed Ian. "Do we make a good team or what? Today was a big day, and we now have a lot of information for the committee to sort through. Thank you, Sara, for being so intuitive and on the ball."

"Think nothing of it," she said. "That's my job. I think that my working in the ER for ten years has helped me sharpen my detective skills."

Harold decided to walk home so he could clear his head. He had taken notes and would go over them again before he met with the other three members of the committee.

Sara took Ian to the emergency room to see if they could come up with a smaller cast for him. "I'm going to leave you in the hands of these proficient professionals," said Sara. "I need to finish my rounds."

But first, I need to sit down with some tea to catch my breath. It has been an exciting morning, and I've been running on adrenalin. I cannot get these Brentville girls out of my mind. "Thank you God for the clues this morning and for all we learned. Now please help us know what to do with it."

Friday night's Bible study/church went well. Ian seemed encouraged by the time spent with other believers. Even though he had been there only a short while, he and Harold had become very close. Harold was easy to love, but this was different. Ian had lost his dad when he was twenty, and Harold seemed to be filling that role for him as well as for Sara.

As Sara was on call for the weekend, she'd decided not to pick up her puppy until the following week. Crystal said that she didn't mind. She had Mary Jane there to help out.

Sara worked all day at the hospital. She was supposed to be at Crystal's shower by seven. At six, she needed to walk Sam and get dressed for the evening's event. Ian had accepted the job of escorting Crystal, Sara, and Mary Jane to Oliver's mother's home. He had also become a big help with the puppies.

"Hi, Doc," greeted Ian as he pulled up in front of her house. He was out and holding her door open before she made it off her porch steps.

"I'm looking forward to this party," said Sara, as she stepped into the truck full of women. Are you ready to be pampered for the evening, Crystal?"

"Yes," Crystal replied. "It will be good just to sit with no children, dogs, or customers. Do you want to come, Ian?"

"No thanks. I'd rather have my fingernails pulled out than attend a bridal shower," he answered. "Just give me a call when you're done. In the meantime, I'll be puppy-sitting."

Jane's living room was decorated with crepe-paper streamers and bows. The dining-room table was set up with her best dishes and silver. She had some beautiful glass plates that had an indentation for the glass cups, perfect for holding a plate and drink on a lap.

There was a card table in the corner for gifts. Because Crystal didn't need much in the way of housekeeping gifts, almost everyone decided to bring things like sexy lingerie and some IOUs for help with babysitting at the hotel to grant Crystal and Oliver some alone time

Sara noticed that Mrs. Morrison was in attendance. *I should probably try to sit near her,* she thought. *I might be able to glean something from talking with her. At the very least, I'll see who she knows and who she seems to be comfortable with. I have a feeling that her friends are her husband's friends. It doesn't seem to me that she would dare form friendships outside the realm of her husband's control.*

There were about twenty women at the shower. Everyone who knew Crystal seemed to love her. As Sara looked around for a place to sit, she noticed that Jane and her helpers were bringing out TV trays. There must have been twenty of them. Sara remembered using a TV tray at her mother's house, but seeing that many coming out all at once struck her as funny. It was as though the trays were taking on a life of their own. *At any moment, I expect them to start marching to the music of the* Sorcerer's Apprentice.

She probably could have asked for one, but the room was so full of wobbly trays, a person had a hard time walking across the room without getting tangled up in one of the flimsy aluminum legs.

TV tray

Those trays must have come with Mr. Brent when he first developed Brentville in the fifties. That was thirty years ago! They've certainly taken good care of them. I wonder if my house has one stashed away somewhere? I'll have to check the downstairs closet and cellar when I get home. Sara smiled.

Finding a seat by Mrs. Morrison, she sat down, balancing her glass plate of food with her glass cup of punch on her lap.

"How are you tonight?" Sara asked Mrs. Morrison.

"Oh, please call me Lisa."

"Okay, Lisa. Are you managing all right with your husband in the hospital?"

"I have three teenaged daughters, and they are a big help. You met Lucy a while back at the hospital."

"Oh, yes," replied Sara. "How is Lucy doing?"

"I think she's all healed up," answered Lisa. "I worry about her though. She seems very melancholy lately." Her comment had come out fast, and Sara sensed that Lisa wished she hadn't said it.

"Well," Sara said in a gentle, caring voice, "Please tell Lucy if she ever needs help or just wants to talk, my office is always open to her. And that goes for you too, Lisa." At that point, she was feeling empathy—or maybe even sympathy—for the poor woman. She would have given her a hug but was afraid of getting into a fight with one of the strategically placed TV trays. Sara reached over and put her hand gently on Lisa's. "Here," she said, "I'm going to write my home phone number down for you. Just in case." Sara smiled.

Lisa gave her a weak but definitely an I've-heard-you thank-you and a weak but definitely I-need-you smile.

The next week was a blur to Sara. Ian helped her get her horse, buggy, and sleigh and showed her how to hook them all up. Having grown up on a farm with horses, she needed no more help in that department.

Ian delivered her new puppy, and Sara had a cage for training purposes. She decided to name the new member of her family Matilda. Ian had already started the crate training, so each time Sara took Matilda out of her crate, Sam and Sara took her out to "go potty." Because Ian had been doing this with the puppy, Sara knew that before long, she would be trained. *What a sweet and playful addition to my household,* Sara thought. Sam seemed happy to have another dog around too, even if the newcomer was a little rambunctious at times.

CHAPTER 15

The Wedding

Wedding bells were ringing. Saturday had arrived. Sara learned that in Brentville when someone gets married in the church, love songs are played all day before the wedding. The music could be heard through much of the village. *I don't know how they do that, but it's quite nice.*

It was Ian's job to get Crystal and her entourage to the church on time. Crystal and her twins, Mary Jane, and Sara made it too many for one trip. He transported everyone else from the hotel first and came back for Sara.

There was a room at the church for dressing the bride, the twins, and the wedding party. The roads were snow covered and would be perfect for the sleighs later. More snow was predicted, but it hadn't started yet.

"Thanks, Ian," said Sara, as she climbed down from the running board. "I pray that we will see and hear things tonight that will help us. We need to keep our eyes and ears open."

"I hear you, Doc," said Ian as he saluted Sara with his good arm. "See you later."

Sara found the right room by following her ears. She could hear Joseph and Jenny running up and down the hallway. "Come on, you guys," she said as she motioned them into the big dressing room. "We need to get you looking your very best for your mama's wedding."

Two hours later, a beautifully dressed group crowded the dressing room. The bride was radiant in her lace mermaid-cut dress. It was strapless and had net flowing out around the knee area. The long, lace-trimmed veil came down to the train in the back.

The four dark-blue velvet bridesmaid dresses were all alike. Sara's dress, cut differently, was made of the same material. All of the bouquets were white.

The twins were dressed in blue and white also. Jenny had a long blue dress with a white pinafore. Joseph had blue knickers, suspenders, and a white shirt and bowtie. The men all had red vests and ties that Crystal had designed and made.

The church had been transformed into a fairytale room, perfect for a fairytale wedding. There were three Christmas trees, all decorated with white poinsettias, and a multitude of lights. There were electric candles in all the windows and in every nook and cranny into which a light could fit.

A white satin rug waited to be rolled out on the middle aisle for the wedding party to walk on. All the pews along the aisles had ribbons, bows, and fresh flowers.

The candles were burning, and the church lights were either off or dimmed. Everyone in the church had been given a candle to hold and to light at the end of the service. The groom, best man, and groomsmen were lined up in front of the church, in front of the altar.

The organ started playing as Joseph, Sam, and Jenny came down the aisle. Joseph carried the rings on a pillow. Jenny was gently scattering blossoms from her basket. Sam sported a big red bow, and his tail was wagging a mile a minute. He was stealing the show.

The beautifully attired bridesmaids gracefully walked the carpet next. Sara followed them. As she started her walk down the aisle, she caught Ian's eye. They exchanged smiles, and Sara could tell that he approved of her beautiful blue dress that fitted ever so perfectly and her hair, in its upswing, with soft, blond wisps showing at her neckline.

The trip down the aisle seemed so long, but finally, I'm in my place.

The wedding party turned to watch Crystal being led down the aisle by Harold. Everyone in Brentville seemed to know him. It was as if he were everyone's father or grandfather. Crystal was not a Christian, and she didn't know anything about the Bible study/church or the committee. She just loved Harold as a grandfather and friend.

Oliver couldn't take his eyes off his beautiful bride. Sara stood by Oliver and Crystal, and carefully pulled back Crystal's veil. The minister asked a few questions, the couple said their vows, the soloist sang a very pretty romantic song, and it was done. That was just what Jenny and Joseph needed—a not-too-long, short-and-sweet wedding.

No mention of God in the ceremony, Sara mused. *It's sad, but I'm not surprised.*

Only candles remained lighted. Everyone lit his or her candle, and the soft glow of candlelight filled the sanctuary. The bride and groom walked hand in hand down the aisle, out the big front door, snuggled into warm capes, and climbed into one of the comforter-filled sleighs waiting in front of the church. Adding to the romance of the moment, snowflakes were beginning to drift down.

Oliver's mother, who was minding the twins, helped them climb into another sleigh. Just as the rest of the guests started leaving the church, more snowflakes floated down to kiss their cheeks.

CHAPTER 16

Invasion of the Mansion

By the time the last sleigh had pulled up to the mansion, the snow was coming down so fast the building was barely visible. The wedding party arrived first, and group pictures were taken as the guests arrived. The twins and Sam were enjoying the whole process. There were tables of food all around them. Between photos, Joseph helped himself, and each time, he took a handful to Jenny. Sam trailed behind, cleaning up the spills.

Mr. Brent spent some time with the twins before Oliver's mother took them home with her. It had been a long day, and they had been on their best behavior. Sam stayed with Sara.

On the first floor was a big reception room in the mansion's left wing that was open to the wedding guests. Most villagers had never before been invited inside. It was comparable to being invited to the White House and having the president say they could make themselves at home. As Sara looked around, she was stunned by the enormous rooms, the marble, the chandeliers, the large stairways leading to rooms in which she wasn't allowed, and the many candles.

After the photographs had been taken, the wedding party moved to the big reception room. The guests were already there, enjoying an open bar and hors d'oeuvres. The band announced the bride and the groom with a drum roll, and the rest of the wedding party followed. Guests were invited to find their seats. Sara was pleased to see that her place card was beside Crystal's. She noticed that Ian and Mary Jane were beside each other at the next table, along with Lisa and her girls.

The groomsman who was sitting on Sara's other side was about forty-five and had planned to be married the previous year, but his fiancée had experienced a change of heart. He explained all this to Sara between bites of the ever-so-tender filet mignon.

The meal was finished, and the cake had been cut. The bride and groom danced the first dance. Listening to the familiar music was making Sara lonely. *I wish I had someone to dance with. Oh, how I loved dancing with Jim!*

Joe, the young man next to her, must have been feeling the same way. He asked, and as she followed him to the dance floor, she felt a little nervous. *I'm used to dancing with Jim. I haven't danced with anyone else since college.*

Sara managed the fast dance reasonably well. Though they were living in the eighties, the citizens of Brentville were stuck in the fifties. The band was playing mostly jitterbug, jive, or slow dances. *If I were back in Harleysville, dancing with Jim, we'd have been doing the funky chicken or the hustle or some such fun dance.*

Walking back to the table, Sara noticed that Ian had asked Mary Jane to dance. *I wonder if he's learned anything new today.*

Mr. Brent had Lisa out on the dance floor. She didn't act as though she was particularly comfortable with the situation.

"May I have this dance?" Ian asked Sara.

"Oh, yes," she replied, and he guided her out to the dance floor.

It was a slow dance, for which Sara was grateful. She had come to know Ian well enough to be very comfortable in his arms. He was a good dancer and led her around the room with grace. The song ended, and he lingered for a second as though he didn't want to let her go.

"Thank you, Sara. You feel good in my arms—or should I say *arm*?" He chuckled. "And by the way, you look very beautiful."

"Thank you, Ian," answered Sara. *It sure is nice to be complimented.*

The reception was a success. Sara thought, *You can say what you want about Mr. Brent, but he does know how to throw a party.*

Crystal said she was pleased with everything. She and Oliver left the mansion, walking outside to a heavy snowfall. The enclosed sleigh was waiting for them by the front door. Off they went to the designated cottage on the lake. Crystal had taken her suitcase over to the cottage earlier in the day.

It should be a perfect setting for their honeymoon, thought Sara.

Guests started riding back to the church. It wasn't a long ride, so with all the sleighs, the crowd was dwindling quickly. Sara and Ian, Harold and Olive and Sam climbed into the next sleigh. "The snow is really coming down now!" Sara commented. "There must have been three inches of snowfall while we were in the mansion."

The sleigh was enclosed, and the driver was sitting on an outside seat, high up in the front, guiding the horses to the church. "I don't think the driver can hear us," said Harold. "Does anyone have anything to report?"

Both men said that they had tried to investigate the layout of the mansion as much as they could. They both had come to the conclusion that the cellar held something of interest. Harold had managed to get down a hallway in the cellar before someone led him back upstairs. "I told them I was looking for the restroom," explained Harold. "I think they bought it."

"I've been so curious about that place. Did you find anything down there?" Sara inquired.

"I saw quite a bit, but at this point I don't know what any of it means," answered Harold. "There were many rooms along this hallway. Most rooms had little windows at the top of the door, but all were locked and bolted shut. Through one of the windows I saw a large auditorium. On the outside wall of the auditorium, I saw a door that I think went outside. Through another small window, I saw a gigantic computer-like machine." Harold added, "I need to go home and make notes on what I saw, so I don't forget some of the details. We'll have a meeting with our committee soon. I'm glad to have you two working with us."

Sara, feeling the chill of the night, was glad to see the church.

"Hop in, everyone," invited Ian. "I'll take you home and will come back for Mary Jane and whoever else needs a ride."

"You won't get any argument from me," said Sara, her teeth chattering.

By the time the truck got to Harold and Olive's house, the heater was blowing hot air instead of cold.

"See you tomorrow," Sara shouted. *What an adorable couple.*

Harold walked in front of Olive, scuffing his feet, making a path for her.

"What a guy!" commented Sara.

In a few minutes, they had reached Sara's house. The warmth from the heater was feeling so good that Sara didn't want to go anywhere. Sam seemed to be quite comfy and settled.

"What?" Ian jested. "Do you want me to scuff a path to your front door?"

"No, I guess I can make it on my own." She pouted mockingly at him. Then Sara smiled as she slid out the door to the running board and stepped into the soft snow. "Thanks! I'll see you tomorrow."

Sara and Sam ran to open the front door and rescued Matilda from her crate. Out the threesome dashed into the snow. Matilda and Sam seemed to be beside themselves with joy. Sara, on the other hand, couldn't wait to get back into the warmth of her house. *I wonder what my Jim and the kids are doing tonight. Wish I could see them. Wish I could tell them about Jesus.* "Dear Lord," Sara prayed, "please open the hearts of Jim and the kids to you and your word. Please draw them to yourself, like you did me. I beg you, Lord, help me find a way back to my family."

"And Lord, if I don't get back to them, please put someone in their lives who can show them the way to you, and your kingdom. In Jesus's name, I pray, amen... and, happy birthday, Lord Jesus!"

Sara had invited Harold, Olive, and Ian over for Christmas Day. *I want to be with other Christians. I want to have them help me put up and decorate my Christmas tree. This will be my first Christmas as a child of God. This baby Jesus is someone to be celebrated!*

After thinking through the day's plans, Sara had decided to invite Mary Jane and her two girls as well as Lisa Morrison and all six of her children. *Why not? Maybe some of the Christian prayers and Bible readings will rub off on a few of them.*

Sara knew that Harold, Olive, and Ian would put all talk of the committee or of the Bible study/church on hold while the other guests were present.

Her guests were invited to arrive around eleven. Everyone was bringing food, and Sara was baking a ham and scalloped potatoes. *I hope that while the women are getting the food organized, the men can get the tree put up in the living room. After Christmas dinner, they can all pitch in and help to decorate it.*

CHAPTER 17

Sara's "First" Christmas

Christmas morning was crisp, clear, and beautiful. Everything outside was glistening. After Sara took the dogs out, she shoveled the sidewalk from the house to the street. The village sidewalk plow had already been by. The roads had been partially plowed, but, as usual, the workers had left a good cover of snow for the sleighs.

Ian was the first to arrive. "Merry Christmas, my friend," Sara greeted, as she shared a lopsided hug. "By the way," she continued, "you did a great job on the dance floor last night. Most people wouldn't have even tried to dance with an arm like yours. I must say, you managed to make me feel like I was floating on air."

A few minutes later, Harold and Olive came, followed by Lisa and her six, then Mary Jane and her two girls. The two men and Lisa's oldest son, Brian, who was fourteen, went outside on the porch to get the tree. Sara had the stand for the evergreen placed on the floor in the living room, in front of the bay window, right where she wanted it to be.

At first glance, the men were sure the balsam wouldn't fit in the living room. "Trees always look smaller when they're outside," Ian mumbled under his breath.

"Well, let's give it a try," suggested Harold.

Harold and Ian carried it in. Brian made sure it fit into the stand then tightened the screws to make sure it wouldn't fall down.

"Look at that," said Ian. "A perfect fit. There's at least a two-foot clearance."

"We'll let the tree sit for a while as we eat," Harold said.

"Holy smoke!" exclaimed Brian as he looked up to the top of the tree.

Sara walked by, appreciating the Christmas tree's aroma. "I love it," she said. "Thanks, guys."

The food, dishes, and silverware were set out on the kitchen counter. Sara invited everyone to come out to the kitchen, make a circle around the kitchen table, and hold hands. Ian prayed, "Thank you, Lord, for this food and for our friends who prepared it. We thank you for sending us your son so many years ago. In Jesus's name we pray, amen."

Sara let the youngsters go first. "Fill up your plates. Then find a seat here at the table."

She had room for twelve at the dining room table and six at the kitchen table, so everyone could sit at a table. The mixed ages of the guests animated the conversation, making it fun. Sara could tell that Lisa and Mary Jane knew each other well. The children, too, seemed very well acquainted.

I don't doubt that there are some deep dark secrets these two women have tucked away. And I wouldn't be surprised to find that the children have a few memories that are so bad, they've buried them forever.

"Let's work on the tree for a while before we have dessert," suggested Olive. Everyone agreed and headed to the living room.

"I love the smell of balsam needles," commented Harold. The whole room was filled with it.

"Okay," said Ian, "Brian and I will put the lights on first."

"I'll put the big star on top," volunteered Harold.

Olive led the rest in opening the box of ornaments. There were plenty, even for that big tree.

"Now it's time for the foil icicles," announced Sara. "This is the hard part, because it takes patience. We need to put them on one by one. Near the end of the process, we're tempted to put them on in bunches, but that doesn't work."

"Holy smoke!" uttered Brian as he gazed at the nearly trimmed tree.

"I found a crèche in the attic," announced Sara. "Would you youngsters like to put it together for me and then place it under the tree?"

The record player was playing Christmas music, and all were enjoying their tasks. Before long, the tree was trimmed, and the crèche was sitting under it.

"Lucy, would you please do the honors and plug in the lights?" Sara asked.

Everyone stood in awe of it all. They clapped their hands, while they oohed and aahed. "Holy smoke!" said Brian again. It seemed that he was really impressed but unable to come up with any meaningful word to show his appreciation for the tree. For him, on that particular Christmas day, "Holy smoke!" seemed to say it all.

"Harold, would you please read us the Christmas story from the Bible?" Sara asked.

"Glad to," he replied, and Sara handed him a Bible. Everyone sat quietly as he read the verses from Luke. Sara noticed people's eyes were focusing on the baby in the manger as they heard the story. She was guessing that most of them had never heard it.

"Thanks, Harold," Sara said. "Now it's time for dessert. I have a birthday cake for Jesus because, after all, today we're celebrating his birthday. Janet, would you please light the candles for me?

Once they were lit, Sara said, "Now, as we sing 'Happy Birthday' to Jesus, you kids gather round and blow out the candles at the end of the song. There are Christmas cookies, pie, and ice cream also. Help yourselves."

She was pleased with the way the kids sang to Jesus. "Please, Lord," she silently prayed, "call them to you. Help them love you as I do."

Harold played some Christmas carols and everyone enjoyed the rest of the day. By four, the celebrators were beginning to leave.

"So nice of you to have us," Lisa said to Sara. "When do you think my husband will be released?"

"Not sure," Sara answered. "It will be a while. He has a couple of bad breaks, and we're watching him closely for infection." Sara thought she sensed some relief in Lisa. *She's afraid of the man.*

Next to leave were Mary Jane and her girls. As she hugged Mary Jane good-bye, Sara thanked her for taking such good care of Crystal. "She's a good girl," said Mary Jane. "And I need her as much as she needs me."

"Let's sit for a while and soak in the peace and contentment that this tree is offering," Sara suggested to the remaining guests.

"Sounds like the perfect ending to a wonderful day," answered Olive.

Olive, gathering Matilda onto her lap, chose the rocking chair. Harold and Ian were on the couch. Sam had his head on Ian's feet. After she'd thrown another log on the fire, Sara curled up in a big soft chair. "Did you notice how the guests listened so attentively to your reading today?" she asked. "Wouldn't it be great if they were to want God in their lives? Wouldn't it be wonderful if, in this community of Brentville, citizens would come, one by one, to know Christ?"

"Yes, the village would be healed from the inside out," said Harold. "We will pray for that tonight."

"We need to be going, dear," said Olive. "Thank you for this joy-filled day, Sara."

"Would you like a ride home?" offered Ian.

"No thanks," answered Harold. "We need the exercise."

Ian was still sitting on the couch, so Sara sat back down too. She asked, "Are you planning to move into your house tomorrow?"

"Yes, and looking forward to it," he answered. "Mary Jane offered to go in and clean for me, since the hotel is closed down for a few days."

"That's good. I'm anxious to see it. Let me know when you're ready for a guest to drop by."

"You never need an invitation. Please come any time."

"Are you planning to get a horse, buggy, and sleigh?"

"I'm thinking of it," he said. "A sleigh might be a better way to get around in the winter."

"I'm glad you could be here to celebrate my first Christmas since I have had Jesus in my life," Sara said. "Words cannot express the love that I have in my heart for God and his grace. Only another who feels the way I do about Jesus could ever understand my feelings."

"I know," said Ian. "Isn't it great? Oh, and I have a little gift for you, Sara—just a little something to let you know how much your friendship means to me. Without you, dear Sara, to guide and help me, I would probably have been killed trying to get over the wall."

He continued, "I had this gift in my truck for my daughter. But it's more appropriate for you. It is always exciting to see other people ask God into their life. The Bible says that the heavens rejoice each time this happens. I'm rejoicing too, and this cross is to help you remember—and celebrate—what you have in Christ."

He went on. "When I get home, I'll buy my daughter another cross. She has known the Lord since she was sixteen. I know she would want you to have it and would be celebrating with you."

He continued. "I think you are aware that I would like to be more than friends. But I respect the fact that you are still a married woman, and I know how much you love your husband." He handed her a little box with a slender gold cross in it. She removed the cross from the box. Her eyes moistened, and she asked Ian to help her put it on.

"I will cherish this cross, Ian. And I cherish your friendship." *Why am I so teary-eyed? I don't quite know. Maybe I'm just feeling blessed to have this person in my life.*

"The present that I'll give you will come tomorrow after you get moved in," she said. "Come to the hospital, and I'll put you in a much smaller and more flexible cast and sling."

"Thanks, Doc. I've already spilled tomato soup all over this one." Ian lifted his foot away from under Sam's head. "Well, Sam, sorry, I had to move my foot. I have to get going." Sam got up and lumbered over to the rug by the fireplace.

Sara gave Ian another lopsided hug, thanked him for the cross, and helped him get his coat on.

"Merry Christmas, dear friend," she shouted as Ian slid across the snow to his cold truck.

The kitchen was all cleaned up. Washing dishes by hand was not something that Sara was used to doing, but she didn't mind it as much as she'd thought she would. Actually, she was finding that when someone helped her with the job, it could be a grand time for sharing thoughts and usually ended up being a time of deep conversation.

The dogs had been walked. Both loved romping in the snow, and they collected large balls of snow on their legs and fur. Sara had learned the hard way that it took a while to remove those clumps and clean up the melted snow. Her cellar had become the perfect place for de-icing the dogs.

Her feeling of peace each time she walked by the softly lit Christmas tree was too much to ignore. *I'll just sit here for a few minutes before I go to bed.*

With Sam resting on her foot and Matilda in her lap, she opened her Bible and read again about how Jesus came to this earth. "Thank you, God," she prayed, "for sending us your Son. And thank you for letting me know that even if I don't get reunited with my family, I will have you forever. What a gigantic gift you have given me. I look forward to being with you in heaven. In Jesus's name. Amen."

"How did your move go?" Sara asked Ian the next morning at the hospital.

"Very well," he answered. "As you know, we don't have much to move."

"For sure," she said. "It was the easiest move I'd ever experienced."

Sara called a couple of nurses and guided Ian into the exam rooms. After they sawed the cast, and took it off his arm, Sara gave him his new cast. "Your arm is looking good," she said. "This new cast probably won't have to be on much longer. You were fortunate. Merry Christmas." She smiled.

CHAPTER 18

Polishing Up the New Sara

Each time Sara needed something, like a haircut, more makeup, or a new pair of slacks, she learned a little bit more about this well-run little village.

Sara had met Janis at the Bible study. Janis's arrival in Brentville happened much as Sara's had. She had been there for four years when Sara arrived. Janis was now an up-and-coming hair stylist in Brentville. The villagers swarmed to her shop because they knew she was up on all the more recent styles. The two other hair shops in Brentville were stuck in the fifties.

On Saturday, Sara was looking forward to her nine thirty appointment with Janis. She and Sam trudged through the soft snow that had fallen during the night. The snow boots she'd purchased at the local shoe store were coming in handy. They went on over her shoes and zipped up the front. They went up a couple inches past the ankle and had faux fur all around the top. She remembered her mother wearing a pair like them in the fifties.

After entering Janis's salon, Sara found a spot where she and Sam could sit. There was a pot-belly wood stove in the front with a sofa and a couple of soft chairs. She found some old newspapers from Brentville and a few old magazines. Everything in the place was of the fifties era, except Janis. Fortunately, she had come with her head full of eighties ideas.

"Hi, Sara," Janis said. "Come on over to the sink, and I'll shampoo your hair."

Oh my, this is heavenly, Sara thought. "I need to be pampered more often."

After the shampoo, Janis pulled the attached porcelain cover back down over the sink, twirled Sara's chair around, and voilà, Sara was looking into the mirror and ready for her new style.

They decided to go short, and Janis was pleased. "You have some natural curl here. I'll give you a razor cut, which always works well with naturally curly hair. I know you'll like it."

And indeed, Sara loved the end result. *Soft, short curls. This is probably more age appropriate.*

"I like the way the soft, perfect blond curls frame your face. It accentuates your beautiful blue eyes," Janis said.

As Sara and Sam left the shop, she realized that she was feeling like a new person. "Maybe we need to find me a new sweater and a pair of slacks," she told Sam. "Then my spirits will *really* be lifted. I haven't done any shopping here to speak of, so this will be my first time in the department store."

It was a good-sized store with a squeaky wood floor. It had a smell that she remembered in the old stores that she had gone to with her mom.

Sara found a pretty pink angora sweater and a pair of gray wool slacks. *These will go with my pearl necklace.* She had been wearing her pearl necklace the day she entered Brentville. The only other jewelry Sara had was her wedding ring, her watch, a few pieces she'd packed for her trip to the convention, and now her new cross.

"Can I return these if they don't fit?" she asked the clerk.

"Absolutely," he said. "Are you ready to check out?"

Sara nodded and handed him the clothes. "One pair of gray slacks," he wrote out on the yellow receipt pad, and "one angora sweater."

"That comes to eighteen dollars and fifty cents before tax—nineteen in total."

Sara handed him a twenty-dollar bill. The man put the yellow receipt and the money into a cylinder that went by way of a pneumatic tube to an office upstairs. While he was waiting for the cylinder to come back, he put the clothes into a paper sack.

A few seconds later, Sara heard the swishing of the cylinder coming back down. He grabbed the tube, took out the receipt and the change, and handed her the receipt and clothes.

"Thank you," called Sara, as she walked toward the door.

Sam was sitting right where she'd left him, on a dry spot in the sun in front of the store. "What a good boy!" praised Sara. Sam responded with a small tail wag.

When Sara and Sam reached home, they invited Matilda to go out for her walk. *What a beautiful day! I think I should test-drive my horse and sleigh today. I want to check out Ian's new house, and it's too far to walk comfortably in the winter.*

After lunch, Sara took Sam out to her garage, and she hooked Nellie up to the sleigh. "Come on, Sam, jump up! We're going to visit Ian before I go to Mary's for my Bible study."

The horse appeared to be well trained and used to pulling a sleigh. Sara was feeling a happy freedom, similar to the day she had obtained the bike from Harold. *What fun! It's exhilarating to be doing something that makes me feel young again. I haven't been near a horse since I lived on the farm as a young girl.*

Most of the houses in Brentville had hitching posts. Sara was glad to find one in front of Ian's house. She carefully climbed down from the sleigh, tied up Nellie, and called for Sam.

Ian was stocking his pantry shelves. Mary Jane and one of her daughters were there, cleaning.

"Smells good," commented Sara.

"Must be the lavender cleaning mixture," said Ian. "I just bought it this morning. I also have a roast in the oven. Want to join me for supper?"

"I never turn down an invitation that smells this good," she replied, grinning. "What time?"

"Why don't you come at around six?" he said.

"I'll be here. Maybe I'll wait to have the house tour when I come back tonight."

Later that evening, as Sara and he sat by the fire, Ian told her of his latest findings. "Last night I sat by this back window in the kitchen for quite a while. Looking into the woods, I thought I could see some smoke and maybe a fire. I don't know if it was my imagination or if I really did see something. One of these days, I plan to hike out that way through the woods to see what I can see."

Sara said, "If it's on a day when I am off work, I'll go too. If you end up going yourself, call me, so I know where you are. If you don't come back, I'll send out a search party to find you. I should be leaving now. Nellie would probably appreciate some oats and the barn's shelter."

"Looks like more snow coming," commented Ian. "Do you want to try some ice fishing with me tomorrow? As it will be Sunday, we'll both have the day off. It might be fun."

"Sure! Pick me up when you're ready."

CHAPTER 19

A Serious Interruption of Plans

The next day, Sara still had to do early-morning rounds at the hospital before she could go anywhere. She was out of the door by eight. The hospital was almost filled to its capacity—mostly with colds, flu, and pneumonia patients.

"Good morning, Mr. Morrison," greeted Sara. "Any improvement for you today?"

He lifted his head from the pillow but didn't have much life in his eyes. He had caught the flu.

Not only that, I'm pretty sure he's also suffering from pneumonia.

"Not so good," he answered in a weak voice.

"I'm changing your medicine," said Sara. "Maybe that will help." She was getting ready to give him the shot when Mr. Brent came to the door. He had another man with him, and Sara recognized the man. It was Frank.

"I'll be finished here in a minute," she said.

The men backed up into the hallway and waited for the okay to enter. "These rooms are under quarantine," said Sara, as she removed her gloves and mask and washed her hands. "Mr. Morrison is a very sick man, and unless this is of the most urgent nature, I would advise you to wait until he is better."

138

Mr. Brent was obviously not used to being told what to do. He bristled and said, "We will take our chances."

"It's not only you I'm worried about," continued Sara. "Mr. Morrison is very weak, and a visit right now could do him in."

"Thank you, Dr. Saunders, but we'll take our chances," said Mr. Brent as he pushed by her.

"Then please take these gloves and masks for your protection, and his," said Sara. She promptly exited the room.

Fuming and a little shaky after her encounter with Mr. Brent, Sara left the hospital and started walking home. As she thought about the situation, she turned around and headed back. *What was so urgent that Mr. Brent and his companion needed to get in right then? Did they want to shut Mr. Morrison up so he wouldn't give away any information while he was delirious with fever?*

With each new thought, Sara walked faster. Running in the front door, she grabbed some gloves and a mask from her office. She hurried to Mr. Morrison's door, gave a few taps, and walked in. The men were gone, and Mr. Morrison was white, limp, and not breathing. "Oh, what did they do to you?" cried Sara.

After asking the nurse to take care of all the details, Sara headed for home. *I need to find Lisa to tell her about her husband.*

Ian was waiting at Sara's house when she arrived. Shaken from the morning's nightmare of activity, she was glad to see him.

"What's the matter, Doc?" he asked when he saw her pale face.

"I think I need a friend," she replied as she took hold of his arm for support.

He led her to the couch, where she was glad to be sitting. Ian sat with her while she verbalized her shock and concern—and yes, anger.

"Come on, Sara," said Ian. "I'll go with you to find Lisa. We can go ice fishing another day."

Driving up to Lisa's front door, Sara was rehearsing what she would say. Ian had prayed with her in the truck before they got there. "Okay," she said, "here we are. God, give me the words."

Ian helped her out of the truck, and they walked to the front door. As soon as Lisa's eyes met Sara's, she knew there was bad news. "What is it?" she cried.

"I'm sorry to be bringing this news," said Sara. "But your husband died this morning."

Lisa dropped into the nearest chair, and Sara and Ian sat next to her. "What happened?" she asked.

"Not really sure, but we think that the pneumonia took him," said Sara. "He was so run down after his accident, and then the bout with the flu. His body just couldn't handle one more thing."

Lisa took a quavering breath and thanked Sara for all that she had done. "I knew that he was very sick," she added. "I was half prepared for this.

"Do you want me to arrange to have the funeral home pick up his body?" asked Ian.

"No. Thanks anyway, but I'll do it." Lisa seemed to be getting her voice—the voice that she could not have when Mr. Morrison was alive.

Back in the truck, Sara broke down and sobbed. "I'm so worried about Lisa and her kids. I worry what Frank and his men may try to do to them. If they think she knows too much, something awful may happen." She added, "It looks to me like the oldest daughter is pregnant. What a mess! Lord, help us know what to do."

"And he will," said Ian gently as he drove up to Sara's house. "God will give us the strength to get through anything."

"Let's walk the dogs, and then let's drop in on Harold and Olive," suggested Ian. "They always seem to be able to add a touch of hope to anything that is going on."

Sitting with Harold and Olive was bringing peace to Sara's heart. They were helping her look at it all from a different angle: from God's angle. She just needed to get her mind off the problem and back to trusting God to help her know what to do.

"I'm telling you, I think that Mr. Brent had something to do with this death," said Sara in a shaky voice. "I will not confront him, and at the moment I won't tell Lisa. But if I feel she needs a push to stand up against the man, I may rethink that decision. I wish I knew how much of this village is under the spell of whatever it is that's going on."

Sara was sitting in the rocking chair. As she thought about everything, her rocking got faster and faster.

Harold smiled over at her and said, "Sara, remember—worry is like rocking. It gives you something to do, but it doesn't get you anywhere."

"Good one, Harold," said Ian, and they all laughed out loud.

"I will report all this to the committee," said Harold. "One day soon, we would like to have you meet with us to do some brainstorming."

"The sooner the better," said Sara with some impatience in her voice.

"We should get going," urged Ian. "We need to tend to our animals and get prepared for work tomorrow."

"Thanks so much for being our friends," said Sara. "I love you and have grown to depend on you in so many ways."

"You're important to us too," said Olive as she gave them both a big hug.

As they reached Sara's house, Ian said, "Since we both have Wednesday off, let's go ice fishing. I will pick you up at six in the morning. No excuses! And bundle up."

"Thanks, Ian," Sara said

"What for?" he asked.

"Just for being you."

CHAPTER 20

Ice Fishing 101

On Monday after work, Sara stopped in at the department store to pick up some long underwear, ski pants, ski jacket, scarf, mittens, and a few other things to help keep her warm on Wednesday.

Early on Wednesday, Sara peered through her front window. To her surprise, Ian was parked in front of the house. It was only 5:55. *He's like a kid waiting for Christmas morning!* She flicked the porch lights off and on a couple of times, so he came to the door.

"Morning, Doc," said Ian, in his cheery voice. "Are you ready for a great day?"

"Can't wait," Sara answered. "Let's agree that the one who catches the most fish has to fry them."

"Why don't we have a fish fry on New Year's Eve?" he said. "I like to be an optimistic thinker."

"What if we don't catch any?" she worried out loud.

"Oh, ye of little faith," he kidded.

"Okay," she answered, "You're on!"

Brentville had been in a cold spell for the last week, but that day seemed a little warmer. "The warmth could be a good thing," Ian said. "Those conditions usually bring on a good fishing day."

It didn't take long to drive to the lake. Ian parked the truck on the shore. "When I'm sure the ice is thick enough," he said, "I'll drive out onto it. Today, just to be safe, we'll carry our equipment out on the sleds."

He's thought of everything—breakfast, fishing equipment—everything.

"I'm not quite sure how they cut holes in the ice in Brentville," he said. "But luckily I had my fishing equipment in the back of my truck when I ended up here. I had just been to an outlet store and had stocked up and replenished all my fishing equipment. I have a new drill that is battery powered, and it can be charged in my vehicle." They had two fishing poles with lines, two pails to sit on, one drill, a battery charger, and lures.

"We will start near the shore and work our way out," he said.

They watched the pink and red sunrise, then Ian drilled a couple of holes, put the pails down (upside down), and told Sara to pick one. She did, and he handed her a pole and a line ready to drop into the hole. Before Ian could sit down to start fishing, Sara's line tugged suddenly in her hand.

"What do I do?" she yelled. Ian showed her how to get the fish out of the water and how to get the hook out of the fish's mouth.

"Doesn't that hurt the fish?" she asked after watching him rip the hook out of the mouth of the poor fish.

"No," he answered.

"How do you know," she asked. "Did the fish tell you?"

Ian looked at Sara with disbelief.

He must have figured I was going to love ice fishing.

"Here's the thing," he said. "If I have a big fish that I'm going to throw back, I don't fight hard with it because that can harm the fish. Then to throw him back is not good. But the fish I'm going to keep, I fight to keep. And that's food for my family," he added. "Does that redeem my fishing priorities at all?"

"Yes, I guess," she answered. "Now if I can just get you to pull the hook out, I won't have to think about whether I'm hurting the fish."

"Okay," said Ian. "I'd be glad to do that." And he did.

By seven thirty, Sara had caught ten large fish and Ian had seven. He was at a disadvantage because he was taking extra time to help her with the hooks. "I think it's time for breakfast," he said as he reached for the picnic basket. He had two thermoses filled with hot chocolate. He also had beef jerky, peanut butter, cookies, cheese, hard-boiled eggs, and apples.

"Let's move out a little," he suggested. He drilled a few more holes, and they sat on their pails.

"Good spot," yelled Sara excitedly. In a half hour, she had four northern pikes and some perch. Ian was so busy helping her he'd only had time to bring in one fish.

"Shall we make one more move?" he asked.

"Sure!" Sara answered. "I'm on a roll!" Ian was happy that she hadn't given up after her first try.

Moving toward the bend, they drilled a few more holes, set up the pails, and started fishing. They'd been so engrossed in what they were doing that they hadn't paid much attention to their surroundings. "Look at that," Sara said, as she pointed to all the icehouses. "Just like a little hamlet out on the lake."

"We were lucky today," said Ian. "It was warm enough that we could be out in the sunshine and not freeze, but those ice houses would help on a dark, cold, windy day."

Men and women were coming and going now. To and from the icehouses they went. Sara noticed Mr. Brent and Frank going in and out of one of the bigger icehouses.

"How about it, Doc." Ian said. "We've been here a few hours. Are we ready to call it a day?"

"Yes," she replied. "I'm feeling cold now, and I think we have enough fish for a nice fish fry on New Year's Eve."

Sara was about ready to pull her line from the water when she felt a heavy tug. "Ian!" she cried. "There's something on my line that doesn't look like a fish. It looks like a big fat snake." Sara didn't know whether to drop her line and run or whack the beast with the pail. Ian saw the fear in her eyes and quickly took her rod. He fought the ugly thing out of the water.

"An eelpout," he said as he killed it. I'll throw it on the truck and dispose of it when we get home. Some might eat them, but I never wanted to bother with the sliminess of it—or the stink."

Sara took a deep breath and was glad they were about ready to leave. "Who will be cleaning all this fish?" she asked, as if she'd forgotten their bargain.

"I'll do it as soon as I get home," answered Ian.

"I'm impressed," she said, grinning. *Glad I don't have to do it!*

"Let's invite Harold and Olive," suggested Ian.

"Anyone else?" asked Sara.

"What about Mary Jane and Lisa and as many of their kids who might want to come," Ian responded.

"Yes, we really should," agreed Sara. "I'll ask them all tomorrow."

"Let's have it at my place," said Ian. "I'm used to frying fish. That was always my job."

"You've got it," said Sara as she pulled herself into the truck. "I loved today, Ian, eelpout and all. Thanks for introducing me to ice fishing."

CHAPTER 21

Fishy Frolic and Buttercups

Everyone accepted Sara's invitation to the New Year's Day fish fry and seemed grateful for the invitation. They had all offered to bring food, and Sara happily accepted. All that was left for Sara to bring was the dessert.

One thing she had wanted to do was take a tour through some of the large greenhouses. Since Mary Jane's two daughters were both working in the greenhouse industry in Brentville, Sara asked Mary Jane if she could set up a private tour for her.

"Both girls work on Saturday," replied Mary Jane. "If you have time, I'm guessing Saturday would work."

"Thank you. I'll wait to hear from the girls as to the time."

Later that day, Sara received a call from Maribelle Ross. "Hi, Sara," said the chipper voice on the other end of the line. "Mom says you'd like a tour. I would be glad to do it tomorrow morning if you'd like. Be at Greenhouse 5 at nine. I'll meet you in the office."

"Thanks, Maribelle," said Sara. "I'm looking forward to it."

Maribelle, an office worker who had just been promoted to office supervisor, greeted Sara at Greenhouse 5. "Good morning," she said with a smile. *Maribelle always seems happy and appears to have a good head on her shoulders. She would do well in anything she decides to do. One thing I've noticed, though, is that she appears to dislike or distrust Mr. Brent. I'll remember that for the future. She might become an ally.*

Maribelle took Sara into a large office. "I brought you here first, because I want you to look at these large maps on the wall." She pointed out where they were starting from and where they would go. "There is way too much to see this morning. I just wanted you to get a feel for how enormous this industry is."

Sara was astonished as they entered Greenhouse 5. It was gigantic and made mostly of glass. *It feels as though it's July instead of almost January!*

"The temperature is regulated very well and always stays at from eighty-five to ninety-five degrees. Greenhouse 5 is our tropical greenhouse. There are orange trees, lemon and lime trees. We also have hibiscus. And anything you'd find growing in a tropical garden, you will find here." She paused. "As you can imagine, there is a lot of upkeep with all these buildings. It's a very well-operated industry. Mr. Brent makes sure that everything is running smoothly, because if this fails, Brentville fails." She added, "There is a natural gas line that keeps these greenhouses warm. In addition, the windmills and rivers are used to generate our electricity."

Sara was processing all of this. *I find Mr. Brent distasteful. I also think he's an egomaniac with an inferiority complex, but I have to admit that he knows what he's doing when it comes to making a successful community—right down to the orange tree spreading above me. He even has the greenhouse stocked with bees* and butterflies, and as Maribelle told me, if I dug into the dirt in the greenhouse boxes, I'd find worms.

"I hope this has been helpful to you," said Maribelle. "It's almost eleven, and I need to get back to work. If you want to, we can tour another greenhouse someday."

Sara thanked her, gave her a hug, and decided to go to the Greenhouse 5 store before leaving. She was elated to find brilliant fresh flowers, hardy-looking vegetables, and fruits. On one side of the room was a space like that of a farmer's market. The clerk explained that Brentville residents were allowed to bring their homemade wares to sell—anything from homemade bread to handmade chairs.

What a find! I'll come here at least once a week. I can't wait to tell Ian about it.

Sara left with her arms full. To get everything out to her sleigh, she had to make two trips.

What marvelous flowers! I can't believe I even found some buttercups. Now that I found that fresh rhubarb at the store, I'm going to make both a carrot cake and a rhubarb pie for the fish fry.

It was New Year's Eve.

Everyone was to meet at Ian's at four. Sara picked up Harold and Olive in her open sleigh. Everyone, including Sam, covered their legs with her blankets. *I hope we won't have snow tonight.*

They were the first to arrive. After letting Harold and Olive out in front of the house, Sara took Nellie out back to the stall in Ian's garage/barn. Ian was getting ready to start frying the fish in a large cast-iron frying pan.

"What can we do?" asked Sara.

"How about arranging dishes, silverware, and napkins here on this counter?" he answered.

"Be glad to," she said, "and shall I put the desserts on this card table?"

"Yes, they look delicious."

Sara found a tablecloth for the card table. She put the pies and the cake out, along with some dessert dishes, silverware, and napkins. Last but not least, she tucked her little arrangement of buttercups into a tiny crystal vase, right by the rhubarb pies.

"Happy New Year," called Harold as he let the rest of the guests in the front door. All ten of them had arrived at once. "Why don't you all leave your boots out on the front porch," he directed. "Then take your coats and put them on Ian's bed. So glad you could come."

Ian didn't have a Christmas tree, but he did have two card tables set up with two separate jigsaw puzzles. He had already started one of them. The puzzles appeared to be popular with all ages. The young people gravitated to one table and the adults to the other.

When the children saw the dessert table, they were excited to find the buttercups. Sara could see that they wanted to take a buttercup out of the vase. "By all means," she said. "Help yourself."

Lucy was the first to take one. She went to Sara and held it under her chin. "Oh, you like butter," she exclaimed after she saw the yellow reflection under Sara's chin. Soon all the children were checking with a buttercup to see if the person they were testing "liked butter."

Sara remembered being at her grandmother's house. *How I loved seeing whether or not my cousin liked butter. Thank you, God, for good memories. How silly that game is! I wonder if there is anyone in the history of this buttercup checking game who didn't reflect the fact that they liked butter. I used to feel so special, because I was found to like butter and so excited when I could say to the person I was checking, "You like butter!" Maybe it's because I fit in when I passed the butter test. I was found normal. Who knows? I'm sure it meant different things to different children.*

But remembering good things like this that go back to our childhood is a surprising moment that pops up every once in a while—an unexpected gift from God.

Buttercup thoughts remind me of the turkey wishbone. Grandma and Mom always saved the wishbone and let it dry. Then they'd invite someone to wish with them. Each person would take a side of the wishbone and pull. Whoever ended up with the longest piece was the winner. Our own children liked doing that too. I wonder if they will pass it down through the generations.

It was fun to do, even though I knew it didn't make a wish come true. It's nice to have those memories. I wonder if whoever cooked the turkey at our house in Harleysville remembered to save the wishbone.

The fish fry was going smoothly. The food was delicious, and the games were fun. Harold played songs that both old and young knew—and they knew every single word.

Soon everyone was content to just sit. Even the kids were getting groggy.

"How about we have a contest to see who can make the best snowman," suggested Ian.

Sara remembered the piece of leather hide draped over a chair in the kitchen. Ian had mentioned hoping to use it to create some kind of belt carrier for his tools. *Oh, this would be perfect*, she thought.

"May I borrow that piece of hide?" she asked him. "I could wrap your arm in some of that wax paper, then in the hide, and then use more wax paper on the outside. Hopefully that will keep your arm dry while we're outside."

"Help yourself," answered Ian. "Don't know what I'd do without you, Doc. Let the party begin!"

Everyone bundled up, even Harold and Olive. Ian brought out some carrots for the noses and scarves for their snow sculpture. Everyone was laughing as they rolled snowballs for snowmen.

It was decided that Lucy and Maribelle had the biggest and best snowman. They had found branches for its arms and some greens for its hair. It did look impressive. Ian ended up with six big snowmen in his front yard.

"Happy New Year, everyone!" he called out as he threw a snowball at Sara. That was it! Everyone let loose; soft snowballs flew all over the front yard.

As Lisa was preparing to leave, she shared with Sara that she was worried about her older daughter, Janet. She had not been feeling well, and Lisa asked Sara if she could make an appointment for her.

"Why don't you have her come over to my house tomorrow," suggested Sara. "I won't be back at the hospital until Tuesday."

"Thank you, Sara," said Lisa as she piled the children into their sleigh.

Sara removed the wax paper and leather from Ian's cast and checked for dampness. "Looks good," she said. "Now we need to get home before the ten o'clock curfew."

Harold and Ian made plans to go ice fishing very soon. Sara thought she might have overheard plans to build a new fish house.

Sam and Sara led Harold and Olive out to the barn, and Sara tucked them into the sleigh for departure. When Ian said good-bye, he added that he was going to watch out the kitchen window for a while. "I'll look to see if there is any unusual activity in the woods behind my house."

Janet arrived at Sara's around ten in the morning on Sunday. Sara invited her in, saying, "So glad you came. I'm happy that you trust me enough to come. I give you my word, Janet, that I'll not tell anyone what you tell me today—unless you give me your permission."

"Thank you, ma'am," said Janet. Sara could hear the fear in her voice and see deep sadness. Janet began to weep.

Her big eyes seem to have been storing these tears for some time. Until now, Janet must not have known who to talk to. She couldn't even be sure that trusting her own mother was an option.

"Come sit with me," Sara said, and she guided Janet to the couch. Reaching for a handkerchief and a box of Kleenex, Sara sat down in the chair next to the couch. "Where do we start? Why don't you tell me your biggest problem? Then we'll back up and fill in the holes."

"I'm pregnant!" Janet blurted out. "It is not the first time. The father's name is Frank. He's a friend of Mr. Brent. I was drugged, and I only remember bits and pieces."

Sara was saddened but not surprised by what she was hearing. "What happened to your other baby?" she asked.

"My mother delivered it. My father gave it to Frank. I think it was used as a sacrifice."

Sara got up from her chair and joined Janet, who was sobbing uncontrollably. She gave Janet a hug and a Kleenex. "Janet, what do you want to do about *this* baby?"

"Even though I hate the father and hate the way this baby was conceived, I want to keep it. It isn't the baby's fault, and I love my baby already."

"Oh, Janet," cried Sara, "I am so sorry you've had all this to go through. You haven't had any support to help you with it. I'm here to tell you that you have me now; I want to help you in any way I can. The first thing I can do is get you away from your home. I know you feel close to your sisters and brothers, but what would you think of coming here, of living with me for a while—at least until after the baby comes? There are two unused rooms upstairs and a bathroom."

Janet's eyes were full of disbelief. "Why would you do this?"

"My dear Janet," said Sara softly. "God loves you, and I love you. You are so worth being cared for. Please let God take care of you now. He is calling your name. He wants to be in your life—and so do I.

"Janet, your life is not a random thing. You were created by God. God has put you right where you are, at this exact moment in time, and he's made you exactly the way you are because he has plans to prosper you and not to harm you, plans to give you hope and a future."[5]

More tears dribbled down Janet's face. "Yes, I think I would like living here with you, Dr. Saunders."

"Oh please, call me Sara. Let's go right now to get your things."

"Okay," agreed Janet. They walked out the back door toward the horse and sleigh. As usual, Sam joined them. And Sara even invited Matilda to come along.

CHAPTER 22

Call for Committee Action

"Please make yourself at home," Sara said to Janet. "And feel free to invite your family over anytime you feel lonesome. I'll make some dinner, and then, since I have to go to Harold and Olive's tonight, maybe you could do the dishes. I'm going to enjoy having some help around here."

"I will be glad to do anything that I can to be helpful," replied Janet.

When the doorbell rang, Sam and Matilda went running to welcome the newcomer. Ian let himself in, said hello to the dogs, and found Sara in the kitchen.

"Hi, Janet!" he said, surprise in his voice.

"I'm almost ready," said Sara. "Sit down by the fire, and put your feet up. You've been working all day and must be tired."

Sara asked Janet to come upstairs for a minute. She wanted to talk with her in private. "Janet, I wanted to ask you something before I leave. I told you this morning that I wouldn't tell anyone anything that you told me, and I will keep that promise. But I trust Ian with my life. He loves God as I do, and he's here a lot. So I would like your permission to talk with him about why you're here. He is on our side and will be a big help in all this."

Janet looked at Sara with tears starting again. "I am surprised and touched to have others helping me. Yes, please tell him. And by the way," she added, "I already know that we can trust Olive and Harold. They are a sweet couple, and I know you love them. You can tell them too, if you want."

Sara hugged Janet and headed downstairs. "I'll leave the dogs with you for company," she shouted up the stairs.

"Oh, good, thank you," Janet answered, looking down the stairway. "I'd love to have them here while you're out."

Sara and Ian sat out in front of Harold's house while Sara told him the details of Janet's plight. This would be Ian's and Sara's first committee meeting. Harold and Olive, Bob and Jan, the couple who put out the weekly paper on their printing press, and Sara and Ian, were the only ones on the committee. The church group had voted them in. They made weekly reports to the church groups. As members of all the groups saw new clues, they reported them to the committee.

"Looks like Bob and Jan won't be coming tonight," Olive said as Sara and Ian entered the house. "One of the girls has a high fever."

Sara left her boots out on the porch and her shoes just inside the front door, and threw her jacket over the bannister. Then she grabbed a blanket from the back of the sofa and wrapped it around her as she sat down by the fire. *It is nice having friends like this. I love just coming in and making myself at home.*

"Well," said Harold, "let's get the meeting started. Bob gave me his findings for the week, so I will start by reading to you what they have found. The biggest thing I see in his report is that someone found a place in the woods where they think there might be the remains of human bones. It's straight out behind your house, Ian."

"Sara has some very sad news," said Ian. "She just told me in the car, before we came in. Go ahead, Sara. Fill them in on the details."

As Janet's story was unfolding, Olive's eyes teared up. "I declare," she gasped, "that poor girl."

"Yes," said Harold, "this is the most concrete piece of evidence we've had. We need to be praying about what to do with it."

"Ian, as you and I pursue our ice fishing project, maybe we could include Mr. Brent in some of it," suggested Harold. "As much as we don't like him, I do think he is a lonely fellow. I'd very much like to get to know him enough to see if we think he is connected to Frank and this satanic worship, or if he is being bamboozled by Frank. I believe Mr. Brent is a controlling person, and he has done some bad things, like keeping us here against our will, but I think maybe he doesn't know about the satanic stuff that's going on."

"We need to keep praying for Mr. Brent," added Harold. "Maybe God is planning to get ahold of him, and maybe God wants to use us in that process. As I've said before, wouldn't it be exciting to see the place healed and changed from the inside out?"

"Let's close the meeting time in prayer," said Harold, "and then, Olive has some peach shortcake ready for you."

As they gathered in the kitchen for dessert, Harold turned the radio on. He had it on the new station, 97 AM, the local station that played music 24/7. Frank Sinatra was singing "Get Happy." For the moment, all was well.

When Ian dropped Sara off, he decided to go in to say a quick hello to Janet. "I just want to tell you," he said to her, "that Sara shared your story with me. I will not tell anyone, and if you ever need me for anything, you know how to reach me." He handed her his phone number.

"Thanks," said Janet. She waved to him as he walked out to his truck.

"This has been quite a day, Janet," commented Sara. "A lot has happened, and it's all good. I'm glad you made the decision to come and stay with me."

Janet sat down on the couch. Clearly, she wasn't used to so much attention. For a moment, she looked as though she might begin to sob again.

Sara said, "Monday, I'll get you in for an examination. We need to start making sure that you are getting proper prenatal care. Do you know what month you are in?"

"Yes, it would be around seven," answered Janet.

"Guess we'd better ask Crystal to make you some maternity clothes," Sara said with a grin.

Janet spoke as she made her way up the stairs. "Tonight I'm going to sleep well. I am lucky to be with you, Sara."

Sara turned out the lights and went to her bedroom. Finding her Bible on her prayer chair, she sat down to talk with God.

CHAPTER 23

Unexpected Ominous and Compassionate Visitors

Sara had enjoyed having Janet with her for a few weeks when it happened. Janet had been feeling very much at home with her new way of life. She loved being surrounded by the caring group. Before meeting Sara, the ugliness had been ever-present and always in the forefront of her mind. Though she'd been there only a few weeks, she was, as she'd told Sara, comfortable, relaxed, and beginning to put the ugly past into the back of her mind.

Something changed that.

When Sara arrived home for lunch, she noticed that Janet was very pale. Sara had always checked her family for fever by kissing their foreheads. So she took Janet's face in her hands and gave her a kiss on the forehead.

"You feel fine," she commented.

All the kind attention was too much for Janet, and she started bawling.

"Come sit," said Sara as she patted the couch with her hand. Hearing the pat, both dogs jumped up too, and Janet had to find a space between them.

By then Janet was breathing more easily and drying her eyes. She began to tell Sara about her horrible encounter. "The morning started normally." "I called to the dogs and told them we were going for our walk."

"With my hand on the door knob, I glanced out the window in the door and saw a man walking up the walkway. He was a big man with a dark overcoat. His scarf was blowing so that I couldn't see his face. He had a fairly small hat, dark, with a brim—a businessman's hat.

"It wasn't until he was stepping up onto the porch that I recognized him. It was Frank, the father of my baby, the man who seems to be the ringleader of the underground satanic activities in Brentville. This is a well-respected, churchgoing lawyer in the community. He's not married, doesn't have a family. He's the person in Brentville I most fear.

"My hand was still on the doorknob. I hadn't opened the door yet. My mind was screaming, 'Run!' But run where?

"Frank was now standing at the door with his hand on the other side. He was turning the knob, opening the door toward me and the dogs! Backing up into the hallway, I dropped the dog leashes and asked Frank why he had come. He smiled, left his galoshes by the front door, removed his heavy coat and scarf, and entered the living room. He made himself at home. I sat on the other side of the room, flanked by the two dogs. Golden retrievers are not known to be guard dogs, but Sara, I sensed that Sam would fight anyone who tried to hurt me.

"Frank told me in a creepily pleasant voice that he had just learned from my mother that I had moved out. He said that he knew how much my mother was missing me and wondered how long I planned to keep punishing her.

"I gave him a weak smile, and I thanked him for his concern, though I know very well that my mother wants me here with you. I also understood that being alone with this man, who would probably rather see me dead than to have anyone find out about the baby and about his actions, was a very dangerous place to be.

"He told me that he could see I was pregnant and that he would like to help me. I thought, *Just like you helped me with my other baby. You scooped it up and took it away before I even saw it. You went off into the night with my precious baby!* But I didn't say a word to Frank. I felt paralyzed.

"Sam and Matilda heard something and went running to the front door. The next minute, the doorbell rang. I noticed a look of concern on Frank's face as I got up to see who might be there. It was Walter. I quickly opened the door and welcomed Walter into the living room. I could tell that Walter was surprised to see Frank, and he asked him why he was there. Frank said that it was nothing important and that he was just leaving. I stayed back in my chair while Frank put on his galoshes and coat. I didn't look his way or say good-bye.

"After the door closed, Walter sat down beside me. Looking troubled, he asked me what was wrong. He told me I looked as though I'd seen a ghost! For some reason, I've always tended to trust Walter. Soon I was weeping, and I told him about the baby and about Frank. Walter was upset, to say the least. He had known Frank for many years. Frank had always seemed to be his father's friend.

"Walter had been totally unaware of any of the information that he was hearing from me. He took my hand and told me not to worry. He said he was glad I had support from you and your friends. He said that he would watch out for me now too. He told me to call him anytime. I truly appreciated Walter's offer to help me. I want to be safe. I want my baby to be safe.

"Then Walter remembered what he had come for. He had to go down cellar to check the line for a gas leak. Before long, I heard his work boots clomping up the cellar stairs. He said that it looked okay down there and that he would check outside too. I thanked him for everything as I opened the front door for him. He even congratulated me on my new baby to come."

Listening to Janet's story unfold left Sara badly shaken. "I think we both need to get out for some fresh air," she said. "Bundle up. We'll take the dogs out for their walk."

Walking rapidly, before they knew it they had reached Main Street, so they decided to stop at the drugstore for some lunch. Sam and Matilda stayed outside. Sara tied Matilda to the post, and Sam waited obediently beside Matilda.

The drugstore felt warm. Sara and Janet took a table near the lunch counter. They both ordered a cheeseburger, fries, and one of the yummy milkshakes that Barbara, the girl behind the counter, was so good at making.

"I must say, you look much better," said Sara. "Your cheeks are rosy from our walk, and your new maternity outfit is very nice." The two-piece outfit Sara was admiring had a moss-green, long-sleeve top with a cowl neck. The skirt was black with a hole in the top front for her tummy. It had a string at the top to tie around the expanding waistline. The hole was a perfect space for the growing baby. The green top was long enough to cover the hole in the top of the skirt.

"You know, Sara," said Janet. "I've been finding happiness and real fun since coming to live with you. It will probably be a while before I can live my life without always expecting the other shoe to drop, but I'm actually thinking that there *is* hope for me and my baby. You tell me about God and tell me that your God loves me, too. I'm beginning to believe you may be right."

"Hey, Doc!" yelled Ian from across the drugstore.

"Pull up a chair," Sara said as he came toward the table.

"I'll take what they're having," he said to Barbara. "But make my milkshake chocolate, please." He sat down. "Love these old-fashioned milkshakes," he commented, as they watched the young waitress scoop the ice cream into the stainless-steel cup and insert the cup into the milkshake machine.

A few moments later, the high-speed whirring stopped. "Voilà!" exclaimed Ian, "the greatest milkshake ever!"

"Glad to see you," said Sara. "You are just in time to hear the latest regarding Janet."

As Ian listened to her story unfold, he seemed to be making mental notes. Sara could imagine approximately what they were: *1. Janet should not be left alone. 2. We can trust Walter enough to bring him on board, so ask him for help in trying to protect Janet.*

Sara needed to hurry back to the hospital. She and Ian said in unison, "Be sure to lock all the doors, and don't let anyone in."

"I'll be careful. Thanks for wanting to protect us," she said, one hand resting on her midriff.

CHAPTER 24

Newfound Happiness

Later in the afternoon, Sara arrived home from work to find Janet, Sam, and Matilda all napping on the couch. After throwing a couple of logs on the glowing embers, Sara headed for the kitchen to see about dinner preparations.

"Hi, Sara," said Janet in a half-awake, husky voice. "Do you have time to talk?" She sat up and pushed the dogs from the couch.

"Sure," answered Sara. "How are you feeling?" She kissed Janet on the forehead. "No fever; that's good."

"Oh, I'm doing fine," answered Janet. "Probably as fine as I've been in all my eighteen years, thanks to you," she said. "I'm feeling relaxed and feeling your unconditional love. And I'm getting a glimpse of what seems to be true happiness. I can see that happiness in you, Sara." Janet sighed. "And I want what you have."

Sara sat very still beside Janet. *Oh, Lord,* she pleaded silently. *Please, give me the words to convey your message to Janet. Please open her heart to your love and your truth.* "Well," started Sara, "since I arrived in Brentville, I have cried out to God. I told him that I needed him. I found out later that God was really drawing me to himself. Even my calling out for help was his doing.

"It is a gift from God, the God who loves us so much that he gave his only son. When I learned how much God loves me—that's where my peace and joy come from. And Janet," said Sara in a soft voice, "God wants to be in *your* life too. Jesus died for *you*."

"Oh, Sara," Janet cried, "I do want to know God! I want what he has given you."

"Then let's pray right now. Let's ask God to be in your life too," suggested Sara.

Sara reached for Janet's hand, and they bowed their heads and closed their eyes. Sara prayed aloud with her: "Dear Lord, we love you and thank you for sending Jesus to us. We ask you to come into Janet's life. She needs you and wants to be forgiven, free, and happy. Thank you for promising to send your Holy Spirit to us. In Jesus's name we pray. Amen."

Janet agreed with an eager "Yes, God, I *do* need you, and I want to *know* you!"

Drying their eyes, Sara and Janet stood up, gave each other a big hug, and Sara said a fervent, silent, *Thank you, God, for allowing me this privilege, for allowing me to be used by you. Amen.*

Sara said, "I have been meeting at Mary's house every Saturday afternoon for a Bible study. If she agrees, would you like to join us?"

"Oh, yes," Janet replied. "I can't wait."

"In the meantime, you can take my Bible and start reading the book of John."

Sam and Matilda almost knocked Sara down trying to get to the door. Someone was approaching the house. They both sat by the door with tails wagging, without barking. Then, like clockwork, the doorbell rang.

"Oh, it's Walter," said Janet as she went to the door. "Come on in," she said, a welcoming smile on her face.

Walter had a giant bouquet of velvety pink roses in his arms. "These are for you, Janet."

Her expression showed that she couldn't believe he'd come back with flowers for her. "Oh, thank you, Walter." Her cheeks were no longer white, but as pink as the roses.

"Before I go," said Walter, "I want you to know that I've alerted the Brentville Police Department to the fact that you had a break-in today. I didn't go into any of the details, since we really don't know who is trustworthy. They will be watching over your house. I won't tell my father about any of this until I can get more information regarding Frank."

"Thanks again, Walter," said Janet, as she waved and closed the front door.

Heading for the kitchen to put her roses into a vase, Janet looked at Sara with happiness sparkling in her eyes. "This has been quite a day. This morning I was afraid of what Frank was going to do to me. I asked the Lord into my life, and now I have received a beautiful bouquet from a very handsome man."

"Quite a day, indeed," agreed Sara as she gave Janet another hug.

CHAPTER 25

Tree House Joys and Pain

"I'll pick you up for church tonight," said Ian. "We have lots to tell the committee."

"Okay," answered Sara, "I'll look for you at around six forty-five." As she put the phone back into the cradle, she noticed the time. *It's three thirty, and I have so much to do. I wanted to check in on Crystal and the twins. I've missed my time with them,* she lamented. *Since Crystal and Oliver were married, I haven't seen much of my little family.*

Walter had become an almost constant part of the scenery around Sara's house. Since Janet had trusted him with her secret, they had become much closer and were seeing each other every day. Sara smiled. *He really cares for Janet, and Janet is certainly enamored with him.*

Janet had been to three Bible studies with Sara and to a couple on her own with Mary. She had read the book of John four times and was excited about her new faith. She didn't hold back in talking to Walter about it.

As Sara walked by the living room, she overheard Janet trying to explain to Walter what she'd found in Jesus. He was telling Janet that he believed in God, but that he wasn't so sure about

Jesus. "Excuse me for interrupting," said Sara, "but may I make a suggestion?"

"Sure," they agreed, and she settled into her soft chair by the fireplace.

"Well, here's the thing," continued Sara. "If you believe in God, you also believe in Jesus, because they are one. You haven't had the chance to learn that yet. Why don't you go with Janet to her Bible study on Saturday? Walter, if you're really interested in getting to know the God you say you believe in, Mary would be a great support and help."

He didn't have an answer or an argument for Sara. He just took a breath, smiled, and said, "I would really like that."

Janet had been very quiet while Sara was talking with Walter, but she just had to add something that Mary and she had been talking about earlier. "On the night before his crucifixion, Jesus told his disciples that he was the way and the truth and the life, and that no one comes to the Father except through him."

Seeing Sam and Matilda standing by the door with tails wagging alerted Sara to the fact that Ian was probably on his way to the door. "Hi there," she said, just as he was ready to open the door. "Do come in and make yourself comfortable. I need to make a quick change out of my hospital clothes and will be ready shortly. Janet and Walter headed toward the kitchen, followed by Ian and the dogs.

As Ian and Sarah tromped through the snow to the truck, he told her what he'd learned from talking with Janet and Walter in the kitchen. "I found them doing dishes and listening to the Chordettes's rendition of 'Mr. Sandman.' I asked her how she was feeling. She said she was feeling great and asked me if I had heard their news. Janet told me that Walter had asked her to be his wife and that she had accepted. I told her that I was happy for them, and said, 'God bless you all!' Janet said that God had blessed them. She said that to have God in their lives, to have each other, and soon to be having a baby was about all the happiness they could ask for."

"How come you didn't tell me about the engagement?" asked Ian as they entered the cold truck.

"I didn't know it when you and I were talking earlier," Sara answered. "I'm surprised, but they have been seeing a lot of each other. And I knew that Walter was really smitten with her. I expect they plan to wait until the baby comes before tying the knot."

She added, "I think that soon we should include them in our Bible study/church at Harold's."

Ian parked in front of Harold's house. He helped Sara onto the slippery sidewalk and held out his good arm for her to lean on. They rang the doorbell and walked in.

Almost everyone was there. They found a seat and settled down to listen to Harold play a few hymns. Some were singing along. Some were just listening. Sara was learning, and appreciating, the words to the old hymns.

After the study, Sara and Ian stayed until everyone else had left. "If you have a few minutes," she said to Olive and Harold, "we would like to stay and bring you up to date concerning a few things."

They smiled and gestured to Sara and Ian to have a seat.

"As you know," Sara began, "Janet Morrison is living with me now, and I already told you about the baby and Frank. Well, he showed up at my house while I was at work. We figure he knows my work schedule and knows when Janet will be there alone. He really scared Janet, and we do think that she is in some degree of danger.

"Walter and Janet are now an item. In fact, we learned tonight that they're engaged to be married. In the meantime, Walter is keeping pretty good track of her. He has alerted the police to be watching my house. He said he didn't go into any of the details with the police—just told them that someone had broken in."

Ian said, "Janet is trusting Jesus now, and Walter may not be far behind her in his wanting to know God. Sara thinks it would be good to invite them to your church, but I think we should wait on that until we know we can trust Walter. He *is* Mr. Brent's son, after all, and we can't take a chance that Mr. Brent might find out about our secret church meetings."

"Praise God!" Harold cried out. "It is always exciting hearing about new sisters and brothers in Christ."

Sara said, "Now I know how you and Olive felt when I came to know Jesus."

Harold asked, "Remember when I said how great it would be if more and more persons in Brentville would come to know the Lord—how the whole village could be changed from the inside out? Well, look. Little by little, it seems to be happening."

"Are you up for some ice fishing, Ian?" Harold asked. "I'd like to work on plans for a brand-new deluxe icehouse. I was thinking again about Mr. Brent. Maybe we should include him in the project."

"Sounds great," answered Ian. "What do you think, Doc? How much longer before I get this cast off?"

"Should be this week," Sara replied.

"All right then," Ian said to Harold. "Sounds like a plan."

"I'll set something up with Mr. Brent, and let you know," said Harold. "Let's keep praying that we will be able to get to know Mr. Brent, that we can be a good witness to him—and that he will trust us and will see God through us."

Then he asked Ian, "Have you noticed any more questionable activities behind your place?"

"Not really, but I have been thinking about building a very tall tree house in back of my home. I think the youth of our church group would enjoy having it, and it would be a great place for me to do some checking.

"I have a pretty powerful telescope that I had in the back of my truck when I arrived. I have just been waiting until I got the cast off to start anything regarding this project. In fact, my neighbor has offered to help me with it. He seems like a nice guy. He's probably just about my age. He and his wife have had me over for dinner a few times."

Ian interrupted himself. "Well, Doc, the ten o'clock whistle is about ready to blow. We'd better get going."

Sara held onto Ian all the way to the truck. "Sure hope Olive and Harold don't fall out here," she said. "We should come over and put some ashes down for them."

"I'll do it tomorrow," Ian volunteered.

"Do you think you could be at the hospital tomorrow at eleven?" asked Sara. "I will see that you get rid of that cast."

"Only if you'll have lunch with me afterward," replied Ian. "You can help me celebrate my freedom."

"You have a date," she said, feeling a sudden smile break through. "Let's go to the hotel for lunch. I would love to say hi to Crystal."

Sara realized she was depending more and more on Ian. *Yet I know I'm not ready to let go of Jim. Although my life in Brentville seems more real every day, my thoughts are still very much connected to Jim and my family back in Harleysville. Ian is such a nice guy; I don't want to hurt him.*

As soon as Ian was free of the cast, he enjoyed a lunch of Crystal's finest lunch menu items with his favorite doc. As they finished the meal, he said, "Now I'm headed home to make plans for my tree house. I've invited my neighbors, Russell and Susie, over for dinner. After the meal, I'll present the drawings to Russell."

That night and on the following evenings, Ian phoned or came by to keep Sara up to date on the tree-house plans. The first night

171

he reported on his neighbor's reaction. "I asked Russell what he thought. Did it look like a project he'd like to be in on? He jumped out of his chair with delight, and said, 'Are you kidding?' He told me that he retired from his teaching job a year ago and was about ready to go stark raving mad. He wanted to know when we could start."

The following evening, Ian checked in with Sara, again. "I picked Russell up this morning. We headed to the hardware store for supplies. I don't know Susie or Russell well enough to have a good idea of where they are with their faith, so I didn't feel I could go into detail regarding the real purpose of this tree house—or as I like to think of it, my lookout tower.

"Russell didn't seem to question the blueprints or the fact that it was going to be extremely high. I think he was just excited about being involved in a project. I have two days off, and I hope to get the project completed in that time frame."

Sara listened carefully as he clearly outlined how the day had gone. She felt as if she had been there the whole time. He added, "Susie made us sandwiches, and then it was time to get started. Fortunately, there are four huge trees that are strategically placed and will be perfect for our endeavor. I've recruited a few of my friends. We need all the muscle power we can get.

"I picked up the large strips of wood at the sawmill. By three thirty, Russell and I had the tree-house materials cut and were nailing the frame of the house together. By five thirty, it was getting dark, and everyone was hungry. We headed to Susie's house for the food you and Susie had prepared. The ham loaf and scalloped potatoes smelled good, and the pies on the counter looked tempting too.

"All five of us men left our boots on the porch, put our jackets into a pile beside the boots, and followed our noses to the kitchen. Most of our conversation seemed to be around how things had gone and what we hope to accomplish tomorrow. I confess, we all seemed quite impressed with each other's work and how the job was progressing."

The next morning, all the men had gathered by eight. Anxious to see the fruit of their labor, they were all in agreement that no time was to be wasted.

Sara decided to go over to Ian's to see what was happening and to cheer the workers on.

By two or so, they were all crowing like roosters at the wonderful job they'd done. And it *was* a sight to be seen. The tree house reached eight feet above the top of the trees, high enough that Ian could see down into the woods for many miles. He would be able to see a bonfire smoking. And he could see many of the trails. It was perfect for his detective work.

The men had created some wooden furniture, a table, a couple of chairs, and a bed. The building had one door, and the top half of the structure was all windows on all four sides. The doors had real glass and screens. As Ian commented, "This isn't your ordinary little tree house."

The house was painted yellow to match his yellow house and barn. The shutters on the house, the barn, and the tree house were white.

Ian had to leave at four. His practice, for the most part, included large animals. Because of the dairy farms and all the horses, the clinic was kept very busy. That day he had some sick cows to look after. "Why don't you come with me, Sara?" he asked. He had been wanting her to ride along with him.

"Okay," Sara said. "I would love to go."

Russell said he'd stay on to clean up the mess so the others were free to go. The three helpers left with Ian.

Ian and Sara returned from the farm call to find Susie walking toward Ian's house. "Hi there, I've lost my husband," she said with a chuckle. I was surprised he wasn't at home when I returned from the grocery store. I knew he was going to clean up after the work on the tree house, but that was a few hours ago."

"Let's check the barn," Ian suggested. "Maybe he started another project." The path to the barn, packed down from all the workers going to and fro, was hardened, slippery snow. Entering the barn, they could hear the horses, but the lights weren't on, and it was otherwise still. Too still.

Now Susie was worried. "Hey, Russell, are you here?" she yelled.

They turned on the light. At first glance, they didn't see anything unusual, but as they walked around the corner to the work bench, they saw Russell's body slumped over the sawhorse.

"Oh, Russell!" Susie cried.

Ian hurried to his limp body, lifted him from the sawhorse, and put him flat on the floor.

"I'm not getting a pulse," Sara said in a low voice.

"Oh no," Susie screamed., "Please, Russell, don't leave me! I need you—I love you," Susie cried.

Sara helped Ian put the body in the back seat of his truck. She jumped into her car and left for the hospital. Ian and Susie drove Russell to the hospital.

Congregating at the hospital, Sara told Susie how sorry she was. "There's nothing more we can do. We think Russell has been dead for a few hours. It looks as though he might have had a massive heart attack."

Susie was very pale, now sitting in a hospital chair, crying. Sara and Ian sat with her. Sara took Susie's hand. "Do you want me to call the undertaker?"

"Yes," answered Susie.

"We'll wait here with you until he comes," Sara said.

Ian said, "After you've talked with him, I will take you home, Susie."

Sara handed Ian a sedative in case Susie felt the need for one. Ian and Susie left about half an hour after that.

Much later, Ian phoned Sara. "Hi, Doc," he said when he heard her voice. "When I picked up the phone to call you, the operator asked me if it was true that Russell had died. I told her he had. I still can't get used to this phone system. The operators know who we are and what's going on before we do."

"It is a little unsettling when we're not used to it," Sara said. "How is Susie doing?"

"On the drive home, she told me that she is thankful that Russell is a child of God and that he was looking forward to meeting Jesus."

"Hallelujah!" Sara responded.

"Then," Ian continued, "she slipped back into fits of crying. Pulling up in front of her house, I turned the truck motor off and ran around to help. Her body seemed to collapse into my arms, so I decided to carry her in.

"I asked her if she was going to be okay, and she said yes. 'Tell you what,' I said, 'I'm going over to my house to get my puppy. I'll feed my horses and will feed yours while I'm at it. Then I'll come back to see how you're doing.'

"When I got back to her, she was sitting in a chair, still whimpering and, as far as I could see, was probably in some kind of shock. I suggested that she get ready for bed and that I'd give her one of the sedatives that you sent.

"She didn't argue, Sara, but seemed glad to have someone telling her what to do. I gave her the pill and told her that the puppy and I would sleep on the couch in case she needed anything. She was out within five minutes."

"Do you think I did the right thing?" Ian asked.

"By all means," Sara answered. "I would be there myself if I weren't working the late shift."

CHAPTER 26

Jealousy Vs. Faith

Harold and Olive's church group members took turns helping Susie. For a week or so, someone stayed with her at night. They fed her and kept her company. They guided her through the funeral and the burial.

The group learned that Susie and Russell had been among the original citizens of Brentville. They had both been in their twenties when Mr. Brent was looking for converts. They were young and foolish and looking for an adventure. They knew they couldn't have children, and they didn't have any family ties.

They also learned that Susie and Russell had a very strong faith in Jesus. Although they had not been with other Christians for thirty years, they had spent many hours together, reading the Bible and praying.

Ian now made a habit of checking in on Susie each morning on his way to work. He later told Sara that he'd informed her about the plan to find out all they could about any possible satanic worship. "I asked her to be on the lookout for any questionable actions in the woods behind her house. And I told her about Frank. She said, 'I'll keep my eyes and ears opened. I know most everyone in this village. I have had some questions myself about certain individuals.'"

On the morning of Bible study/church, Ian invited Sara to ride along with him again. Although he practiced animal medicine and Sara, human medicine, their studies and practices allowed them to share conversations that others might not find interesting. He was also hoping that they would learn something new about Frank.

He told Sara, "The first farm had thirty milk cows with some young stock. Most farms have a bull or two. A couple of the cows have mastitis. One is having trouble delivering her calf." By the time they got there and out of the truck, the farmer came running for help. The calf was a breach delivery. Ian got it positioned so it could be delivered. Shortly after birth, the slimy little critter stood up and hobbled around.

They spent some time visiting with the farmer before packing up the truck. "Do you see much of your neighbors? Ian asked. Knowing that Frank had the small farm a short distance down the road, he was hoping to gain some valuable information.

"The man next door is Frank," said the farmer. "He hires workers to take care of his pigs, chickens, eggs, and beef cows. He stays pretty much to himself. I don't see much of him. I know he's a lawyer and has a practice in the village, and I see him at the Brentville Church."

"Now that I think about it," he continued, "I do see a lot of activity over there. I sometimes wonder what's going on. So many coming and going, and some nights there might be fifteen or twenty cars parked or horses tethered by his house, depending on how much snow there is on the road. They seem to have a lot of their gatherings at night and usually out in the back yard. Seems they like to party, and they often have bonfires."

He added, "It beats me as to how they get away with being out so late. Their parties seem to go into the night. Me, I'm an early-rising dairy farmer. I'm usually in bed by nine."

"Well, sir," Ian said, "please call us if you need any further assistance."

"Thanks," he said as he looked fondly at Lucky.

Ian introduced his pup Lucky, and explained that she'd discovered that she'd rather ride along with him than stay home alone.

After Ian and Sara jumped into the truck and got the heater going, Lucky settled down with her hindquarters on Sara while her head rested on Ian's leg. Ian purposely drove very slowly as they passed Frank's farm. "We've got to get to the bottom of this," he told Lucky. Lucky just looked up at him with her beautiful golden retriever eyes. "Boy, she's a lovable dog!" said Ian. Sara smiled.

Ian knew it was church night at Harold's, but he needed to make one more stop. A farmer had a cow that had tangled with a barbed-wire fence. "Most of the farmers in Brentville have their cows in stanchions in the barn for milking, and most of the farms have milking machines," he told Sara. "In the summer, the cows stay outside all day and some nights. If the pasture area is across the road from the barn, it's not an uncommon occurrence to have to wait as the cows cross the road from the barn to the pasture."

As they went around the bend, there were at least thirty-five cows crossing the road to the farm. It was taking more than a few minutes. "Wouldn't you know it?" Ian sighed. Usually, when they're anxious to be milked and fed, they don't dawdle. The farmers have dogs to help with the herding of the cows, but today, the dogs don't seem to be working very hard.,"*Finally*, we're on our way home. I will take you home first. A quick walk with Lucky, a shower, and I'll pick up Susie. See you soon."

When Ian and Susie arrived at Sara's, she didn't wait for them to come to the door. She had been watching for them, so when they arrived, she blinked the porch lights and came right out to the truck. The Big Bopper was singing "Chantilly Lace" on the truck radio.

1970s truck

"Hi, Doc," Ian said as he opened the door to the back seat for her. She'd known that he would be picking Susie up first. In fact, it had been her idea, but she was experiencing an uncomfortable feeling as she sat in the back seat.

It was almost as if Sara had claimed some kind of ownership of that seat in the front—that seat beside Ian, that intimate spot where she felt safe, protected, cared for—and, yes, loved. She realized that she was feeling a twinge of jealousy about someone she had no right to be feeling jealous over.

"Here we are," announced Ian. "Hope you will like our Bible study/church, Susie. It's important to keep the true meaning of this gathering a secret," he reminded her. "We don't know who we can really trust in Brentville."

Climbing the steps to the front door, the three could hear Harold playing the piano. Sara thought, *For the first time in thirty years, Susie will be hearing others singing the old hymns that she learned as a child.*

Susie very softly sang some of the words in the midst of the welcoming, warm group. She had met most of them already. They had all been showering her with love and helping her through her time of grieving.

Mary invited Susie to sit with her. Susie slipped quietly into the chair, her Bible in hand and tears shining in her eyes. She looked as though she was feeling an overwhelming feeling of peace and acceptance—as though she were finally home. *She must also be feeling a great sense of loss,* Sara thought. *Russell, her soulmate for the past forty years, is gone.*

Ian and Sara found a spot across the room. Settling in with Bibles on their laps, they silently listened to the glorious music. *Please, God,* Sara silently pleaded, *help me know what to do with these feelings about Ian.*

At nine thirty, Sara, Susie, and Ian climbed back into the cold truck. "If I were a real gentleman," said Ian, "I would have come out at nine fifteen to start the truck to get Humphrey warmed up for you."

Susie laughed and asked how he ever came up with the name Humphrey for his truck. He said that he'd been investigating his heritage and had found that there was a chieftain in his Scottish clan named Humphrey.

"Very good," said Susie. "I am impressed."

Sara was sitting in the back seat, fuming. *What is the matter with me? Here I have just experienced an inspiring worship service, and somewhere between Harold's house and Humphrey, I have completely lost everything I gained in the service!*

But wait, I see I'm undergoing some jealousy concerning Ian and Susie. To acknowledge that is a good thing. It's what I actually do about this feeling that's most important. I can't fix something until I see what needs fixing.

So, thank you, God, for helping me to recognize this feeling for what it is.

Sara had been so deep in thought that she hadn't noticed that Ian had driven Susie to her house first. He jumped out and opened Susie's door and walked her to her house. Ian then ran to his house, picked up Lucky, returned to the truck, opened Sara's door, and guided Sara to the front seat. With Lucky on her lap, she leaned back with a sigh. *Now this is more like it.*

It was nine forty-five, leaving Ian only fifteen minutes to get back to his house. "What an idiotic rule," he complained. "Here I am a grown man, being treated like a child."

"I know," Sara said. "Just one more reminder of why we need to keep working on our escape."

Ian leaned over and gave Sara a kiss on the lips. He had kissed her on the cheek before, but this was a different kind of kiss. "You mean so much to me," he said. "I thank God that you have been here to guide and direct me."

Sara was surprised by the fact that it felt so pleasant to be kissed. She plunked Lucky down on Ian's lap, opened her door, and ran to her front door. She turned and waved, and Ian drove off.

After talking to God, Sara turned off the light and laid her head down on the pillow. *I need time to process all this. Maybe I need to talk with someone about my predicament.*

"Oh, Jim," cried Sara aloud. "Why did this happen? I loved you so much. I still do."

I think I need to visit Harold and Olive, thought Sara, as she drifted off to sleep. *They will help me.*

CHAPTER 27

Where's Lucky?

Ian told Sara that he and Harold had met a couple of times to discuss the plans for the new icehouse *and* to pray about and think about whether to include Mr. Brent. "One morning, we were discussing just how we could approach the man. Harold said that he feels Mr. Brent is a lonely person and is searching for ways to fill that vacuum. I told Harold that I don't know Mr. Brent, and to me, he still seems like an egomaniac with an inferiority complex. Harold added that he has always gotten along with Mr. Brent, so he wouldn't mind just telling Mr. Brent about our project, and asking him to join us in the endeavor."

Ian smiled. "I said that sounded like a great idea. I knew that with God's help, I could follow this plan with Harold, but I was relieved to know that I won't have to be the one to start the ball rolling. Harold thinks that even though Mr. Brent doesn't know it yet, there is a crack starting to develop in his wall. He thinks Walter is almost ready to ask the Lord into his life. The crack has begun, and it will be growing."

He was silent for a moment then added, "Sara, I feel grateful to have Harold, such a wise, fatherly figure in my life. I thanked him for getting it started and asked him to let me know what's happening."

Sara was very pleased to hear Ian's news.

Ian and Sara both had the day off. He had persuaded her to go ice-skating, but he needed time to take his plow out on the ice to plow a spot for skating. So he made it to Sara's house about two hours late.

"Sorry," he said as he entered the house with his backpack and Lucky. "Let's have some hot chocolate while I tell you what happened."

Pouring the drink from his trusty thermos, he started to tell her his tale of woe. "I stopped at my house to pick up my skates, some hot chocolate, and cheese and crackers. Tucking the things into my backpack, I headed toward the truck. I called for Lucky, but there was no response. You know, she's been pretty good about staying close, so I was concerned when I couldn't locate her right away.

"I decided to climb up into the tree house to get an overview of the area. To my shock, I noticed a man on one of the trails in the woods. He was all bundled up, and it looked as though he was carrying a dog. I grabbed my hunting rifle from the rack in the back window of the truck, put some ammunition in it, ran to the barn, and jumped on one of the horses.

"We went flying out the barn doorway. I'd taken time to bridle the horse, but I was riding bareback. My gun was strapped around my shoulder. I started at a slow pace and then, when I was sure I was on the right trail, I sped up. Seeing no sight of the man, I decided to work up to a gallop.

"Before long, I'd caught sight of a figure down the trail. Not wanting to alert the man to the fact that I was coming up behind him, I slowed down again—always keeping him in my sight and always gaining ground, but very slowly. The wind was blowing toward me, so I knew he probably wouldn't hear me approaching until I caught up with him.

"I was within several feet of the man. Lucky spotted me before he did. She jumped out of his arms and ran toward me. I dismounted the horse, got my gun ready, and aimed it at the man. I had no intention of shooting, but I wanted to scare some information out of him.

"'Why did you take my dog?' I asked. 'Who put you up to this?' I really don't know, Sara, who is trustworthy in the police station, so I thought maybe I should get him to talk and then just let him go.

"So I got right up close to the man and said, 'It's jail or talk. If you tell me what I want to know, I'll let you go.' I was pointing the gun right at his face.

"'Okay, which is it? If you wait too long on my questions,' I said in my most powerful voice, 'this rifle could accidently go off. Who put you up to this?' I demanded.

"'Frank,' the man said, and he gulped.

"'Where were you going with the dog?'

"'To Frank.'

"'Are there others working with you?'

"'Yeah.'

"'Okay,' I said. 'Now get! And if I ever see you around here again, I will shoot.'

"The man went running down the trail and into the woods. No telling what he might have done with the dog. But, hey, with a name like Lucky, I guess I shouldn't worry too much. Maybe I need to get a watch dog to teach Lucky to bark." Sara and Ian both laughed.

"Oh, by the way," Ian added, "do you think I could have a rain check on the skating date?"

"Of course. Let's go over to Harold's to see what he will say about all this," suggested Sara. "I like the way he thinks. And good work, Ian!"

Sitting around the fireplace in Harold and Olive's living room felt good. "Nice seeing you youngsters," kidded Harold. "We haven't been able to do this for a while." He paused. "By the way, Ian, I set up an appointment for both of us to meet with Mr. Brent next Tuesday. He seemed interested, and said we could use any of his tools."

"Oh good!" exclaimed Sara. "The sooner we get to know him, the better."

"I'm hopeful that we'll find a nice man buried down under that ego," added Harold.

"Well," said Ian, "I have a farmer wanting me to stop in to help with some of his cows' horns. If I don't get them off, they're apt to hurt each other. Guess I'd better get going."

"I'll stay here," said Sara. "I'll walk home. It will be good for me. Thanks for offering to take me skating, Ian. We'll do it another time."

After Ian left, Sara looked at Olive and Harold and said, "I want to be just like you guys when I grow up."

"And now I want to ask you for some advice. I trust and respect you both and I know that you try to do God's will in every action you take. I could use some guidance regarding my relationship with Ian."

"Yes, dear, what is it? Tell us what's happening," said Olive.

"I've grown to depend on, and am enjoying being with, Ian more each day.

"As you know, he's a terrific person. In fact, I haven't found anything that I don't like about Ian. But, I'm still married, and I love my husband and pray that I can be reunited with him and with my kids.

"Some days I think that I will never get out of Brentville. But, most days, I'm filled with hope that we will find an escape. And here is the tricky part—Ian is part of that hope of finding my means of escape.

"He is so dedicated to the idea. I feel I need him for my survival here, but I don't want to lead him on.

"I am so in love with my Jim, and I don't ever want that love to fade."

She sighed. "I don't know if I'm making any sense. I'm confused and frustrated and even a little jealous of Susie. I don't understand how I could be feeling that way. It's probably good for me to be talking about it."

"Yes, dear, I believe it is," Olive said. "As for me, I don't really have any words of wisdom, but we do need to keep praying about it. God will help you sort through your feelings, and before long, I think you will know what you need to be doing."

"What about it, Harold? Do you have any thoughts on the subject?" Olive asked.

"Only that we've grown to love you both," he said. "You are like our children. So come back anytime to talk and pray. I'm positive that God will show you the way."

Walking back to her house, Sara felt about ten pounds lighter. "Thank you, God, for these beautiful friends. Please help me as I struggle with what I should do about Ian."

It was early spring, and most of the maple trees in Brentville had been tapped. Some of the buckets hanging on the trees were galvanized steel, and some were older and wooden. Sara found herself checking the buckets as she walked to and from work. The clear sap was dripping into them, and she always wanted to see how full they were getting.

Mr. Brent had an efficient and workable plan for the maple-syrup processing industry in Brentville. Instead of all the small, family-owned sugar houses—or sugar shacks, as some were called—he had created a large factory where those who wished could convert the sap into syrup. They had big wood fires with large vats over the fires.

The people took horse-drawn sleighs or wagons around to the trees. There were empty sap buckets on the wagons. They took each filled bucket to the wagon and replaced it with an empty one. Then the wagons took the sap to the sugar factory.

The sap was poured into the vats and boiled until enough of the water had evaporated. When it was at just the right temperature and consistency, they bottled it. This produced enough to last the community a year or more.

Ian told Sara that he remembered going to his uncle's sugar house in Minnesota when he was a boy. They had parties in the little sugar shack. "Uncle Mike would fill up some big pots with snow and tamp it down," he told Sara. "When the syrup came to a point where it would hair, they drizzled the hot syrup over the snow. *To hair* means that when a half teaspoon of the hot syrup was put into a cup of cold water, it formed hair-like strands.

"We all took a fork and dug in. Winding the sweet candied syrup around my fork is something I love to remember. It was so sweet it made my teeth hurt.

"After we'd eaten so much sugar that we couldn't eat anymore, my uncle would pass around the dill pickles. That would take the sweet taste away. Then we could usually go back to twist more of that sweet-tasting stuff onto our forks."

Sara smiled and thought, *That might be a fun thing to do with our church group.*

CHAPTER 28

Snowmen, Sugar, and Fish

On Tuesday morning, Sara's phone rang unexpectedly. It was Ian. "Hi, Sara! I was on my way to pick up Harold for our Tuesday appointment with Mr. Brent. Lucky was looking out the window, watching the windshield wiper throwing the slushy snow off the truck window. I told him we'd have to build a snowman when we got home. His tail was wagging, so I guess he agrees with me.

"Anyway, as I walked up Harold's steps, I got this idea: I'd invite friends over this afternoon to roll out some snowmen. After that, we can have some maple sugar on snow. I asked Harold if I could use his phone before we left. When I told him what I was planning, he caught my excitement and said he would ask Olive to make some phone calls."

Ian paused. "So, Sara, I'm calling you and a few others and leaving the rest of the calls to Olive while Harold and I go to meet with Mr. Brent. I asked her to invite a few of them to bring a big laundry tub to hold the snow for our Maple Sugar on Snow party."

Sara replied, "You must be a mind reader. I was just thinking that we should have one of those parties. I'll do my part. See you later."

After meeting at the mansion, by the time Ian and Harold got to Ian's house, most of the guests had arrived. Sara greeted Ian at the door.

"This is the way to have a party," laughed Ian as he walked into his house. "I arrive after all the work is done!"

"Yes!" Sara said as she joined in his laughter.

"Everything is all set up for boiling the syrup. The big laundry tubs are outside, waiting to be filled with clean snow," reported Olive. "By the way, how did it go at the mansion?"

"It went surprisingly well," answered Ian. "We will tell you all about it later. Let's get some teams together for our snowmen. We probably won't be having many more of these perfect snowfalls this year. Let's make the most of it."

Olive brought out a wooden crate full of things that she thought would go well with the snowmen. There were carrots, coats, pipes, scarves, hats buttons, sticks, and gloves. "One thing about being in Brentville—" Sara said to Olive, "it forces us to use our imaginations."

"Yes, with no television or other modern things like that, we have to get out and do more," Olive responded.

Sara and Susie were partners for the snowman-building project. They decided to make it in Susie's yard. The snow was perfect—just right for packing. They had their first big snowball rolled out and placed where they wanted to put their snowman. Then they proceeded to create a snowman.

"Perfect," they agreed as they rummaged through the crate for accessories.

Janet and Walter were busy making one right next to them. Janet's three brothers were making a couple of snowmen in Ian's yard. Harold had taken them under his wing; he had been trying to do more with them recently.

Janet's sister, Sue, was there also, but Sara didn't see Lucy, the fifteen-year-old, or Lisa, her mom. *I must make a visit to that household,* Sara thought. *My chief inspector antenna is going up. I'm concerned about how they're doing.*

After praising everybody for their unique snowmen, the group decided that it was too cold to be out any longer. As they entered the house through the basement bulkhead door, they left their snow-laden coats, hats, and mittens on wooden racks and put their boots over a big drain. Even the adults, with their noses tingling from the cold, felt like kids again as they tromped up the stairs.

A few of the guests had gone back inside earlier to get things started in the kitchen. There were four big laundry tubs full of clean snow. The maple syrup gently boiling on the stove was almost ready to be drizzled on the snow.

Olive had a glass of cold water in her hand, into which she dropped a little of the hot syrup. "I declare," she said with a big smile. "It's ready to go. Do you see?" she asked, holding the glass toward the people who were standing around her. "It has formed what looks like stringy hairs in the glass."

When she started to drizzle the hot syrup onto the snow, everyone grabbed a fork. They had three tables set up, so almost everyone could sit. The mood was festive and the conversation enjoyable as they twirled the sticky lines of candied syrup around their forks.

"I think it's time to pass the dill pickles," announced Ian. He had a big dish of pickles ready. He walked around, offering them to the guests. By then, most of indulgers were in a sugar coma, and a dill pickle sounded like a good antidote.

Olive showed them how they could make maple sugar candy by boiling the liquid a little bit longer. She then put it into another bowl and quickly stirred it as it thickened. Then she put it onto wax paper in one-inch drops, so she had enough candy to give everyone to take home.

"Thanks, Ian, for reminding us to relax and have fun," she said.

Most of the guests had gone, and Olive and Harold were about ready to leave. Walter was going to take them home, along with Janet, Sara, and the dogs. He was using the mansion's big horse and buggy, so there was plenty of room for everyone, even Sam and Matilda. They wagged their tails excitedly.

Later, when Janet was in her room, Sara tapped softly on her door.

"Come in!"

Sara entered the room to find Janet in bed, her Bible on her lap. "Sit here," Janet said as she motioned Sara to the end of her bed.

"How are you feeling?" asked Sara.

Janet sighed, "I feel full, and I feel fat."

"I know what that's like," Sara responded, "but in a short time, you'll have this little one in your arms. It will be much better very soon."

"That's right," responded Janet, remembering her other pregnancy. "But I didn't get to hold the other one."

Sara could hear Janet's grief. "I'm so sorry that you have had to go through all this. This time will be so different."

Janet agreed. "I've been asking God to help me forget the nightmare of the other birth."

"Yes, Lord, please help Janet to be a whole, healthy person, with freedom from past hurts," prayed Sara aloud as she rested her hand on Janet's shoulder. "Please help Janet to be the wife and mother that you want her to be."

"Amen," they said in unison.

"After the baby comes, I want to give you a baby shower," Sara said. "For now, I'll give you some money. I would like to have you go to the department store to buy a few baby things. We have the bassinet and crib set up already, but you'll need some nightgowns and undershirts and rubber pants and blankets and other things."

Janet was touched. "I can't begin to tell you what you mean to me, Sara. I owe my life and my baby's life to you. I can never repay you."

"Yes, you can," Sara said with a smile. "When people who need help come into your life, you can give it to them. That will be my payment." Sara walked toward the door. "Time for me to get my beauty rest. Good night, sweet girl."

The phone rang just as Sara snuggled into bed. She knew it was Ian, keeping his promise to let her know what had happened at the mansion. She pulled the quilts around her as she listened.

Ian said, "While you and Olive were issuing invitations for us, it was, as Harold said, time for us to get down to business. When we pulled up to the mansion, Harold prayed, 'God, give us the words.' I added a heartfelt amen.

"Maggie answered the door. She welcomed us as she wiped the flour off her hands. Her apron was spattered with flour, so Harold asked, 'Do I smell one of your apple pies?'

"'You betcha,' she answered. 'If you stay long enough, I'll bring you a piece. Just head on into the living room, and I'll call Mr. Brent.'

"Sara, the mansion is very impressive. Harold agreed with me as he settled himself into a large, plush leather chair. 'Guess we'd better not get too comfortable,' I told him with a chuckle. 'Need to keep our minds on business.'

"Harold reminded me that it was okay, saying, 'God had it covered.'

"Mr. Brent came into the room with a tray full of goodies— some crackers, cheese, apples, and cookies. He said that he thought we might need something for energy as we worked on the icehouse.

"He carried the tray into the den, and we followed. We each grabbed a chair and pulled it up to the big, round table. Mr. Brent put some large drafting paper out in the middle of the table and made sure we each had a pencil. Then he said he'd love to hear about our ideas.

"Harold told him that we were just beginning with our thoughts and plans, and that's why we wanted him in on it too. The three of us sat at that table for a couple of hours. All kinds of ideas came forth. We debated and poured over the plans. When we'd finished, we had begun to design the biggest, most deluxe fish house that any of us had ever seen. Maggie was in twice to bring food and drinks.

"Suddenly realizing the time, I explained that I had a previous appointment and should be on my way. Mr. Brent was surprised that the two hours had flown by. He said that he was going to enjoy the time on this project—and with us. He added that most people in Brentville called him Mr. Brent. He said that he had never had many friends and asked us to call him Jack.

"'I extended my hand to him, and said, 'Okay, Jack.' Harold asked if it would be the same time, same station next week. Jack said that he was looking forward to it. He seemed genuinely happy about it.

"'Well, that's encouraging,' Harold enthused as we climbed into the cold truck.

"Sara, I never thought I would enjoy two hours with Mr. Brent."

"You mean Jack?" Sara asked with a smile.

"Oh yes, Jack." They both laughed.

"I couldn't believe that I'd let my guard down this much with Jack. Keeping my mind on my priorities on this case is going to be more difficult than I thought. It's hard not to like the guy."

"We'll have to be careful," Sara replied. "Thank you for telling me what happened. God bless your sleep. Good night, Ian."

CHAPTER 29

Love Is Strong

Sara left for work before Janet was up. She put fifty dollars out on the kitchen table with a note that read, "Dear Janet, Enjoy your baby shopping. Love, Sara."

Unfortunately, that didn't happen.

Sara was in the ER when Walter carried Janet in. "What happened?!" she asked.

Walter began his story as Sara went about seeing to Janet's needs. Sara asked the nurse to get Janet settled into a room.

"Apparently, Janet ate breakfast, walked the dogs, and hitched up the horse and buggy. She has been feeling pretty heavy these days and decided against walking all the way to the store in the slush and ice. Having arrived at the village's center, she tied the horse up to the hitching post in front of the department store. She was looking forward to purchasing a few baby things. Entering the store, she asked the saleswoman where she could find some baby outfits.

"Janet told me all this on the way here." He paused and said, "She had spent a couple of hours looking at all the sweet baby things. It sounds like she was able to purchase quite a bit with the money you gave her. On her way out of the store, she looked to her left and caught sight of Frank. She could see that he was heading her way.

"Frank told her she was looking good and asked her when the baby was due. She was feeling panic and was remembering what happened with this man and her last baby. She said that she looked at him with eyes of steel. She said she didn't know where she got the courage, but she was able to tell him that if he came any closer, she would scream.

"She walked rapidly to the door. But in hurrying to her buggy, she slipped on some ice and went flying. Both sacks full of baby things fell to the sidewalk, and she rolled toward the curb.

"Apparently Frank was watching the whole thing and must have decided he could talk her into letting him take her home. But when Janet saw him standing over her, she screamed. The saleswoman came running from the store. She bent over, told Janet to be calm, and said she would call for help.

"Shoppers were starting to crowd around Janet. I arrived right after that. Frank disappeared.

"I ordered everyone to stand back. The saleswoman and I helped Janet up and gently put her into her buggy. I wrapped her in a blanket and headed here as fast as I could."

Hearing Walter tell the story was making Sara's blood boil. "We need to take care of this man," she muttered. *But first things first*, she thought as she concentrated on Janet.

Janet was admitted into the hospital at noon. Sara had checked her over and nothing was broken. The baby seemed fine and had a good heartbeat. However, after she'd arrived at the hospital, Janet's water had broken, and she was having some bleeding.

"You're in labor," announced Sara.

"I know," replied Janet. "My contractions have started. They're coming every twenty minutes now."

Sara called Olive to ask if she and Harold would tend to her dogs. "It may be a while before I get home. Would you call the church group to ask them to pray?"

"Willingly, dear," replied Olive. "As soon as we hang up, I'll do it."

This experience was all new to Walter. And Sara could tell that hospitals didn't agree with him. "Would you mind taking my horse and buggy home?" she requested. "And maybe you could give these baby clothes to Olive and ask her to wash them for us."

Walter seemed very happy to have a job and to be heading out to the fresh air.

"We'll take good care of Janet," promised Sara.

By six, Janet was having contractions every ten minutes, and they were getting stronger. She was dilated only to three centimeters. Sara was beginning to be concerned. By eight o'clock, the contractions were every five minutes, and Janet had dilated to five centimeters.

When ten o'clock rolled around, the contractions were coming every three minutes, and she was at nine centimeters. Sara worried. *Why isn't this baby coming?*

After more prodding and checking, Sara was sure that the baby was in the birth canal, but it had decided to come feet first. *Too late for a Caesarian section.* Sara gave Janet another whiff of the anesthesia and eased the baby along to birth as best she could.

Miraculously, the five-pound girl was perfect in every way. Sara decided to put her into an oxygen tent because the birth had put so much stress on her little lungs. Other than having a few stitches and being very tired, Janet was perfect too.

"Your little miracle girl," said Sara, as she presented the baby to Janet. Janet took the black-haired little one into her arms and cried. She and Walter had decided that if it was a girl, they would name her Jackie, after Walter's father, Jack Brent.

Walter had been pacing the floor in the maternity waiting room and was finally allowed in to see Janet. "Meet Jackie!" said Janet as he came toward the bed. "Would you like to hold her?"

"Of course," he replied as he lifted the baby into his arms.

"Our Little Miss Jackie," he declared. "Welcome to Brentville. I'm your dad."

CHAPTER 30

Joining Forces

Janet and the baby were in the hospital for five days before Sara let them go home. Sara had arranged to take a week off work and expected to enjoy being at home with Janet and this sweet infant.

Their first night went smoothly.

When Ian stopped in on his way to work, he found Sara sitting in the living room, holding Jackie. "Well, if you don't look like the youngest grandmother I've ever seen," he said.

"Thank you, kind sir," replied Sara. "This is just the most perfect little thing. I'd forgotten how good they smell. Do you want to hold her?"

"Thanks, but I'll wait until she's a little older—old enough for me to know she won't break, anyway. I have something in the truck for Jackie. I'll bring it in."

Sara could tell that he was excited about whatever it was.

A few minutes later, he came in with a rocking horse. It wasn't a little rocking horse, but a huge rocking horse, which was mounted on a steel frame and attached to the frame with four big, heavy springs. Sara remembered having seen ones like it in the fifties and sixties. Her sister had one that she rode for hours.

"I had one of these as a kid," said Ian. "I couldn't resist it when I saw it this morning. Someone was getting rid of it, and I just knew I had to get it for Jackie. It seems to be in very good shape."

"Thank you, Ian. I think Jackie will love it when she's old enough." *How sweet that Ian is so excited about his gift for Jackie.* "Just put it in the corner of the dining room," Sara said. "That should be a good spot."

Ian said, "Harold and I have another meeting with Mr. Brent today." "This will be our third, and we're really encouraged to see how receptive Mr.—or, I mean Jack—is to our reaching out to him."

"That's fantastic, Ian," said Sara. "I think I'll go over to see the Morrison family this week. I still feel that place must be full of clues. I'll go before we have our committee meeting at Harold's. I hope I'll have something to report."

"I'm off to work," announced Ian. "See you later. Oh, Susie would like to come over to see Jackie. Would you mind if we come over later?"

"That would be nice," answered Sara. "I'm sure Janet would love to see you."

Sara sat holding Jackie for quite a while after Ian left. She had done a lot of praying about her feelings for Ian. *The best thing right now is to pull back a little. Maybe I could include Susie in more of the outings that I have with Ian. Tonight may be a good start. As they spend time together, who knows, they may discover that they are attracted to each other.*

I know it will be hard. I'm already missing him, but it's the right thing to do. I'm not ready. Jim is still my true love, and I will not give up my hope of returning to him.

Sara's week seemed to be flying. She decided it was time to get over to see how Lisa was doing. Lisa answered the door and invited her in. "I haven't seen you in a while," said Sara. "I was disappointed that you and Lucy couldn't make the Maple Sugar on Snow party at Ian's last week."

Lisa looked pale and worn. "Is everything all right?" asked Sara.

"Not really," answered Lisa. "As you know, since my husband's death, I've had to work to make ends meet. That means I'm not around much for my kids. The boys seem to be doing fine. Harold has given them so much of his time, and he even gets his friends involved with the boys. But the girls are a different story.

"I've just found out that Frank has been coming to the house when I'm not here." Lisa sighed. "The kids are afraid of him, and to tell you the truth, so am I. It's a relief to know that Janet is with you and that she has Walter now. I'm sorry I haven't come to see Janet and the baby. I'm so angry at Frank for what he has done to Janet. I don't know if I could see that baby without thinking of him!

"I think Sue has the personality and determination to fight for her rights. So, if Frank came around, I think she would kick and fight and even shoot him if she had to. But Lucy is more like Janet—and, I suppose, like me. We don't fight, and we don't see our worth."

"Interesting that you would say that," replied Sara. "I think you're right. Did you know that Janet has God in her life now? Her life has been totally turned around. She is a new person."

Lisa's eyes were filled as she heard Sara talking about Janet. She said, "Oh, thank you for telling me. And thank you for caring enough about her to take her in like you have."

"If I could find housing for Lucy and Sue, do you think they would be open to making the change?" asked Sara.

"Oh yes, absolutely," answered Lisa with hope in her voice.

"I will see what I can do. I am so disgusted and upset with Frank and all that he has done. If you know anything about him that would help me put him away forever, please let me know."

"Okay," replied Lisa. "It goes beyond Frank. He seems to be the ringleader, but there are others, like my husband, for instance, who are involved too. There may be as many as thirty."

"If you ever feel afraid and need help, please call me," offered Sara. "Or if you ever think of anything that might prove or lead us to proof of any wrongdoing, please let me know. Lisa, what is your opinion of Mr. Brent? Do you think he knows about any of this?"

"From what I've seen of Mr. Brent, I really don't think he knows. I am afraid that he has trusted Frank for so many years that he has a film over his eyes when it comes to judging him."

Sara thanked Lisa and told her that she would be in touch. She couldn't wait to talk with Ian and Harold. In fact, she stopped at Harold's on her way home. She told Harold, "Lisa thinks that Mr. Brent doesn't know anything about the satanic worship or about Frank's being involved in it. Now that you guys are friends with Mr. Brent—Jack, that is—do you think that it's safe to talk with him about it? With his power, we'd have a much better chance of figuring all this out."

"You're right about that," said Harold. "We need to bring it to the committee."

"What would you think about my asking Mary to take Lucy and Sue for a while? I feel very strongly that we need to get them out of that house. They're just not safe—especially Lucy."

"By all means," answered Harold. "If Mary is on board, please make it happen."

By six that evening, Sara had done what she needed to do to put the move into action. Lucy and Sue were at Mary and David's by dinnertime. Sara could get to the committee meeting on time, if she hurried.

After the committee discussed it, they decided that it would be good to talk first with Walter. "It's agreed, then," Harold concluded. "Walter must be asked what he thinks about the relationship between Jack Brent and Frank." They needed to find out if Walter thought his father could be part of the satanic movement that they were seeing.

When asked, Walter told them, "I still live at the mansion, but I have my own quarters, so I don't know about everything that's happening there. Even so, I'm pretty sure my dad knows nothing of this dark side of Frank. I think he should be told. We should all join forces."

Harold, Ian, and Walter were appointed to be the ones to tell Jack, as some of his new friends were calling him.

"Dad is pretty loyal to his people," said Walter. "We have to get our facts straight and to have as much proof as we can. My father and Maggie have been having an extremely busy life over these past two years. It has not been officially announced, but Dad has adopted a little boy. He is just about two years old now. It's something Frank arranged for Dad a couple of years ago. Frank said some girl had a baby out of wedlock and couldn't keep him.

"My father and Maggie have been quietly raising this little boy in the mansion. I'm happy to have the child around. I've never questioned Dad about the particulars of the adoption or the reasons for it. With my father's busyness and my own responsibilities, there are days when I don't even run into my father at all.

"I confess that this whole thing feels strange. I feel a little like I may be betraying my dad by talking with you before discussing it with him. Yet I don't know what else can be done. To complicate the situation, I haven't talked to Dad about Janet, the baby, or my newfound faith. I guess it will all come out tomorrow. It will be a relief to be able to talk with him about it."

The appointment with Jack Brent was made for the very next morning.

Knowing how concerned Sara would be, Ian checked in with her after the mansion meeting. Before he went home for a much-needed post-meeting nap, and not trusting the phones, Ian dropped by for a private conversation with Sara. As accurately as possible, he gave a play-by-play account of how the meeting had gone. "Harold and I were already sitting in the living room with Jack when Walter arrived from his part of the mansion. Jack got up and welcomed him with a handshake. Harold started talking first. He explained why we were there—being his articulate self. I shared some of my experiences with Frank.

"Next Walter told of his involvement with Janet. He also told his dad what he had learned about Frank. It was Walter's story that seemed to be bringing Jack over to our side. We could see that he believed him.

"After a couple hours of talking and hashing things through, we were emotionally exhausted. Jack said that he needed time to process it all. He suggested that we resume our conversation in a couple of days. He also said that he would not say anything to Frank. He was afraid that it might be true, and he wanted to make sure we planned it out carefully. Jack then invited us back on Friday morning to continue our journey toward justice.

"After we'd left the mansion, Harold and I agreed that Jack wasn't the only one who was worn out by the meeting. When I said I needed a nap, Harold said he had the same plans and added,

'Working out in the fields all day wouldn't be half as tiring as what we just went through!'

"Most importantly, we both agreed that it had been a wise decision to meet with Jack. Having him on our side, along with Walter, who knows the ins and outs of Brentville, will make it easier to bring Frank and all his cronies down."

Ian yawned, apologized, and headed to the door, escorted by Sam and Matilda. Sara thanked God that progress was being made.

CHAPTER 31

SOS!

Sara had been thinking about Lisa and her situation. *Maybe I'll give her a call this morning before I leave for work.*

"Hello," Lisa answered.

"Good morning, Lisa. This is Sara. I wanted to see how you're adjusting to not having the girls around."

"I'm missing them," Lisa admitted, "but I know it's for the best. Now I wonder if the boys are safe here. Frank seems to be obsessed with all of us."

"Oh my," said Sara, "that doesn't sound good. I have an idea of someone who might be willing to take the boys for a while. Do you want me to look into it?"

"Oh, would you?" cried Lisa. "It might be a smart thing to do."

"I'm on it," said Sara. "I'll get back to you as soon as I know anything definite."

"Thank you, Sara."

Sara decided to make a quick stop at Harold's before work. *I want to tell them about my phone call with Lisa. I wonder if they might be willing to take the boys. Harold seems to have bonded with them, and Olive loves kids. And they have three empty bedrooms and a bathroom upstairs.*

"Good morning, Sara," Olive said as she greeted her at the door.

"Hi! Do you and Harold have a few minutes?" Sara asked. "I want to ask you something."

"Yes, dear," said Olive. "Harold just went out for more wood for the fire. Come sit, and I'll bring you some hot cider."

Harold came in and headed toward the fireplace. "To what do we owe the pleasure of this visit?" he asked as he threw a log on the fire. "I know there must be something important on your mind for you to be here before work."

"You know me well, don't you, Harold," Sara said. "Yes, I do have something weighing on my mind. I talked with Lisa this morning, and she seems to be worried about the boys being left alone for so many hours. I have been thinking about who might be able to take them for a while, and naturally, I thought of you."

Olive and Harold looked at each other and laughed. "Funny thing," said Harold, "but we've had a few discussions about this on our own. Seeing the boys there alone so much of the time is worrisome, and it's not good—especially with the likes of Frank on the prowl."

"I'm thrilled to hear that you might be able to do it," Sara responded. "It would be so good for the boys to be under your care and influence."

"My stars!" exclaimed Olive. "What are we waiting for? I'll call Lisa this morning before she heads out to work. I'll invite them to come."

"I love you both," said Sara, and she gave them a hug. "Congratulations on starting a new family—and at your age. Who would have thought?" she said with a giggle.

As she walked to work, Sarah thought, *One more thing I can cross off my list. I hope it won't be too much for Harold and Olive. The boys do seem nice and may end up being a help to the older folks. There are lots of chores they could help with.*

Later that afternoon, Sara's phone was ringing as she walked into her office.

"Hi, Sara! Harold is moving the boys in as we speak," Olive said with excitement in her voice. "We're both ready for this and feel that God is going to work through us to help these kids."

"I'm sure he is," agreed Sara. "Thanks for being so willing to help."

"Harold is helping Brian, who's fourteen, and James, who's twelve, and Johnny, who's ten, to choose the room they want to claim. They've never had a room of their own. In fact, they're used to being squeezed into one room. It is a privilege to have them here. They're good boys. We'll need to find a few chores for them; they're used to hard work."

"I'll stop in after my shift is done to check on how things are going," said Sara. *I'm glad Janet has decided to stay with me for another month. When Janet, Walter, and Jackie move into the mansion after the wedding, I'm really going to miss them. I've grown fond of them.*

When Sara reached home, Walter was in the living room with Janet and was rocking Jackie.

Cute little family, thought Sara. They seemed to be in a conversation about what Mary had said at their Bible study.

"Did I hear you say that you have asked God into your life?" asked Sara.

"Sure did," replied Walter. "I'm very excited to be your brother in Christ."

"Oh, Walter!" Sara exclaimed. "I am so happy for you. I've been hoping and praying that I would be hearing these words. This calls for a hug." It was a three-way hug, with a cooing Jackie in the middle.

Sara sat down with them in the living room. "I have something to share with you both. This can't go any further than this room." She had their attention. Even Jackie was still. "We have a secret church in Brentville. You have met many of our members because they are our friends. It's secret because the church in Brentville is very liberal—a social club, really. And Mr. Brent seems to run the church. We're assuming he would be against true Christianity."

Walter was nodding.

"I think you've probably heard about all the book clubs in the village," Sara continued. "Well, they are a cover for our Bible study/church meetings. The one I go to is at Harold and Olive's house. We meet every week, on Friday night. We'd love to have you guys join us. And, I'm sorry, Walter, but until we are more certain about your dad's attitude and what he might do, we would ask that you not give him any of this information."

Janet and Walter had surprised looks on their faces. "I would love to join you, Sara," said Janet. "It would be nice to be around other Christians."

Walter seemed excited to know about the group too. "I'm interested in learning all I can about my God and my Jesus and the Holy Spirit, Three in One," he said, smiling at Sara. "So count me in."

"Come over here on Friday night, Walter, and we'll all go together," said Sara. "You can bring the baby, too, Janet. You'll find quite a few other children attending. In fact, you'll probably see your brothers there."

Janet and Walter thanked Sara. Their excitement at being included in the church was obvious.

Jackie was stirring in Walter's arms. "Is it time for a bottle?" asked Sara.

"Not quite yet," Janet answered. "I'm following your suggestion with the schedule thing, and it looks like we have another hour to go."

"You're going to be a good dad," Sara commented as she watched Walter with the baby.

"I hope so," he replied. "I know it's a big responsibility. This beautiful little girl with her black hair and pink cheeks deserves the best." He paused and muttered, "She reminds me of someone, but I can't for the life of me think who. I guess they all look pretty much alike at this age."

"Actually," said Sara, "I think Jackie looks just like her mom!"

Sam and Matilda, tails wagging, scrambled to the door; their bodies seemed to be filled with anticipation. A few moments later, Ian walked in, right on cue. "Hi, Doc, how's everyone doing?" he asked. "That sure is a beautiful little girl you have in your arms," he said to Walter. Ian paused. "Something happened today that I am hoping Walter will be able to help me with."

"What is it?" asked Walter.

"Well, on my way to work this morning, I caught sight of the man who took Lucky. He was just getting into his car, so I followed him to what I think was his house. I thought if I showed you where it is, maybe you would know who lives there. Then we would have located another of the thirty or so who are involved."

"No time like the present," said Walter. "Take me to his house, and I'll tell you if I know who lives there. I do know most everyone in Brentville."

"Do you want to take the next turn?" Walter asked Sara, as he handed the baby over to her.

"As a matter of fact, I do," she answered. "I haven't had my Jackie fix yet today."

Having a baby in the house had certainly changed the household dynamics. It was clear that they all loved the presence of the infant. From the crying in the night to the sweet smell and feel of the soft-skinned infant in their arms, it was one big miracle wrapped in a pretty pink blanket.

Sara's phone rang. She picked it up to answer, but there was no one on the other end of the line. She clicked the cradle switch a couple of times and got the operator. "Hi, Mabel," said Sara. "Do you know who just tried to call me?"

"Give me a minute. I'll see what I can do," answered Mabel.

After a minute, Mabel said, "Yes, funny thing—it was from Lisa Morrison, but as soon as I put the call through to you, the line went dead. And it wasn't just a hang-up—it is now out of service."

"Thanks, Mabel," said Sara, as she replaced the handset into the cradle. *I need to get over to Lisa! I gave her my number and told her to call if she needed anything. This may be a time when she needs me, and I would never forgive myself if I didn't go.* "I'll be right back," she said to Janet. "I won't be gone long."

She saddled the horse, and was off.

Sara, the police, Walter, and Ian all arrived at Lisa's at about the same time. Sergeant Hanratty told his men to cover the doors and windows, and Walter and Ian were to push in the front door. Sara was following Ian to the door when they heard a gunshot.

Lisa's body had slipped to the floor. Frank was placing the revolver in her hand as Walter knocked down the door. Frank ran for the back door, and two police officers grabbed him and handcuffed him. They deposited him in the police car and headed to the jail.

Sara ran to Lisa to feel for a pulse. "She's still alive," Sara shouted. "Looks like the bullet went straight through. Let's get her to the hospital."

Sara held Lisa in the back seat, and Ian sped to the hospital. He told her quickly about how he and Walter had been checking out the house of the man who had stolen Lucky. They'd recorded the name for Harold and the committee. "As we drove past Lisa's house, we noticed Frank's car parked in front of it. Walter wanted to stop at a friend's home down the street to make a call to the police station. There are a few there he seems to trust. He wanted to have them here for backup. That's how we happened to arrive when you did."

"I am truly thankful to God that we were all there at the right time," said Sara as they arrived at the ER doorway. She held the door open as Ian hurried in with Lisa in his arms. He found the nearest gurney and gently placed her on it. "Okay," said Sara, "I'll take over from here. I need to help with the care of Lisa."

She asked Walter to ride her horse home and tell Janet about her mother. "Reassure Janet that I'll call her as soon as there's something to tell."

Lisa seemed a little groggy, but she wanted to tell Sara what had happened. She whispered, "When I got home from work the house was dark, something that I'm not used to. It felt lonely, but I knew it was the best thing for the kids. I opened the door and felt around for the light switch. Turning to hang my coat on the coat rack, I was startled to see a man sitting in the chair by the window.

"My first impulse was to run, so I headed toward the door, but Frank jumped up to stand in front of it. 'Lisa, Lisa, Lisa,' he said to me, frowning. 'What am I going to do with you? Giving away all your children. Now I'm wondering what you may tell others about me. I've taken such good care of you and your family, and you don't seem to appreciate it.'"

Lisa took a deep breath. "I was very fearful of what Frank might do. I could sense the color draining from my face; my body was feeling weak. I tried to call you, but just as I told the operator to get Sara Saunders, Frank jerked the phone line from the wall. He cornered me and pushed me to a chair. He said that he thought I must be very lonely, that I must be so despondent about not having my kids that I wanted to end my life."

Lisa paused. "Handing me a pencil and paper, he ordered me to write. He ordered me to leave a suicide note to the kids saying I wasn't strong enough to live for them and that I was sorry. He told me exactly what to write, word by word. As soon as I'd finished, he took the paper and pen from me and placed it on the table." Lisa's voice was hoarse.

Sara reminded her that she had come in just after the shot had been fired. "There's no need to say any more now. You are to rest and get better. Doctor's orders!"

Sara arrived home a few hours later. "Your mom is going to be fine," she told Janet and Walter. "As would be expected, there is some minor internal damage, but the bullet went in and out, straight through, missing her heart and major arteries by a fraction of an inch. She will need to be in the hospital for some time, but she is one fortunate lady."

Janet started to cry. "Thank you, God," she said. "And thank you, Sara. Once again, you have saved someone I love."

Sara didn't find it necessary to give Janet the details of her observations and what she'd learned when Lisa was barely able— but eager—to talk. *Lisa can tell Janet as much or as little of her story—if and when she is ready to do so.*

"Thank you, God," Sara prayed aloud as Walter, Janet, and she sat in the warmth of her home. "Thank you for bringing us together in time to save Lisa's life."

Walter and Janet joined Sara in the amen.

"Maybe Walter could take you over to the hospital tomorrow," suggested Sara. "Jackie and I will be fine here by ourselves."

CHAPTER 32

Junior Detectives' Success

The next morning, Janet fed the baby and got dressed to go to the hospital. She hadn't seen her mom since she had moved in with Sara. When she got back to Sara's, she found her giving Jackie a bath. The kitchen sink was filled with warm water, and Sara was holding Jackie in the curve of one arm in the water, washing her with the other hand.

"I don't know if I dare to do that," said Janet.

"Oh, you'll get the hang of it," Sara said. "The next bath we will do together. Hand me that towel please. We'll wrap her up in it."

Janet wrapped Jackie in the towel and held her close. "I'll take it from here," she said with newfound confidence.

Sara had a blanket set out on the sofa to lay Jackie on, and the clothes were laid out beside the blanket. There were baby oil and baby powder containers on the floor beside the couch. Sara and Janet were thankful for the talc mine in Brentville.

After Janet had dried Jackie, she put some baby oil on the baby's head to help with cradle cap. She powdered her up, pinned the cloth diaper together, and covered it with the protective pants. They were made of a material that someone in Brentville had invented—something similar to plastic, but heavier. They weren't as good as the plastic ones Sara knew were available in her world, but they were better than nothing.

Janet gently pulled an undershirt on Jackie, topping it with a nightgown that tied at the bottom. She carefully combed Jackie's hair and cuddled her in a receiving blanket. She swayed with Jackie in her arms as she quickly told Sara about her visit to the hospital. "Walter drove me there but said he would give me some time alone before he went in. I found Mom's room and peeked in the door. Mom started sobbing when she saw me. She said she was sorry she didn't come to see me when Jackie was born. She admitted she had been selfish, thinking about how she felt instead of thinking of me and what I was going through. I just gave her a big careful hug and told her that I understood.

"I told her that we have a lot of catching up to do and that as soon as she got out of this place, she needed to come and meet Jackie. She's my miracle baby, and I'm thanking God every day for protecting her."

Janet paused. "My mother said that she doesn't know my God, but she's glad I have him. I told her that she could have him too. I told her that if she wanted me to, I could introduce her to him. Sara, I felt *so* good as I smiled and put my hand over Mom's.

"After visiting for a half hour or so, I decided it was time to leave. Mom was looking tired, and I was feeling kind of wobbly. She said she was looking forward to meeting her new granddaughter.

"That's all the good news for now. I'm going to go upstairs to put this sleepy darling into her bassinet."

Janet tenderly began to sing her own version of Frank Loessner's popular fifties song "I Love You a Bushel and a Peck."[6] Janet's gentle "doodle, oodle, oodle, doodle, oodle oodle, doodle, oodle oodle, oo" trailed down the stairs.

"You should take a nap too," Sara called softly up the stairway to Janet. "You've had a busy morning. I'll be back soon. I'm going over to see Olive."

As Sara walked toward Olive's front porch, she could see boots lined up by the front door and a sled leaning against one of the trees out front. *Nice to see those reminders of children in their midst. Harold and Olive seem to be looking and acting younger since the arrival of the boys. Parenthood appears to be agreeing with them.*

"Hello," called Sara as she opened the front door.

"Oh, hi, Sara," responded Olive from the kitchen. "Come in and pull up a chair. Sit with me while I finish up this pie. I've just put three loaves of bread in the oven. It's a thrill to have these three hungry boys to feed. I love it!"

"I wonder where you get all your energy." Sara commented. "Where's Harold?"

"He's up in his little house, working on a song that he's composing," answered Olive. "He's lucky to have that quiet place to go to. He's enjoying having the boys here, but when it comes to his writing or reading or thinking, he likes to retreat to his place."

"Where are the boys?" asked Sara.

"They're out somewhere playing. It seems that even in the winter, they love being outside. They have their BB guns, toy guns, holsters, hats, boots, bows and arrows, and so on. They're probably out in the woods somewhere."

Olive added, "We include them in our Bible reading and prayer time every morning. So far, they haven't rebelled. In fact, this morning, Brian wanted to pray for his mother. They are full of questions about God."

"Terrific!" said Sara.

"My stars, what's all the commotion?" asked Olive.

The boys were running up the back steps, loudly discussing something about bones. They had finally gotten all the wet clothes off and came padding into the kitchen in their stocking feet and long underwear.

"Olive, where's Grandpa?" they asked.

"Oh—hi, Sara!" Brian said as he noticed her sitting with Olive.

"We need to see Grandpa," said James.

"We need help interpreting our findings," added Brian.

"What findings might that be?" asked Olive.

"Well," said Brian, "we were playing way out in the woods, and we came across a place that looks as though someone has cleared the trees away."

"In the middle of the clearing," James said, "there are rough benches in sort of circles."

"And," Brian added with breathless excitement, "in the middle of the circles there is a huge fire pit with a big iron shelf."

"Slow down," pleaded Sara. "Is there anything else?"

"Oh, yes," James added. "We found some bones in the ashes of the fire pit."

"My goodness! This calls for more investigation," Sara said. "Let's find Harold, and you can take us to the spot."

"I'll stay here with my baking," said Olive. "You boys can find dry boots and clothes down in the cellar. I have your other snow gear drying on the line by the furnace."

"Wow," exclaimed Sara. "This may actually be the clue we're waiting for. If this is the place where some of the Satan worshippers are meeting, it's a big break in our case. We could have men waiting on guard to see if anyone shows up there. If they do, Mr. Brent might have a full jail."

"Let's not get ahead of ourselves," warned Olive.

"I'll go up to get Harold," said Sara. "Send the boys out when they're bundled up and ready to go."

Sara followed the narrow, shoveled path out to Harold's getaway. Smoke was coming from the chimney, and the place looked quite inviting. There were even some curtains—Olive's handiwork, Sara suspected.

"Knock, knock," said Sara as she opened the door to the little building.

"Hello there," said Harold with a smile. "What brings you to this neck of the woods?"

"I'll tell you in a minute, but first you tell me about this adorable kitten." Curled up in front of the stove sat a beautiful tiger kitten. "I didn't know you had a cat!"

"We didn't," said Harold. "This is Jessie, and he belongs to the boys. They were so attached to him that we didn't have the heart to say no. To tell you the truth," said Harold, "Olive and I are enjoying his presence. We had cats years ago, and we'd forgotten how much fun it is to have them around."

"I was just down visiting with Olive," said Sara. "The boys came home all excited because they found a place in the woods, a place that has been cleared. It has benches and a big fire pit. Harold," she added, her voice sad, "they found bones in the ashes. This could be the break we need. The boys are getting into dry clothes and will be here in a few minutes. They're anxious to show you what they found."

Harold put on his coat, grabbed his hat, and checked the stove. Sara picked up the kitten, and they headed toward the house.

The boys were still arguing over which boots were theirs when Sara and Harold arrived.

"Oh, there you are," said Brian when he saw Harold. The boys all started talking at once, trying to tell him about their findings.

"Whoa, Nellie! Slow down and let me hear you one by one," Harold proclaimed. They told their story.

Harold said to Olive, "We'll leave Jessie with you, Mama. Do you have any old flour bags handy? I need something to hold possible evidence."

Finally, everyone was ready.

"How far away is this place anyway?" asked Sara.

"Don't know for sure, but it took us quite a while to get there," answered Brian.

"Maybe we should ride the horses," suggested Sara.

"Fine with me," said Harold. "I'll get our two, and we'll ride over to your house to pick you up." Then he suggested, "Brian, you can go with Sara. You can ride one of her horses, and the two younger boys can ride together on one of mine."

"Okay," answered Sara. "Let's go, Brian. See the rest of you in a few minutes."

Harold smiled as he looked at the boys. "Boy, when you start growing up, you don't waste any time, do you?" They appeared to relish Harold's fatherly approval.

Sara and Brian stopped in to see Janet before going out to get the horses.

Janet was rocking Jackie. "Hi, Brian," she said. "Come say hello to your new niece. And Jackie, meet your uncle Brian."

Brian's eyes softened as he saw the sweet little black-haired bundle.

"Would you like to hold her?" asked Sara.

"Sure," he said, nodding excitely. He quickly took off his mittens and coat and sat down beside Janet. She put the baby into his arms.

Brian smiled and said, "Hi, Jackie. I'm your uncle. You have two more uncles, and we will always protect you," he added in his protective uncle voice.

"I'll saddle up the horses," said Sara. "Brian, you come out in a few minutes."

"Yes, ma'am," he answered. "I'll be right out."

When Brian joined them, they were all there and ready to go. "Okay, guys," said Harold, "lead the way."

Brian and Sara were in front, followed by the two boys on one horse, with Harold bringing up the rear. After riding for ten minutes or so, Harold told Sara that he was glad she had thought of bringing the horses. "I know," she agreed, laughing. "The boys would probably have had to go back for help to carry us out of the woods."

"We're almost there!" yelled Brian. He had been following the markers the boys had left in the snow to help them find their way home. The boys had explained that when they played in the woods, they always left markers. Brian always carried a compass too. Their dad seemed to have taught them good outdoor skills. They knew their way around the woods.

"There it is!" cried Johnny.

As they approached the area, Harold suggested they get off the horses and tie them to trees outside the clearing. "Then we can walk quietly toward the large fire pit," he said. "I don't think anyone would be here in the daytime, but you never know. We need to be careful."

The boys appeared to be in awe of Harold. Everything he said seemed to be important to them. They hardly dared approach the area, and when they did get up as far as the benches, they sat down.

"Shush," said James. "Don't talk. Just whisper."

"Be still," they said to each other.

"You boys look around the bench area," said Harold. "See if you can find anything that might have been dropped. Sara and I will check out the bones."

"I see something there on the ground," yelled Johnny.

Brian came up behind him and put his hand over Johnny's mouth. "Quiet," Brian said. "Whisper, remember?"

It would be funny if it weren't so serious, thought Sara.

While the boys tiptoed around and tried to be quiet, Sara headed toward the fire pit. Harold was already there, picking out a few of the bones. "What do you think, Sara?" he asked as he held up one of them.

"We'll take them back to the lab," she answered. "I fear that these may be baby bones," she added, saddened and angry. Soon she found what looked like a crude burial ground just behind the benches. "Look, Harold," she yelled, forgetting about his instruction to be quiet. "Come and look."

Harold did some digging and found more bones. After they had a good sampling, they headed back to his house. The boys had a few things in their pockets that they could inspect at the house.

Sara took the flour bag's precious contents to the hospital. She went right to the lab and called for her most trusted coworkers. "I want you to examine these bones," she said to the two physician's assistants. "This is very confidential, so be discreet with your findings. For now, this will be between you and me—no one else."

When Harold phoned her a few minutes later to bring her up to date, Sara found he had been saying something very similar to the boys. "I talked with the boys while I tucked them into bed. All three had congregated into one room to talk. They were so used to being together in the same room that, since they came to stay with us, they usually start the evenings in Brian's room. They were all sitting on the full-sized bed with Jessie on Brian's lap. I pulled up a chair beside the bed and asked them what they thought of our day. They all agreed that it had been quite an adventure.

"All the boys had to realize that something was going on, but they couldn't know the depth of it all. Even though they had been brought up in a home where the dad was involved in terrible things, they seemed to know nothing of it——in fact, they are very innocent in their thinking.

"Johnny had tears flowing down his cheeks as he asked me about the bones. He wondered if they could be from someone's dog. I told him that we won't know for sure until we get the lab reports, and I agreed that it is an awful, gruesome thought. I suggested that after we say our prayers, we try to put it all out of our minds and let God help us figure this out. And when we know, he will help us deal with whatever it is we're facing.

"I praised them for doing such a good job today. I told them, 'You found some clues that may help Mr. Brent in an investigation that he's pursuing. So you are officially on the team now—and a very important part of the team rules is that this has to be kept quiet until we come to some conclusion. If you have any questions, please come to Olive or me.' I also warned them, 'Please don't talk to anyone else about what we found today,' and I had them shake on it.

"I recommended they go to their individual rooms to crawl into their own beds. I said a prayer with each boy in his own room and they seemed to settle quickly.

"'Good night, boys,' I said as I carried all the findings down the stairs. They all answered good night in unison.

"I've called Ian and asked him to come over. I've also called Jack Brent to see if Ian and I could go to his place to talk about what had happened, and he's waiting for us to come." Harold looked up. "And I see Ian outside now. We'll head to the mansion, and the planning will begin. Remember us in your prayers, please. Sleep well, Sara."

CHAPTER 33

Emergency in Brentville

Walter let Sara know that Mr. Brent had called in some of his best workers and created Operation Woods. He had round-the-clock surveillance covering the area in question.

Walter's orders to them had been clear: "Stay out of sight if the suspected cult members come back. Watch and take careful note of what's happening. Then go back with more officers the following week. If my father is right, they'll be meeting again the same night of the week. It's just an educated guess, but we're hoping that it will come to fruition.'"

The next morning, Sara met with the two physician's assistants at the hospital. They had their report written and wanted to talk with her. "Come to my office," Sara said. "We can discuss it there." When they entered, she said, "Please close the door. Have a seat, and thank you for your prompt attention to this matter. What do you think?"

"Some of these are definitely human bones," one of them said. "We are shocked and wondering where they came from, and what's going on in Brentville."

"I sure do understand your concern," answered Sara. "But right now, I'm not at liberty to divulge that information. Please remember that this has to stay here. No one else can know. This is a very serious problem, and Mr. Brent is working on it. I'll let you know as soon as I get the okay to do so."

They both said she could count on them keeping quiet.

As soon as the PAs had left the office, Sara called Ian. "Could you come to the hospital to get the PAs' report?"

"Sure, Doc, I'm on my way. I'll see you in your office in about ten minutes. Oh, and Sara, I'll bring our lunch."

Their lunch ran longer than she'd thought it would, but it was nice catching up with him. He and Susie were taking care of Lisa's horses and the few farm animals she had. "Thanks," said Sara. "I was thinking about that yesterday and then got so busy, I forgot to do anything about it. How is Susie doing?"

"I think she's doing as well as can be expected," answered Ian. "Probably better than I did at this stage of the game. I was a mess after my wife died."

"It's good that you're there to help her. You're better equipped to help her than someone who has not experienced losing a spouse." She changed the subject. "Janet and Walter are coming to Harold's tonight. I will ride with them, so you won't have to pick me up this week. And Lisa's three boys will be there."

"Our group is growing," said Ian. "Harold's idea of changing Brentville from the inside out is beginning to happen. I'm praying that Harold and I can help lead Jack to the Lord. Now that we've all become pretty good friends, I'm hoping it can happen. I am praying that God's Holy Spirit will show Jack that he really does need God.

"Being betrayed by Frank has affected Jack. He had trusted him so fully—and for so many years. But as you know, sometimes

God uses our times of trouble and anguish to reach us and to show us that we need him. Please keep praying for that on Jack's behalf."

"Will do," answered Sara. "And now I would like a ride home, please. I want to check on Janet and the baby."

Later Sara called Olive to see how they were doing. She told her what Harold had been talking to the boys about. "Because it was church night at our place," Olive said, "Harold knew that he needed to talk with the boys about it. 'I don't want to be devious,' he said to me, and was wondering how he should handle the situation. 'The truth is always best,' he decided. 'These boys are old enough to understand,' he said, 'and as soon as they come home from school, I'll talk with them.'"

Olive added, "I could hear them coming though the cellar. Bursting through the kitchen door, they looked ready for their snack. Usually, by the time they've left their wet outer clothing down there and run upstairs to get into dry clothes, I have glasses of milk and something yummy out on the table for them.

"The boys seem to appreciate being loved and cared for by us. They seem to be more peaceful and to feel safe. Brian told me that they'd never before been around anyone who prayed. Now they're included in prayer time every morning. He said that they'd never seen a Bible, but now Harold is reading to them every morning from this book that is so new to them."

She continued. "Today, as soon as the boys had said grace and were munching, Harold asked them how school had been. Johnny said he got into a fight with Mark Green. Mark said something about his mom getting shot and made it sound like it was her fault. So Johnny said that he bopped him in the nose. Mark started to fight back, but the teacher broke it up.

"Then Harold agreed that it's hard when someone says something mean about someone we love. Johnny looked at Harold and said, 'Yes, sir, I just wanted to bop him.' Then Harold told the boys he had found that it isn't wrong to have an angry feeling. It is what we do with those feelings that counts. He suggested that next time Johnny feels mad, he could stop and ask God for help—then find someone to talk to about the problem.

"Harold also said, 'You really don't know Jesus very well, but the more we read together about him, the more you will like him. He's my good friend, and he wants to be yours too. I go to Jesus for help all the time.'

"Harold also told the boys about our Friday-night group of friends and how they come over to sing and to learn more about God and Jesus. He asked them to join us tonight. He told them other children their age would be here. He added that even though we want to tell others about Jesus, we are keeping our meetings a secret for now and that there are Brentville residents who might hurt us if they knew about our church meetings. He also told them to call it a book club."

Olive concluded her account. "Harold also said, 'We *are* reading a book. Our book is from God—*The Bible*.'"

Promptly at seven that evening, Walter arrived. He'd brought the big horse and sleigh from the mansion—plenty of room for everyone. Sara could see Janet was learning that traveling with a baby was more complicated than she'd expected it would be. Walter helped to collect the blankets, baby bottles, diapers, clean set of clothes in case Jackie spit up, and other bits and pieces. He wrapped Jackie in a warm blanket and headed for the buggy.

"Come on, Sam," Sara said. "Bring Matilda. We're going to Harold's."

Jackie was welcomed with much excitement. Everyone had a chance to see her and greet Janet and Walter.

"You can put her on the baby blanket on our bed," advised Olive. "She's too young to go anywhere, and I'm sure we'll hear her if she cries. And you boys can keep an ear open for your new niece. You can let us know if she is unhappy."

The boys were glad to have an assignment, and they were feeling a little important too. Olive had just pointed out that this beautiful baby belonged to them. They were her uncles.

Harold played hymns on the old piano as worshippers were finding seats. Brian, James, and Johnny sat with Ian. He showed them how to look up the Bible verses and to find the hymns in the hymnbook. The sermon was geared to new Christians.

It's a good thing for all of us, Sara thought, *to hear the gospel preached again and again.* It washed over and through her, reminding her of God's goodness. Sara was feeling very cared for and at peace—and yes, even happy. "Thank you, God, for helping me live above my circumstances," she prayed. "I know that, without you, I'd be wallowing beneath them."

On the ride home, Sara asked Walter what he thought of the group. "I'm so excited to know that all those people trust God, just as I do now," he answered. "I can't wait until next week. I feel as though I finally belong. This is my new family. Thank you for inviting me."

Sara had the bottles washed and filled for the night feedings. She had the dogs walked and was finally ready to jump into her inviting-looking bed. She and Janet prayed together, and Sara said, "We have to hurry and get some sleep before Jackie wakes up." They both groaned and laughed, then dropped into their beds.

At around three in the morning, the Brentville whistle started blowing—the same whistle that shrieked out at ten every night to get everyone off the streets. The only other time it was heard was for fires and emergencies.

Sara, as a doctor, had been taught the code. Actually, everyone in town knew it: If it was a fire, two shorts and a long meant the trouble was on the north side of Brentville. Four shorts and four longs meant trouble on the south side. This time, it was the full emergency code. It just kept blowing short whistles. Sara knew this meant that all the policemen, firemen, and doctors were supposed to call headquarters.

Sara jumped out of bed and stumbled to the phone. "This is Dr. Saunders," she reported. "What's going on, and am I needed?"

"Frank escaped from his cell," answered the officer on the other end of the line. "Someone found him on the outskirts of the village by the wall. Apparently, he tried to dig under the wall, but was electrocuted. He mustn't have known that Mr. Brent had a live current reaching down ten feet under the wall. So, as soon as he cut through the electrical cable with the spade, he was fried. If you could go to the hospital, we'll need you for the death certificate and all the other papers to be signed."

"Okay," answered Sara. "I'll be right there. Where is the body now?"

"Being transported to the hospital as we speak."

The hospital was crowded with firemen, policemen, Mr. Brent, Harold, Ian, Walter, and now Sara. After taking care of her official duties, she invited the four men to come in and use her office. She thought they might need a private place where they could talk.

"Good idea, Doc," said Ian.

"Why don't you join us, Sara," said Harold.

They sat in Sara's office for an hour or so, talking about the next step. Jack was pale and shaken. For the first time since she'd met him, Sara sensed that he was feeling a lack of control.

"Well," said Harold, "God is in complete control of this situation. We need to trust that he will show us the way."

"Amen," said Ian.

"I've never trusted God for anything," said Jack. "I'm sure he wouldn't want me anywhere near him."

"*Au contraire*," Sara responded. "God takes us just the way we are. He knows all about us, and yet he still loves us and wants us to come to him."

Jack just sat there with his head in his hands. "I've never felt such despair. We all need to go home and go to bed," he said. "Let's meet at my place tomorrow morning at eleven."

It was five thirty in the morning when Sara crawled back into her bed. *Jackie has just been fed, so we should have a good four hours before she is ready to eat again. What a night!*

"Please, Lord," she prayed. "Draw Jack to you, and soften his heart."

CHAPTER 34

Too Late

At eleven that morning, Sara, Walter, Harold, and Ian were sitting around Jack's big round table in the den. "I was hoping," started Jack, "to get more information from Frank. I had planned to do that today. Obviously, it's no longer an option. So, what I'd like to cover at this meeting is how to find out who in the jail system is corrupt, and, secondly, how we can keep working on Operation Woods. Any ideas on any of this or anything else I should know would be greatly appreciated."

He paused. "I must admit I didn't expect this ugliness when I created Brentville. I think I overlooked man's sinful ways. I trusted the wrong ideas, and I was very naïve. In fact, I'm questioning now whether I should have trusted myself."

The faces of the four sitting at the table showed signs of disbelief. Could it be that this man they knew as a controlling and strong-willed person, an egomaniac, was having second thoughts and doubts?

Sara silently asked God to help her with her words. She knew that Harold and Ian were probably asking for the same guidance. "As much as I disliked Frank," she began, "I don't like seeing anyone die as he did. I now understand that if I die without Jesus in my life, I will live into eternity without God. That means forever. Forever is a long time. It is too late for Frank now. It is sad to think of anyone in that predicament, even Frank."

Ian and Harold and Walter nodded, while Jack just listened quietly.

"Do we know anything about how Frank got out of jail?" Harold asked Jack. "I know that you had your best men assigned to this case."

"Good question," Jack replied. "I think I have it narrowed down to two officers who might have helped him in his escape. That's two too many, but I'm pretty sure that the rest of the force is made up of good, honest men."

"I agree with you on that point, Dad," said Walter. "I've been your eyes and ears around here for fifteen or so years, and I haven't heard anything about any of the others." Then he added, "I must admit, I was beginning to wonder if you were aware of the satanic worship that Frank was leading."

"Son, I can understand why you would think that, given my close relationship with Frank," Jack responded. "I do have some news from Operation Woods. Last night, before Frank escaped from jail, the group met in the woods. They didn't see our watchers, but our men recognized many of them."

"That's great," said Ian. "Now we just have to hope they'll come back next week on the same night."

"If all goes well, your jail will be full next Friday night," predicted Harold.

It was one in the afternoon, and the meeting was about to end. Maggie had served them lunch. Jack had introduced them to his two-year-old son, who had black hair and beautiful big eyes.

"What a darling boy," commented Sara.

Jack explained that a young girl had become pregnant and couldn't keep the baby. He felt very lucky to have had the chance to adopt him. He had named the boy Carl. "It was all arranged through Frank," said Jack.

Sara stopped to see Crystal after her meeting at the mansion. "Hi, stranger," Crystal said in greeting.

"Oh! It's good to see you, Crystal," said Sara, as she gave her friend a hug.

"I've been thinking about you," Sara replied. "I just never seem to find a minute to get to see you. Lately Jackie has been keeping us pretty busy. Regardless, I love every minute! How's married life?"

"I'm deliriously happy," answered Crystal. "Oliver loves the kids as though they were his own. He loves me in a way that I didn't think it was possible to be loved."

"And," she added in a hushed voice, "I think I'm pregnant."

"Oh my goodness!" cried Sara. "That is big news. I'm so happy for you!"

"I haven't told anyone yet," said Crystal. "Not even Oliver, but I've missed two periods now."

"Come to the office on Monday," said Sara. "We'll get you some answers."

"By the way," "I'm planning a baby/wedding shower for Janet. It will be on Sunday. We hope you can come."

Mary made a house call to Janet and Walter for their Saturday-afternoon Bible study. Sara was thrilled to hear Walter sharing about his faith. She could relate. *It hasn't been that long since God gave me that same thirst,* she thought.

Sara was enjoying planning the shower for Janet. Maggie wanted to help, so they'd agreed to have it at the mansion. It was decided that since Janet would have everything she needed as far as household things were concerned, guests would give her personal items along with baby gifts.

Ian had called Sara earlier to see if she would help at Lisa's that night. Lisa was still in the hospital, so Ian and Susie were still doing her chores.

Sara found Susie and Ian in Lisa's barn. There were a few barn cats scurrying around. One, in particular, seemed extra sweet. He just sat right there on Ian's shoulder as Ian moved carefully around the barn.

Susie explained, "The first day we came, Ian made friends with this little black-and-white love. Now the kitten waits for him and jumps up on his shoulder the minute we arrive. He stays there until he has his chores finished. Then Ian has to detach the kitten from his shirt."

"I like your fur collar," kidded Sara.

"I know," laughed Ian. "I may have to take this one home with me. I wonder how Lucky would feel about having a cat around the house."

Later Walter dropped by Sara's to speak briefly with her and Janet. "As you know, members of the committee are keeping an eye out for any unusual happenings. When I was doing an unofficial patrol, I cut through the graveyard. I glimpsed my father behind some pines. Instinct told me not to disturb him, so I came up quietly behind him and stopped.

"Dad had made arrangements to have a headstone made for Frank. He told me that no one else would do it, and he felt like someone should. He'd left Frank's ashes with the undertaker and asked him to dispose of them. The headstone had already been delivered to the cemetery.

233

"My dad stood by what I realized was Frank's headstone, staring at what he'd told them to inscribe on it—Frank Todd—no dates, no verse, no nothing. 'No, Frank, you don't deserve anything more,' Dad said out loud."

Walter paused. "Dad was obviously very troubled. I remained there, mesmerized, as he continued to speak aloud, sorting things through. He stood in the snow and looked around at all the headstones in the cemetery. They were all people he'd known. Most of them he'd pursued, organized, and eventually brought with him.

"I heard my dad mutter, 'I wonder where they all are now. What did Sara mean about it being too late for Frank? I've never thought about death like I'm thinking about it today. Is there a God? I'm beginning to think there *is* something much bigger than I am.'"

Walter shook his head. "I breathed in sharply. This was a new concept for the father I've known. He was too absorbed in his thoughts to hear me. Dad sat on Frank's headstone and said, 'Frank, we need to talk. The anger I feel toward you right now is indescribable. I'm filled with rage and shock over the dastardly things you have done here in Brentville, the community I've tried to make so perfect. I guess I'm angry at myself too, because I let you fool me. And if I'm honest, I'm sad over the loss of what I thought was a good friend and confidant.' Dad's head dropped down and he swiped his gloves at his eyes.

"'What's the matter with me?' he mumbled. 'I don't cry.' I wanted to put my arms around him, to comfort him, but I felt guilty about eavesdropping. I slipped away behind the hedge and continued my patrol. Janet, Sara, please pray for my father. I feel he's closer to knowing God than he has been in his whole life."

CHAPTER 35

One Wall Crumbles

The shower was to start in an hour, and Sara was just getting home from the hospital. "I'll make a quick change," she said to Janet, "and will be ready to ride with you and Walter in about forty-five minutes."

Sara was looking forward to the party. *Maggie has done most of the work and will be doing most of the cleanup. I can relax.*

It's such fun to see Janet with Jackie. So many wonderful things have been happening—the miracle of my own relationship with my Lord and Savior, then the same awe for Janet and Walter, and last but not least, the beautiful baby Jackie.

Jackie's conception was hardly under the best of circumstances. Her birth was a hard one. It could have killed her and her mother. The fact that Janet and Walter have chosen to "forget" who the father was and see Jackie as their own precious gift from God— surely that is a miracle too!

"Thank you, God," Sara prayed aloud. "And if I have some time to talk with Jack today, please give me the right words."

Sitting on the kitchen shelf was Sara's gift to Janet. She grabbed it, called Sam and Matilda, and ran out to the buggy.

I'm so glad I thought of Jeremiah 29:11.[7] It's perfect for a plaque for the baby's room. I knew Harold would want to help. He's so creative, and he did make it special. His decision to print the verse out and then use decoupage to put it onto a piece of sanded maple wood was ideal. Now that I've wrapped it in a new cloth diaper and tied it with pretty ribbon that Janet can use on Jackie's beautiful black hair, it's made to order.

Sara repeated the verse to herself as she ran: "'For surely I know the plans I have for you,' says the Lord, 'plans for your welfare and not for harm, to give you a future with hope.'"

The shower was a success. There were no wobbly TV trays at this party, for which Sara was grateful. They served the food on pretty glass plates with recesses for matching glass cups. There were no spills among the adults, although Carl did pull a tray of deviled eggs off the table. Sam and Matilda seemed happy to have the extra protein. Carl seemed to be taken with the dogs and the baby.

When the festivities were ending, Sara walked into the bedroom where Jackie was sleeping. She asked Janet if she were ready to leave.

"Almost," Janet replied. "Sara, I came in to check on Jackie and found Carl snuggled up to her, sleeping. At first, all I thought was *Oh, how cute!*' Then I was struck by something. Look at these two, sleeping next to each other. Do you think Jackie looks like Carl?"

Sara took a moment to study the little boy beside Jackie. "Well," she said, "they do have the same coloring, for sure. And yes, now that you mention it, I do see the resemblance. When he was awake and watching the dogs, his eyes reminded me of someone, but I didn't know who. Maybe we can ask Jack for some baby photographs of Carl."

"Better still, I think I saw one in the living room," said Janet. "Stay here with the kids."

As Janet returned with the baby picture of Carl, she exclaimed. "Sara, look! They could be twins." She added in a soft voice. "I think I've found my son! I thought he was dead." She began to sob. "Whatever will I do? Never in my wildest dreams did I ever think that I'd see the baby born to me two years ago!"

Sara could see that Janet was shaken to the core, so she said, "Why don't you get Jackie bundled up? I will take Carl to Maggie. It's probably best if we keep this to ourselves. We will talk with Walter about it before we go to Jack."

Jack called to Sara when she was passing the den. "Would you please join me for a few minutes?"

"Certainly," she answered, saying a silent prayer for Janet, who was waiting. "What's up?"

"I've been thinking about what you said," replied Jack. "That it was too late for Frank. What did you mean by that?"

When Sara sat down across from Jack, he got up and closed the door. "Well," she said, "God tells us that if we haven't trusted Jesus Christ before we die, it's too late. If I died tonight, and God asked me why I should be allowed into his heaven to spend the rest of my life with him in eternity, what do you think the right answer would be?"

"You could tell him that you've been a good person," Jack answered. "You're a doctor, helping patients every day."

"Yes, I try to be a good person," said Sara. "But I've learned from the Bible that God cannot tolerate our sin. In God's eyes, a bad thought is a sin. So, the bottom line is that, on my own, I can't be good enough to get to heaven. I need Jesus."

"Well, how does it work then?" asked Jack. "Why does God make it so hard?"

"It may seem hard, but it's simple, really. In fact, when I first learned about it, I thought it was too simple—too simple to accept." She paused for a moment. "Here's what God did for you,

Jack. He sent his son, Jesus, to die on a cross for your sins. If you accept and believe what God has given to you, you are forgiven; you are his child, and you will be with him forever. It's done. It is a free gift to you, Jack. You can't earn it. Neither you nor I deserve it, but it's yours if you want it."

"May I pray with you before I leave?" asked Sara.

Jack nodded sheepishly, and she began. "Please, Lord, be with Jack as he learns about you and your plan for him. Thank you for drawing him to you and for putting these questions into his head. In Jesus's name, amen."

Jack hesitated for a few seconds, then said, "Thanks."

"Let's keep talking about this," suggested Sara. "Ask Walter tonight if you could use his Bible and read the book of John. Then talk with Walter about it. I'm sure he would love to tell you what he has learned."

"I think I will," replied Jack, and Sara got up and left the room.

Janet and Walter were almost ready to leave and were waiting with Maggie in the hallway. "Thanks, Maggie," said Sara. "You have made this a wonderful evening for all of us."

As soon as they all got settled into the buggy, Janet told Walter her thoughts about Carl.

"I had been thinking that Jackie reminds me of someone," said Walter. "It was Carl all along, and he was right under my nose. I guess it's no surprise that you would recognize your own baby boy, Janet."

When Sara told Janet and Walter about her conversation with Jack, they were ecstatic. "Wouldn't it be tremendous if Jack is going to know God as we do?"

The next morning, Walter couldn't wait to tell Janet and Sara about his dad. Entering Sara's front door, he caught Janet up in his arms and danced her to the kitchen. "Sara," he called, "come hear my news."

Janet and Sara sat on the kitchen chairs as Walter enthusiastically began. "When I returned to the mansion last night, Dad came to my apartment and asked for my Bible.

"He said that he was curious about this God of mine and was hoping that we could talk about it tomorrow. I told him that would be great. I gave Dad a big hug, something I haven't done often. He looked a little surprised, but it was good surprise—he was smiling.

"Early this morning, my father came scuffling down the hallway in his slippers and bathrobe. He said that he couldn't wait to see me and said he wanted what I have. He said, 'I want your Jesus in my life too.'

"We talked and prayed, and talked again. Having God in our lives is adding a dimension to our relationship that I like. I told him that I've always loved him, but now that we both love God, our love for each other is stronger and seems brand-new. And he agreed.

"When I invited Dad to join me in Mary's Bible study, he replied that he couldn't wait. I told him that we meet once a week, so he would have to wait almost a week. I assured him that in the meantime, he could meet with you guys, Harold, and me, of course. We'll be able to answer questions that he has."

Sara agreed with a grin. "We'll invite Jack over tomorrow morning. I'll ask Mary for another Bible. We can present it to him then."

Jack and Walter arrived early the next morning. Jack was anxious to get started, and he also wanted to spend some time with Jackie.

"Good morning," greeted Sara. "Welcome to our home."

Janet had been giving Jackie her ten o'clock bottle and was burping the baby. Jack sat down next to Janet and looked lovingly at her daughter. "It wasn't very long ago," he said, "that we were doing that with Carl."

"When I met Carl yesterday," said Janet, "I couldn't believe how much our children looked alike. Then, when I saw that baby photo of Carl, I was almost positive that these two little ones are actually brother and sister."

"I think you may be right," said Jack. "When I was introduced to Jackie, I also was struck with the similarities in the two children. It was all arranged through Frank. So these beautiful children must have the same father."

"It was Frank," confided Janet. She told him briefly of her nightmare experiences with Frank.

"Oh my dear child!" cried Jack. "I am so sorry that you had to go through this. I am sorry I trusted Frank." Jack sat quietly for a few minutes, watching Janet as she held Jackie.

"I'm glad that Frank is no longer with us," he said. "But I am really grateful to have these two delightful children in our midst. When you and Jackie move into my house, I think you and Walter should raise Carl as your own. He will still have Maggie, and I will be his loving grandfather instead of his loving dad. What do you think?"

Janet was speechless and wiped her moist eyes with Jackie's burping diaper. Sara could see that Walter was smiling.

"Thank you, Dad," Walter said. "I know how much you love Carl and that can't have been an easy decision for you."

Harold and Ian arrived just as all were drying their eyes. Ian said, "I hope we're not interrupting."

"No," said Sara. "These are happy tears." She proceeded to tell them the news of Jackie and Carl.

"Well," said Harold, "I think it's time to welcome Jack as our new brother in Christ. We have a Bible for you, my friend, and we thought maybe we could read a couple of chapters. Stop us at any time, and we can discuss what we've read and address any questions you might have."

After prayers of thanksgiving and for guidance, they spent an hour or so reading and discussing what they had read. Jack said, "the last few years have been years of searching for me. Although, I never talked with anyone about my discontent, these feelings of emptiness had been with me for a while now. Maybe it's my age, maybe it's because I've had Carl around, I don't know. But I do know that I had been thinking about God more. Wondering if he exists. Wondering what he thought about me. I am so thankful to God that Sara was here. She showed me God's truth, and led me to other Christians. Sara didn't worry about saying too much concerning God. She just told me the truth." Then they sat and chatted for a while.

Harold asked Jack what he thought of the idea of a Bible study at the Brentville Church. Jack thought a minute. "That sounds like a good idea. It's funny, but once you get the love of God inside you, it seems that you want everyone to have it."

CHAPTER 36

Rolling Along

"So," Ian said to Sara, "I've invited Jack to join a group of friends for our indoor roller-skating party. As you know, we have reserved the whole rink for Thursday night. Jack doesn't know yet that it is our church group he'll be joining."

Sara had learned that, in Brentville, roller-skating was a much-enjoyed activity. In the summer, the kids all donned heavy ball-bearing roller skates that strapped right over their shoes. Many an hour was spent skating on the sidewalks of Brentville. That simple round key was something that the kids had to keep handy in order to adjust the skates to their shoes.

Almost everyone in the community had both a pair of ice skates and a pair of roller skates. Before Jack had closed the gates to Brentville, he made sure that they had a good supply of both.

People were arriving at the rink. This was the once-a-month get-together for their church group, where all the "book clubs" could gather together. Everyone enjoyed these outings. That night was a little different because Mr. Brent, as most knew him, would be in attendance.

The group had received word that Jack seemed to be more human and that he had even surrendered his life to the Lord. Most of them would have to see it with their own eyes before they would believe it.

Skaters were circling the rink, keeping time with the music blasting from loud speakers. *What fun!* thought Sara. She'd never been on roller skates, so she was sticking to the beginners' corner. Jack stuck right there with her, as he had never tried roller-skating either. Ian helped Sara, and Susie took hold of Jack's arm. A few spills, a few laughs, and soon they were hobbling around, hanging on very tightly to their partners' arms.

"Look at Harold and Olive!" Sara exclaimed, as the older couple whizzed by. They were arm in arm, and every step was synchronized to the other's movement.

"Beautiful!" said Ian with a chuckle. "They've been practicing for a few years."

"Let's sit this one out," suggested Sara.

"Love to!" the others, including Harold and Olive, answered.

"Maybe we could sit at the snack bar for a while," said Jack.

Sarah admitted, "As much as I am enjoying this, my feet and ankles are ready for a rest." Jack didn't comment, but Sara assumed that he might be hurting as much as she was.

"Nice group of friends you have here," said Jack. "They all seem so genuinely happy."

"They all have their problems," said Harold. "But most of the time we can remember that God is in charge and that we don't need to worry or fret." He added, "All of them are your brothers and sisters in Christ, Jack."

"I'm astonished to think that there are this many Christians in Brentville," Jack replied. "I'm happy to know them."

"I imagine you've heard of our book clubs," said Harold. When Jack nodded, Harold explained about the weekly meetings. "We meet at my house on Friday nights, and we'd be honored to have you join us. They are actually Bible studies."

"That would be nice," replied Jack. "I'll be there."

At around nine, Jack thanked everyone for the good time and excused himself.

"Inside out," said Harold after Jack had gone.

"You're so right," agreed Sara, a smile in her voice. "It is happening, isn't it?"

CHAPTER 37

Tying the Knot

It had been six weeks since Janet had given birth to Jackie. She and Walter had decided to have a small wedding at the mansion. Mary's husband, David, was going to officiate. The few guests were arriving, and thanks to Maggie, everything looked perfect. She had created an altar covered with flowers. Seats were set up in front of the altar. In the middle of the seating was a short aisle for the wedding party's entrance.

Walter and his best man, Jack, stood at the altar, waiting for Janet to appear. Carl, the ring bearer, and Sam, his assistant, came in first. Carl was carefully carrying a pillow with the rings attached. He carried the pillow to Jack and then followed Sam to a seat right beside Maggie.

Sara, the matron of honor, walked in next. She looked stunning in her new lavender dress. Her short blond curls framed her face, and her blue eyes were smiling.

As soon as Sara took her place at the altar, Janet started her walk down the aisle. Harold was at her side with her hand resting on his arm. Crystal had created a dress for Janet that was beyond words. As Janet swished by the guests, Sara sensed that she was thanking God for this day, for Walter, and for her new life.

As Janet had said to Sara before their tiny procession had started, "All of this is something that I would have considered an impossible dream."

The music stopped, and David started the ceremony with a prayer. "Thank you, Lord, for this couple, Walter and Janet. And thank you for drawing them to you. Please guide them in this marriage and help them to remember to always put you first. Amen."

Janet and Walter said their vows, and soon the music was playing again. They walked down the aisle and left the room with big smiles on their faces.

Maggie had a beautiful reception planned. Carl was a big help, and Sam did his job well too. Matilda, on the sidelines, also did her share of crumb finding. When everyone had gone, there was not a crumb to be found.

For the honeymoon, Janet and Walter were to travel by horse and buggy to Jack's charming cabin on Brent Lake. It was more like a luxurious home than a cabin. Sara, Olive, and Maggie were going to take care of Jackie, while the bride and groom enjoyed their time away.

Harold and Sara were deep in conversation the next morning. Sara had been wondering when, if ever, they could talk with Jack about escape routes that he might be secretly hiding. "I will never give up hope," she said. "It's all I can do to keep quiet about it when I'm around Jack."

"I know," agreed Harold. "But we need to proceed with caution. Jack is a Christian now, and he's a changed person. But, as you know, we don't change completely overnight. It is a process. The Holy Spirit shows us our defects one by one, as we are ready to see them. Then he helps us to change. It can be a slow process with some of us."

"I know I need to be patient," Sara said. "Did I tell you that when Jack heard about our church group and how it was being run, he offered us the use of the mansion and the Brentville Church for our meetings?"

"That will be a big improvement for us," said Harold.

CHAPTER 38

Good-bye, Dear Friend

Harold stopped in to tell Sara what he had learned. "I know I told you that we have to wait, but after I thought some more about it, I decided that the next time I was with Jack, I'd bring up the subject. I didn't have to wait long. I heard the doorbell ringing, and it was Jack. I invited him in. I asked him how his ankles were feeling. Jack said he was fine, but the day after the skating party he felt like doing no more than sitting with his feet up. He laughed as he said that Carl is not fond of sitting around. Then he said, 'I have a couple of Bible questions for you. Do you have a few minutes to hear me out?'

"'Always." I replied. 'Come over to the couch, and I'll get my Bible too.' We sat for a couple hours, reading God's Word. Then, as Jack was preparing to leave, I decided to make my move. I asked him if he ever thinks about leaving Brentville."

"With a startled look, Jack asked me what I meant and added, 'Aren't you happy here?'

"I replied, 'It's not that I'm unhappy, but no one wants to be held against his will.' Jack half admitted I was right, but said that he always assumed individuals who arrived as I did would come to love it here. I've never had a reason, or desire, to return to my old world, added Jack. Good thing too, because, though I did leave one option open, something foiled that. So now I can't. I have come to realize that my dream of a Brentville utopia was a bad idea. I guess I had talked myself into believing that everyone would be happy and would prefer never to leave.

"Jack said that he had a room downstairs in the mansion with computers and equipment in it. There is a way, but only one person knew. He was a genius with those 1955 computers. Unfortunately, he died a few years ago, taking his secret with him.

"I was glad I'd asked, Sara, but I didn't feel any better off for it. As soon as Jack left, I ran over here to fill you in."

"I will not give up," said Sara. "There has to be someone in Brentville who's smart enough to figure out how those computers can help us reach our old world."

Harold replied, "Time for me to get home to check on the boys. Keep trusting." He stepped down the porch steps and headed home.

Later that afternoon, because Sara had been thinking about what Harold told her, she walked back over to his place to see him. Finding no one in the house, she went out back to see if Harold was in his little backyard house. The afternoon sun was fading, and darkness was near. Sara didn't really think she'd find him, because the lights weren't on in his house. *Still,* she thought, *I'll look as long as I'm here.*

She opened the door and had just enough light to see Harold on his cot.

"Hey, you," she said, "no fair taking a nap."

Turning on the lights, Sara noticed how peaceful Harold looked. He had the notes and music for his new song under his hand. She could see the words to the song over on his trusty manual Underwood typewriter.

But as she stepped closer, Sara was aware that he hadn't moved at all.

"Harold," she cried. "Oh, my sweet friend. You can't leave us now. You just can't!"

There was no pulse.

He's been dead for a while. I need to find Olive.

Sara's tears wouldn't stop, and she finally sat down in the kitchen and sobbed. Harold would always be with her. He had taught her so much, and he had helped lead her to the Lord. But right then, she was in so much pain. *I must pull myself together. Olive will be home soon, and I need to be strong for her.*

Sara phoned Ian. After he expressed shock and sorrow, he said, "I'll call the ambulance, and I'll try to find Olive."

Right after she'd replaced the receiver, Olive came in the back door. "Hi, Sara," she said in her cheerful voice.

"Oh, Olive, I have some bad news for you."

"What is it dear?" asked Olive.

"It's Harold," said Sara. "I found him up in his house. There was no pulse. He probably died a couple of hours ago. He may have had a stroke."

When Olive went limp, Sara guided her to a chair. "Where is he?" asked Olive.

"Still in his house," answered Sara.

"I have to go to him. I need to talk with him!"

"If you feel strong enough to walk out there, I'll walk you out."

"Yes," answered Olive. "Please."

Olive went in and knelt down by the cot. She spoke half to herself, half to Sara. "After he returned from your place, Harold said to me, 'It has been a busy week. I'm going up to my house to work on my latest song.'

"When I replied 'Okay,' he said, 'How about a hug to hold me over until dinner?' We made a rule when we were first married

250

that we would hug each other at least a couple of times a day. All these years—and it has still been an important part of our day. Those hugs from Harold have always given me a feeling of contentment and of being loved.

"'Someone will call you when dinner is ready,' I said to him, and off he went. I didn't realize that Harold might need me. For some time, the boys have been eager to show me how well the pigs are doing and how cute Brian's goat is. Since those animals are so important to them, I decided to go with the two younger boys to see their prize pets.

"'Do you think we could bring our pigs and Brian's goat over to your house?' James asked.

"'You could milk the goat,' Johnny added, sounding hopeful. I smiled at that idea, but said they'd better talk with Harold about it. Now they can't." Olive's eyes teared.

"The boys stayed with the pigs. I walked over to the greenhouse to pick up some vegetables for dinner." Her voice thickened. She bent her head.

Sara said, "I will leave you with Harold now. I'll be right by the door in case you need me." Sara waited silently outside, praying for Olive. She knew that Harold had been her only love. They had married young, had no children, and were as close as two people could be.

Inside Harold's little house, Olive cried out softly. Her voice rose somewhat as she spoke to him. "I knew this would happen someday, but I'm not ready. I know that right now you're rejoicing in heaven. You've seen Jesus, and I'm happy about that. But, Harold, I love you so, and I don't feel I can live without you. I'm not ready."

When Olive's cries became sobs and her sobs became screams, Sara went in to hold her and to try to calm her.

Ian came running up the little walkway. When he came in and saw Harold, he teared up. His Brentville dad was gone.

Olive looked up at Sara and Ian, who were both crying. "My stars," she said. "Our crying doesn't seem to be bringing him back. He's really happy in heaven. We'd better face it, dry our eyes, and prepare ourselves to break this to the boys." Olive knew that she would have many a tearful night alone in her room.

That's Olive, thought Sara. *Still Mrs. Practical and always thinking of others.*

The hearse was just pulling away as all three boys were returning. "What happened?" cried Brian, when they walked up the steps.

"It's Harold," said Olive. "He died up in his house this afternoon. Now he's in heaven with his heavenly Father."

"Oh no," they all cried.

"He was our one and only grandpa," Jim said.

"I know," replied Olive, as she walked down the steps of the porch and onto the lawn. "And how he loved his three grandsons! And I'm your one and only grandma. We are all going to miss your grandpa. We will need to stick together and ask God to help us. With God's help and with the help of our friends, we will get through this." She wiped away her tears. As she headed for the swing to find a place to sit, she added, "Go ahead and cry." Her own tears were not stopping, and she needed to catch her breath.

"Oh, Grandpa," Johnny cried, "I love you."

The funeral arrangements were made. They would have the service in the Brentville Church. Many would be coming, as Harold was known and loved by just about everyone. The women in the Brentville Church planned a luncheon, to be held in fellowship hall directly after the funeral.

"Someone needs to stay here tonight with Olive and the boys," Sara said to Ian. "I have Jackie tonight, and I'm wondering about asking Susie to do it. Do you think it's too soon after the loss of her husband?"

"I will ask her," said Ian. "I think she'll want to do it."

"Jackie and I will stay here now, and until Susie gets here," said Sara. She got dinner for Ian, Olive, and the boys. It was a very quiet meal. Sara broke the silence. "Olive, do you need something to help you sleep?"

"I don't think I'll need anything," she replied. "I'm going to bed now. I'm feeling very tired."

Sara asked Ian to help get the boys ready for bed. As he left the doors open, she snuggled Jackie in her arms and listened from outside.

Ian spent time with the boys in Brian's room first. They talked and had questions about where Harold was now. Ian assured them. "Harold is in heaven right now, right this minute. Let's look up some verses in the Bible that tell us that this is true." They all thought that sounded like a good idea.

Ian called the verses out and helped the boys find them in the Bible. Then they took turns reading the verses. They started with 1 John 5:11–13[8] and finished with John 5:24.[9]

Ian said a prayer with them all just before he tucked them into their own beds. "It's good you are living with Olive," he said. "She's going to need some help, now that Harold is gone."

Susie arrived soon after she'd heard, so Sara and Jackie left.

There were many sad hearts in Brentville. By the time morning came, almost everybody had heard about Harold's death.

Everyone from the barber to the telephone operator was passing the sad news along.

Janet and Walter came to pick up Jackie. As this was their first stop back in the village, they had not heard about Harold. Walter was devastated. He had grown to love this man as a Christian brother. And Janet said, "Oh, Sara, what are we going to do without Harold?"

As she hugged Jackie tightly in her arms, Janet exclaimed, "How I missed my little girl! I could barely stay away the whole week. But I did, and we had a wonderful honeymoon."

"Thank you so much for giving us this week away," said Walter. "It was a good way to start our life together. With two little ones around, we probably won't be getting much alone time," he said with a laugh.

"I'm always here to babysit," Sara said. "In fact, you should probably schedule a getaway every few months." Sara picked up all the traces of Jackie's visit, washed a load of diapers, and cleaned up the bedroom that Janet had been using all those months. *I will miss them*, she thought. *Having a baby around is good for the soul.* Then she rounded up the dogs and headed to Olive's house.

"How did you sleep last night?" asked Sara.

"Pretty well, until around four o'clock," answered Olive. "Then I just lay there counting the chimes as the church clock hit every hour and every half hour." She rolled her eyes.

Neighbors were beginning to deliver food to Olive—more than she could possibly use. But she and Sara understood that people wanted to do something. *It will be nice to have food all prepared for the next few days*, thought Sara.

"Heavens to Betsy," said Olive. "Look at all this food!"

"Yes," replied Sara, "you and Harold sure have lots of friends."

That afternoon, there were visiting hours at the funeral home with an open coffin. When the boys walked in and saw Harold, they started sobbing.

Sara, Ian, and Olive had all done the same thing. There was just something so real and so final about seeing that body lying so still. It looked like Harold; he appeared to be sleeping.

In reality, he's no longer here, Sarah thought. *No amount of crying or being sad or wishing can bring him back. He's gone from this earth forever. But I know our existence never ends. Harold will be with Jesus throughout eternity. What a gift! What a miracle!*

The funeral service for Harold was beautiful—a celebration of the man and the life he had lived—and a celebration because God had prepared a place in heaven for him. Many people got up and shared about their times with Harold. Some were funny, but all were full of love for him, and they all pulled at Sara's heartstrings. The man all the kids called Grandpa would not be forgotten.

The sermon was filled with God's plan of salvation, something that many at the service had never heard. David, who was officiating, wasn't holding back. He was telling the truth about God's wondrous grace. He told about why Harold was in heaven, as he presented the gospel message.

Sitting in the pew, Sara was thinking about her friend. *Even though I'm grieving your loss, I can honestly say that I am happified. I have the Lord, and I know you have him too. It is well with our souls.*

Sara had looked up the word *happified* the first time she'd heard Harold use it, but she couldn't find it. When she'd asked Harold about it, he told her that it was an old word from the seventeenth or eighteenth century, meaning "to make happy."

The song Harold had just written was used at the funeral. He had enough of the music written out that the organist could play it. Cheryl, the soloist, introduced the song by the title they'd found on the paper: "Forever." [10] She sang it with much feeling as the congregation listened intently to the words.

Forever

Verse 1:
I thank you, Lord, for life on earth; your promises
    are true.
I cannot earn and don't deserve; it's not the things
    I do,
But your sweet gift of grace, your death upon that
    tree.
You saved my soul, you made me whole; you did
    all that for me.
My hand is in yours; I want you to know, I'm
    eagerly waiting for you.
I love you so, to you I will go. There's nobody else,
    Lord, but you.

Verse 2:
When my death comes, I'll see your face. I'll be
    with you in heaven.
In the twinkling of an eye, you say, 'Oh, what a
    gift I'm given.,
No pain, and no more tears. I'll live so close to thee.
No greed or fear in heaven; no, none of these I'll see.
So praises I'll sing as I worship and bring my love
    and devotion to you.
I'll never grow tired of singing to you, my beautiful
    Savior, and King.

Chorus:
Al-le-lu-lia and amen. My life with you will never
    end. Thank you, Jesus.
Al-le-lu-lia. Amen.[11]

Throats were cleared, and handkerchiefs were pulled from purses and pockets. People wept. Nobody seemed untouched. But the tears were those of joy as well as of sadness. Many had heard the hope of the gospel message preached. They would be hearing it again if they decided to attend the new Bible study with David.

Sara thought, *I can just hear Harold saying, "You see, it is happening—from the inside out."*

After the reception at the church, a few of Harold and Olive's friends came to the house. They stayed for a while but could see that Olive should be getting some sleep. "Call us if you need anything," they all offered.

Sara and the two dogs stayed the night. The dogs and the cat slept with the boys, one animal on each bed. Sara went downstairs, got ready for bed, and curled up on the couch—the same couch on which she'd spent so many hours talking to Harold. That night, she had insisted that Olive take a mild sedative before she went to bed.

The next morning, Olive seemed rested and in relatively good spirits, considering the situation. The boys came down to breakfast one by one and wondered who would lead the prayer and Bible time in the dining room every morning, now that Grandpa was gone. They had come to like kneeling and using the chair as their table.

"We will do it together," answered Olive as she looked up a few verses for them to share. "Harold would be happy to see that you want to do this. Even though he's not here to lead us, he would definitely want us to do it."

"Lisa is supposed to be released from the hospital tomorrow," said Sara. "What would you think of having her come here for a while?" Sara's thoughts drifted before they answered. *Lisa needs* counseling and help before she will ever be able to care for her family in a healthy way. By not standing up to her husband, by doing what this evil man told her to do, she was a part of the problem.

"Hurt people, hurt people." I need to get help for Lisa, so that she can help her children. If Olive is willing, then Lisa being with her should be a good start toward her healing process.

James broke into her thoughts. "Oh, could we have her come?"

"How about it, Olive?" asked Sara. "Would it be too much for you?"

Olive didn't have to think very long about the request. "Yes, that would be nice," she said in a soft, thoughtful voice. "I would be honored to have Lisa come."

Sara said, "I was thinking that Johnny and James could sleep in the same room, and then Lisa could have the extra room.

The boys could hardly contain themselves. Johnny said with an irresistible, sweet little-boy smile, "Thank you, Sara, for thinking of my mom."

The next night, Sara received an exciting phone call from Ian. "Harold's prediction regarding Jack's jail being full has come true! The group did come back to the woods for their meeting. As soon as the fire got going, everyone on the police force came quietly out of their hiding places and put handcuffs on the men and women. They were taken to the jail, and Jack was called. He will now decide their fate."

"Thank you, God," responded Sara, and she fell back into bed.

The following evening, after those emotionally wearing days, Sara decided that she needed to go to bed early. Since Harold's death, she had been running full steam ahead. *I know that I need some quiet time. I need to be still and know that God is God, and that he has a plan.*

"Help me, Lord," she prayed, "to feel this sadness and to get out to the other side of it. I know that the only way out is through, and I know that I can't keep burying my grief in work. I have never been very good at living my way through my feelings, Lord. Please help me with that now.

"I love you, dear heavenly Father. Please be with my Jim and our family. Amen.

CHAPTER 39

Breakthrough

Sara was hearing hospital sounds, but her body wasn't moving. *I want to see what's going on. Why can't I open my eyes? I can hear voices in the distance. Why can't I recognize them? Why can't I understand their words? I feel so heavy and tired.* She slipped back into a deep sleep.

Then Sara heard a voice that was very familiar to her. It brought her back to her old world with a jolt. Opening her eyes, she could see Jim sitting by the bed. He looked blurry at first, but within a few moments she could recognize his features.

Yes, there he is. It's Jim, all right, looking as handsome as ever. He's holding my hand, and those expressive eyes of his are filled with tearful joy. That's my Jim. He's never been afraid to show his feelings.

As Sara returned to a deep sleep, she thought she could hear the voice of a doctor. "Don't worry, Mr. Saunders. Your wife is finally coming out of the coma she's been in for the last several weeks."

Sara awoke again. She'd had time to realize that she was hooked up to all kinds of tubes and wires, and her right wrist was in a cast. A male voice was speaking. Confused, Sara looked around.

A nurse turned down a radio that was by Sara's bed. "The radio has been turned on daily to provide sound stimulation, to help with easing you out of your coma when your body was ready," she explained.

The station softly declared itself to be "KTIS 98.5, the Good News station."

An announcer spoke again. "Here is an often-requested favorite. The lyrics were originally written by Elvina Hall; the music, by her church's organist. From the album of the same name, here are the Angelic Gospel Singers with 'Jesus Paid it All.'"[12]

Before she left the room, the nurse explained, "Your husband has just gone to phone your family members to let them know that you've come out of the coma."

By the time Jim got back to sit by Sara's bed, she was full of questions. "What happened? How long have I been here?"

"Your car was found by the highway here in rural Wisconsin," answered Jim. "They think you must have gone to sleep and lost control of the car. It had flipped on its side, the driver's side, and crashed into a tree. They had to get the local fire department to come to cut you out. They brought you here, the nearest hospital in Wisconsin. You had a broken wrist, a couple of broken ribs, and a laceration on your head. You've been in a coma ever since. After examining you this morning, the doctor thinks you'll make a full recovery. In fact, he thinks we can take you home very soon."

Jim couldn't seem to quit smiling. "David, Debbie, Susan, and your mom and dad are anxiously awaiting your return."

Sara noticed something moving on the foot of her bed. It was white, the same color as the sheets. She moved her foot a little, and the white fluff-ball started to move toward the head of the bed.

"Well, if it isn't Marshmallow!" she cried. The happy dog, tail wagging, snuggled up to her and rested her head on Sara's arm.

"I brought her here a month ago," said Jim. "She has been with you on this bed most every day. I take her back to the motel at night. It will be good for all of us to get home again. We've missed you, my darling Sara."

After Jim and Marshmallow had left for the evening, Sara began thinking about what had happened. She didn't remember anything about the car accident, but she remembered a lot about her journey to Brentville. The citizens of Brentville were very clear in her mind: Crystal, Ian, Harold and Olive—everyone. Most clearly, Sara remembered Jesus, her new friend and Savior.

Sara was a little confused and tired. She couldn't seem to stay awake long enough to think things through.

When the night nurse came in, Sara asked her to see if there was a Gideon Bible in the drawer of the bedside table. "Yes," she said. "I've been reading it aloud some of the time on night duty, while I sat by your bed and prayed for you. Here it is."

"Thank you for the Bible and the prayers," said Sara as she held God's Word with both hands. *Tomorrow morning,* she thought, *I'll read the Gospel of John to see if it is the same as it was in Brentville.*

Hospital noises woke Sara up by six the next morning. Picking up the Bible, she opened it to the Gospel of John.

Yes, as in Brentville, John's Gospel told her that Jesus Christ is the son of God. Because Jesus is God, he lives forever. It explained that the Holy Spirit will indwell, guide, counsel, and comfort those who follow Jesus. It confirmed Jesus's death and his resurrection.

Oh, what a Savior! Sara thought. *He figured out a way to save me, even in a coma.*

She was just finishing breakfast when Jim and Marshmallow came. Marshmallow cleaned up the crumbs she found on Sara's bed. Jim sat down by the bed and sipped his coffee. He had one for her too.

"Oh, *yes!*" Sara exclaimed. "It's from the Donut Shop."

"Sure is nice to be together again," sighed Jim with a huge smile on his face.

"I know. And I have so much to tell you about my journey. I want you to meet my new friend, Jesus—and I really want us to find a Bible-believing church."

I see a little concern in Jim's eyes, but I'm not worried. I know the mighty God can reach my husband just as easily as he's reached me. Marshmallow has no concern in her eyes. She just seems happy to be back on my lap.

Jim bent over Sara's bed and kissed her on the forehead. Then his lips met hers. She felt the excitement and love that she had been yearning for, waiting for, and hoping and trusting for, all melting together into one warm, awe-inspiring miracle.

"I love you, Jim. We need to get started on our new journey. Please take me home."

"I'm already on it," said Jim. "I'll get the car and pick you up by the front door."

Helen, the nurse on duty, helped Sara dress and get into a wheelchair and then pushed it toward the elevator. Sara had become quite a celebrity on the second floor. Many of the nurses and doctors came to say good-bye and to wish her well.

Sara couldn't wait to get home as Helen propelled the wheelchair through the front doorway. Sara could see Jim waiting in a large, black Suburban. Getting out of the wheelchair, she glanced down at the grass by the sidewalk. She spotted a four-leaf clover. *Oh, Harold, I've found one. I just had to look.*

"No more little cars for you," Jim said as Helen helped Sara into the vehicle. "Hope you like your new car," he added with a grin.

Sara smiled and settled back into the plush leather seat. "Oh, it's so good to be with you, Jim," she sighed. "Home, James!"

They laughed together at their old joke.

Epilogue

Sara and Jim are enjoying life back in Harleysville, Pennsylvania. They've found a Bible-believing church where they're very happy. Jim is beginning to understand more about Sara's newfound faith.

Sara is thinking about changing careers or, at the very least, cutting back on her hospital hours. She no longer wants to be too busy to look at the clouds or build a snowman.

Jim surprised Sara with a couple of beautiful horses. They are enjoying riding around the countryside. And they are relearning the art of having fun.

Sara realizes that she doesn't have to be afraid of tomorrow, because God is already there. She is also learning that it is God who gives her life meaning. It isn't her work, her looks, or her worldly possessions. Her worth now comes from how God values her and what he has done for her, rather than what others may think.

Jim and Sara's three children live nearby. So far, David, Debbie, and Susan don't understand Sara's newfound love for Jesus. In fact, they don't really want to hear about it. Sara is learning, that God doesn't always bring people to put their trust in him as quickly as he did in Brentville. When she begins to worry about her children, she picks up her Bible, flips the pages to the book of Philippians, and reads the following verses:

Do not be anxious about anything, but in everything, by prayer and petition, with thanksgiving, present your requests to God. And the peace of God, which transcends all understanding, will guard your hearts and your minds in Christ Jesus. (Philippians 4:6–7 NIV)

Then Sara whispers, "Amen."

ADDENDA

Forever

ad Lib, Moderately Slow

Cindy Kilpatrick
July, 2016

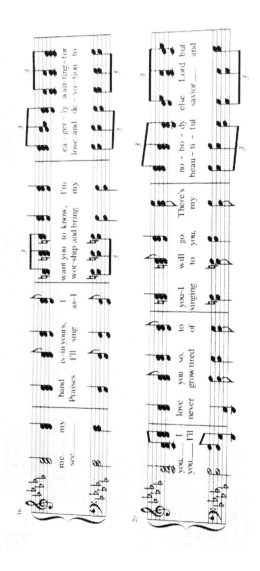

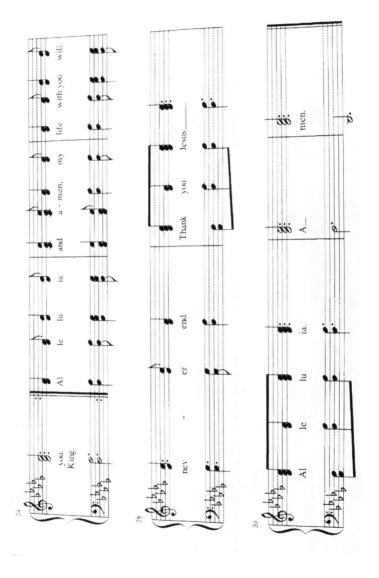

AFTERWORD

People have said to me, "I never knew." Well, I never knew either. I had occupied a pew in a church since I was a baby. But it wasn't until I was in my forties that I knew—I knew for sure and beyond a doubt—there is a God.

I am humbled and grateful to God for softening my heart. And I am thankful for the people he used to teach me the wonderful truth of the gospel. Yes, he is mine, and I am his. Forever.

How then, can they call on the one they believe in? And how can they believe in the one of whom they have not heard? And how can they hear without someone preaching to them?

—Romans 10:14 NIV

ENDNOTES

1   Cru (known as Campus Crusade for Christ until 2011) is an evangelical Christian organization. It was founded in 1951 at the University of California, Los Angeles by Bill Bright as a ministry for university students. Learn more about it at https://en.wikipedia.org/wiki/ Cru_(Christian_organization)#History,

2   "What a Friend We Have in Jesus," Joseph Scriven, 1855, Lyrics can be found at http://library.timelesstruths.org/music/What_a_Friend We-Have-inJesus/.

3   The Gospel of Matthew is the first of the four Gospels in the New Testament, though not the first of them to be written. For a breakdown of the book's contents and meditations, see the World Council of Churches publication at http://www.rc.net/wcc/readings/matthew.htm.

4   1 Peter 1:3-9: Praise be to the God and Father of our Lord Jesus Christ! In his great mercy he has given us new birth into a living hope through the resurrection of Jesus Christ from the dead, and into an inheritance that can never perish, spoil or fade. This inheritance is kept in heaven for you, who through faith are shielded by God's power until the coming of the salvation that is ready to be revealed in the last time. In all this you greatly rejoice, though now for a little while you may have had to suffer grief in all kinds of trials. These have come so that the proven genuineness of your faith—of greater worth than gold, which perishes even though refined by fire—may result in praise, glory and honor when Jesus Christ is revealed. Though you have not seen him,

you love him; and even though you do not see him now, you believe in him and are filled with an inexpressible and glorious joy, for you are receiving the end result of your faith, the salvation of your souls.

[6]   Frank Loesser, "Bushel and a Peck," Lyrics © Kobalt Music Publishing, 1950. To hear Doris Day sing the song's original words, go to https://www.youtube.com/watch?v=aw2phldcmCQ.

[7]   Jeremiah 29:11: "For I know the plans I have for you," declares the LORD, "plans to prosper you and not to harm you, plans to give you hope and a future."

[8]   1 John 5: 11-13: And this is the testimony: God has given us eternal life, and this life is in his Son. Whoever has the Son has life; whoever does not have the Son of God does not have life. I write these things to you who believe in the name of the Son of God so that you may know that you have eternal life.

[9]   John 5:24: "Very truly I tell you, whoever hears my word and believes him who sent me has eternal life and will not be judged but has crossed over from death to life."

[11]   C. Kilpatrick, "Forever." See song text and music in the addenda.

[12]   Elvina M. Hall, "Jesus Paid It All," 1865, originally five stanzas, now four, some of which are considerably altered. Its theme is the completeness of Jesus's work on the cross and the fact that humans have done nothing to merit such mercy, placing us forever in debt to Christ. The tune "All to Christ" is by John T. Grape, 1868. See Tiffany Shomsky, https://www.hymnary.org/text/i_hear_the_savior_say_thy_strength_indee. The 1980s version, which Sara could have heard in hospital, is "Jesus Paid It All," Margaret Allison and The Angelic Gospel Singers, "Lord, You Gave Me Another Chance," released November 13, 1989. A video of release, published February 20, 2013, can be found at ***https://www.youtube.com/watch?v=W76rujcTWuo.***

Modern versions of "Jesus Paid It All" can be found at Joey Feek, "Jesus Paid It All," February 12, 2016, Farmhouse Recordings, https://www.youtube.com/watch?v=y9DUKhFhD74; and the Gaither Vevo, https://www.youtube.com/watch?v=38EVco7eba0.

1. I hear the Savior say,
"Thy strength indeed is small;
Child of weakness, watch and pray,
Find in Me thine all in all."

o Refrain:
Jesus paid it all,
All to Him I owe;
Sin had left a crimson stain,
He washed it white as snow.

2. For nothing good have I
Whereby Thy grace to claim;
I'll wash my garments white
In the blood of Calv'ry's Lamb.

3. And now complete in Him,
My robe, His righteousness,
Close sheltered 'neath His side,
I am divinely blest.

4. Lord, now indeed I find
Thy pow'r, and Thine alone,
Can change the *leper's spots [*leopard's]
And melt the heart of stone.

5. When from my dying bed
My ransomed soul shall rise,
"Jesus died my soul to save,"
Shall rend the vaulted skies.

*alternate text, alluding to Jeremiah 13:23
Source: Hymnary.org (http://www.hymnary.org/
text/i_hear_the_savior_say_thy_strength_indee)

6. And when before the throne
I stand in Him complete,
I'll lay my trophies down,
All down at Jesus' feet.

7. I hear the Savior say,
"Thy strength indeed is small;
Child of weakness, watch and pray,
Find in Me thine all in all."

o Refrain:
Jesus paid it all,
All to Him I owe;
Sin had left a crimson stain,
He washed it white as snow.

8. For nothing good have I
Whereby Thy grace to claim;
I'll wash my garments white
In the blood of Calv'ry's Lamb.

9. And now complete in Him,
My robe, His righteousness,
Close sheltered 'neath His side,
I am divinely blest.

10. Lord, now indeed I find
Thy pow'r, and Thine alone,
Can change the *leper's spots [*leopard's]
And melt the heart of stone.

*alternate text, alluding to Jeremiah 13:23
Sources: Hymnary.org, http://www.hymnary.org/
text/i_hear_the_savior_say_thy_strength_indee.

11. When from my dying bed
My ransomed soul shall rise,
"Jesus died my soul to save,"
Shall rend the vaulted skies.

12. And when before the throne
I stand in Him complete,
I'll lay my trophies down,
All down at Jesus' feet.

Printed in the United States
By Bookmasters